Hindustānī Music
and
the Aesthetic Concept of Form

New Vistas in Indian Performing Arts; no. 1

Hindustānī Music and the Aesthetic Concept of Form

Anjali Mittal

D.K.Printworld(P)Ltd.
NEW DELHI - 110 015

Cataloging in Publication Data — DK
[Courtesy: D.K. Agencies (P) Ltd. <docinfo@dkagencies.com>]

Mittal, Anjali, 1949-
Hindustānī music and the aesthetic concept of form.
(New vistas in Indain performing arts ; no. 1).
Includes bibliographical references (p.).
Includes Index.
ISBN13: 9788124601341
ISBN10: 8124601348

1. Music, Hindustani. 2. Form (Aesthetics).
I. Title. II. Series: New vistas in Indian performing arts; no. 1.

ISBN13: 978-81-246-0134-1
ISBN10: 81-246-0134-8
First published in India in 2000
Second impression in 2009

Published and printed by:
D.K. Printworld (P) Ltd.
Regd. office : *'Srikunj'*, F-52, Bali Nagar
Ramesh Nagar Metro Station
New Delhi - 110 015
Phones : (011) 2545 3975; 2546 6019; *Fax* : (011) 2546 5926
E-mail: dkprintworld@vsnl.net
Web: www.dkprintworld.com

Dedicated to

the memory of
my Parents

Preface

As I begin this preface, my first impulse is to thank my stars on the completion of this work. The subject it discusses is by no means very easy, and I have indeed been lucky to receive, all along, kindly encouragement from my colleagues at the University where I work; and abounding help from my exceptionally sympathetic Guru, Professor S.K. Saxena, to whom I am inexpressibly grateful.

My colleagues and friends, namely, Najma, Sunita, Anupam, Vijaya, and Gullu in particular, have all been very actively helpful, in different ways. They goaded me to keep going whenever I seemed to wobble in my course; and the first four of them never failed to make such adjustments in our teaching work as could release a little more time for my research.

Professor V.K. Aggarwal, our Dean and Departmental Head when I wrote this work, has helped me in many ways. Without his blessings it would have been clearly impossible for me to achieve my purpose, and so I greatly value his help. As for Professor Debu Chaudhari, our internationally famous *sitār* maestro, he not only gave me one helpful hint in connexion with my treatment of *rāga-rūpa*, but has even been impatient for, and not merely interested in, the completion of the present work.

Next only to what Prof. Saxena has done for me, active and substantial help has been received from my *dīdī*, Prof. Krishna Bisht, who is herself a vocalist of no mean merit. When I was finding it difficult to really settle the question of the **comparative** value of *vādī-samvādī* and the 'catch-phrase' in the context of *rāga-rūpa*, she provided me with some excellent material for thought. Further, it is she who picked for me the *khyāl-tāna*s to be analysed, and drew my attention to a clear defect in one of the compositions I had analysed — a defect which was promptly remedied. I therefore feel impelled to acknowledge my indebtedness to her, even at the risk of embarrassing her.

In respect of notations, the compositions analysed in this work have been checked by the late Dr. (Mrs.) Lalit Mathur; and from the viewpoint of rhythm, by the late Ustad Chhamma Khan (*tablā*) and Pandit Tej Prakash 'Tulsi' (*pakhāvaj*). I feel beholden to all of them.

It would perhaps look odd to thank my family too. But I must at least acknowledge the help I have received from my husband, Shri S.P. Mittal, and my daughter, Meghna. They happily did quite a few household chores which were really my duty; and so provided me with more time to concentrate on my work.

I cannot help recalling, at this point, the debt that I owe to my teachers in vocal music: Pandit Sita Ram, who initiated me into the art, and the late Ustad Naseer Ahmad Khan who took me further on the course, and whose exquisite eye for the beauty of little details will for ever remain a source of inspiration to me.

As for the content of the work, it is clearly different from what we commonly find in books on music. The viewpoint is neither historical nor grammatical, but aesthetic. It is only in the field of aesthetics that we find serious reflection on concepts like **form** and **expression**. The present work seeks to do the same in relation to Hindustānī music.

I do not, however, make any claim to exceptional achievement.

I must add, in the end, that barring the *khyāl*-s, all the rhythmic (*tablā* and *kathak*) and melodic compositions I have discussed in the fifth chapter, *The Knitwork of Musical Form*, have been provided by Prof. Saxena; and that the *dhruvapada, dhamār* and *tārāna bandiśa*-es are his own creations.

I expect this modest essay to promote interest in the aesthetical study of our music.

October 19, 1999 **Anjali Mittal**

Contents

1

Philosophical Aesthetics
Approaches and Concepts

THE subject, it is obvious, requires us to study the concept of **form** in *Hindustānī Music* from the viewpoint of **philosophical aesthetics**. The three concepts here involved, which alike need some explanatory comment, if not in equal measure, are: form, Hindustānī Music, and philosophical aesthetics. Of these three, the last one may be taken up first for explanation, for neither its own nature nor its relevance to our music has so far received, in our country, the attention it deserves.

Philosophical Aesthetics

What is philosophical aesthetics? How, if at all, is aesthetics related to philosophy? Can it be regarded as a part of the latter?

Such questions, it may at once be said, need careful attention. For, unlike other accepted branches of philosophy like metaphysics, ethics, logic and epistemology, aesthetics has come to be regarded as a branch of philosophy only in comparatively modern times. Aesthetical **thinking** has always been there since the days of Plato. But the thought that the aesthetic consciousness is a distinct kind of consciousness; and that, as a study of art and beauty, aesthetics may be regarded as a distinct discipline, emerged only in the writings of Baumgarten and Kant. However, the thought that aesthetics is a distinct subject of study is not the same as the thought that it is a branch of philosophy. It is with the second that we are presently concerned, and we have to give it some pointed attention.

All aesthetics, be it noted, is not a branch of philosophy; only philosophical aesthetics may be said to be so. Therefore, it would help understanding if we first say something about non-philosophical aesthetics, and then turn to see what philosophical aesthetics itself is.

NON-PHILOSOPHICAL AESTHETICS

Now, non-philosophical aesthetics may be psychological, socio-cultural or metaphysical. Psychological aesthetics discusses questions of the following type:

> Does the excellence of an artist's work depend on his intelligence quotient?
>
> Is creativity in any way related to the use of drugs?
>
> Is it helpful for the creation of a great work of art if, before he begins the creation in question, the artist is enabled to enjoy a brief period of rest and relaxation?

Aesthetics which is done from the socio-cultural point of view discusses such questions as the following:

> What are the socio-cultural factors which have led to the sudden popularity of *ghazal/bhajan* singing in India?
>
> Why is it that the best *ghazal* singers still come from Pakistan? Is it because the cultural setting of that country is more conducive to the proper cultivation of this art?

As for metaphysical aesthetics, a good deal of traditional Indian aesthetics may be said to be a good specimen. Perhaps the most important concept of older Indian aesthetics is *rasa*; and *rasa*, as we know, has been regarded as a close approximation to the experience of ultimate reality. Even generally, according to our ancient point of view, all artistic activity is a pathway to ultimate reality. It is, in this connection, interesting to note that the traditional Indian definition of *svara* as "स्वयमेव राजते" is very similar to the characterisation of ultimate reality as *svaprakāśaṁ*.

Now we may turn to see what philosophical aesthetics positively is. This may be done in two ways. We may say that philosophical aesthetics discusses the major traditional questions of philosophy in relation to art; or that it does philosophy in relation to art in precisely those ways in which philosophy is today generally done. Both these ways of answering the question, what is philosophical aesthetics, deserve our attention; for both may be expected to help us in our study.

AESTHETICS AND THE TRADITIONAL QUESTIONS OF PHILOSOPHY

Now, to begin with the first approach, philosophy has been traditionally concerned with questions of truth, knowledge, reality and meaning. Therefore, philosophy of art, or philosophical aesthetics, is nothing but the discussion of such questions in relation to art. This must, however, be developed at some length to clearly bring out what philosophical aesthetics is and what it does.

Here, we would do well to begin by reflecting that of all the questions that we have listed as the traditional concern of philosophy, the problem of meaning, which contemporary philosophy emphasises, is perhaps the most important. We say so because we cannot set out to answer **any** question properly unless we first take care to determine what that question **means**. This is exactly why it is a basic concern of contemporary philosophical aesthetics to think out and determine the precise meanings of the various concepts which we use in talking about art and beauty. What do we here mean by words like **art**, **expression**, **feeling**, **creation**, ***rasa*** or **aesthetic experience**? This is indeed a very important question which is discussed by philosophical aesthetics today. Nor is this question in any way artificial. For the fact indeed is that what these words mean in relation **to art** is, in many cases, different from what they mean **in daily conversation**.

Take, to begin with, the word **art**. It is true that even in everyday conversation this word is used in three distinct senses: art as **an object** of art, art as a distinct kind of **activity**, and art as signifying **all objects of a particular kind**. But, everyday talk does not try to think out how art, as an object of art, differs from the objects that we deal with in daily life. But philosophical aesthetics is not so indifferent. It points out that, though we can certainly speak of a work of art also as a thing — as when we are asked to merely put a painting in a corner of the room — a work of art is not a mere thing, because whereas things are important because they can be used for practical purposes, art is significant primarily because it opens up for our contemplation a whole new world of feeling, form and images which is quite independent of the considerations of truth, reality and utility.

Let us turn now to the word 'expression'. That art is essentially a matter of expression is perhaps the most commonly accepted definition of art. Among Indian musicians this is certainly a very popular view. But, here too, a question may well be put with regard to the meaning of **expression** in relation to art. Does the word here mean exactly what it does in daily life? What is commonly meant by 'expression' is either the expression of our thoughts in words or the expression of our emotions in terms of bodily behaviour. Now, whatever be the words that we choose in daily life to express our thoughts, they can all be replaced by synonyms from a different language, and with a different sonant character. What I am presently writing in English can just as well be expressed in Hindi. When I make this change, the sound of words will certainly be altered, but the meaning will remain absolutely unchanged. But in the case of an art like music or poetry, the moment we change the sound of *svara*s or words, the significance of the music or the poem in question will at once be changed. In other words, whereas in the case of everyday expression of thoughts, what is expressed is separable from the medium in terms of which it is expressed, in the case of artistic expression such separation is impossible. Therefore, expression in art is different from the everyday expression of thought in language.

Take, now, the case of emotional expression. When I get angry my face turns red and my muscles are tightened. But all these bodily changes which constitute the expression of the emotion in question take place automatically. I do not have to make any effort to so produce and organise the bodily changes that they may come to express the emotion I experience. In other words, ordinary emotional expression is automatic and not consciously organised. On the other hand, when the musician, or in fact any artist, tries to express an emotion, two distinctive features are noticeable. First, he does not himself feel, but only **imagines**, the emotion he sets out to express; and second, he has to consciously **organise** the melodic and the rhythmic aspects of the music, so that he may be able to bring about the expression in question.

It is just as proper to ask what **feeling** means in relation to art. In everyday conversation, we take the word to mean emotions which bear clear-cut names, such as joy and sorrow, anger and jealousy. But, in art 'feeling' is not confined to these emotions. Music, for example, may easily project such feelings as poise, and liveliness which are not commonly regarded as emotions.

Our next word is **creation**. It is different in meaning from the word **making**. The difference is recognised even in daily conversation. Thus, we commonly speak of **making** a table or a chair. Works of art, on the other hand, are commonly said to be **created**. We compliment an artist on being creative, not on being a maker. In the region of an art like music, however, the word **creation** has quite a few different meanings which may now be distinguished. First, a musician may be said to be creative if he comes to develop a style of his own. Thus, Kumar Gandharva may be said to be creative in so far as the way he projects a *sthāyī* is different from the traditional way of the Ustāds which would be distinguished by what is called *kaṇ bharṇā*. Thus understood, **creation** stands for newness or originality. He who creates **new** *rāga*s is said to be creative. However, it is important to note that in this sense of newness, creation or creative quality cannot be regarded as a **necessary** mark of good music. For it is a matter of common experience that those of our musicians who come from *gharānā*s take pride in being able to sing **exactly in the way of their forefathers**. A measure of originality may well be said to enhance the excellence of a singer, but we cannot categorically say that there is no good music without originality or newness. That which makes music necessarily creative is not the newness of a composition or style, but its ability to conjure up such a world of *svara* and *tāla* that a *rasika* may be able to contemplate it — nay, even to dwell within it — in disinterested delight. Such delight, we may add, is the joy that we take in attending to a thing of beauty without raising any question about its reality or utility.

The basic question that philosophical aesthetics puts about **reality** (when art is said to relate to it in various ways) is about the very meaning of the word. It is surely proper to put such a question because the word 'reality' is in fact used in many senses. Its most familiar meaning is: our everyday or empirical reality of things, persons and happenings. This is the reality in which we live and move about, and with which we have to deal in the way of meeting challenges and overcoming difficulties. Reality, thus understood and experienced, is opposed to what we experience in illusions and hallucinations. The other meaning of the word in question is reality as metaphysical which may be spoken of as God, *Brahman* or the Absolute. This is not the reality with which we deal in everyday life; it is rather the Reality which we come to realise, if at all, by practising disciplines of various kinds.

Now, to begin with the second sense, if we discuss the question as to how an art like music is related to ultimate reality, we would be doing, as pointed out earlier, metaphysical aesthetics, which is not what we mean by philosophical aesthetics today. So we may turn straightaway to the first meaning of 'reality'. Here our question is obvious. Is an art like music **real** or **unreal** in the everyday meanings of these words? Is listening to music similar to dealing with an everyday happening? Or, is it unreal like an illusion or hallucination?

Now, it is easy to see that actual music cannot be said to be totally unreal in the sense of mere privation. For when we listen to music we perceive real sounds which can be recorded, and which, as the *svaras* of a *rāga*, are perceived in essentially identical ways by different listeners, so that they can be said to be objectively real. What is more, listening to music can bring about tangible improvement in our ability to make subtle distinctions in the region of sounds, and can so liberate our imagination that we may ourselves become capable of composing new patterns. The cultural effect of good music, even if it is wordless, can be considerable. It is a verifiable fact that where the arts are not given the importance they deserve the popular expression of emotions is often quite chaotic.

Yet, on the other hand, music cannot be said to be real like a thing or an everyday happening. We do not **use** music as we use tables and chairs. And where we do employ music for a practical purpose, as in the case of musical therapy, we do not really attend to music as art; we rather look upon it as a kind of **medical treatment**. Nor can listening to music be regarded as a dated event in the same sense in which one's marriage and graduation are. One does not include the number of concerts attended in one's bio-data.

At the same time, it would be wrong to assume that the art of music has nothing to do with real life. The various suggestions of emotions that we find in music are identified as such only on the basis of our everyday experience. What is more, the intensity which a musician is able to put into his music may be directly related to some personal tragedy. On the other hand, we must not ignore the many clear differences between the real world and the world of music. The former comprises things, people and events; the latter is the world of *rāga*, *tāla*, *svara* and *bandiśa*. The roominess that we may 'see' in the *vilambit* singing of a great singer is not meant to accommodate people and things. Nor is musical time measured and experienced in the same way as time in daily life. To determine time in music we use beats and claps, not watches and clocks; and whereas the filling of real time is provided by the actual events of individual and social history, the content of musical time is provided by the ideally apprehended flow of *laya*, *beats*, *bol*s and the numberless patterns of varying extent, pace and design. The truth indeed is that, categorically, music can neither be said to be real nor unreal. It is certainly real in some senses of the word, but is just as clearly unreal in some others. In fact, when we listen to music we just do not raise the question as to whether it is real or unreal; our judgement is suspended, and we only contemplate the music. Music liberates us, if only for a short while, from considerations of reality and unreality, and of utility and disutility. This is an important meaning of the traditional Indian emphasis that aesthetic experience or *rasānubhūti* is *vitavighna* or transcendent of obstacles to the realisation of the one seamless Reality.

'Truth' has been taken in quite a few ways. The best known views here are: truth as correspondence, and truth as coherence. According to the first of these, being true is to be true to **some objective** norm, fact or situation; and, according to the second, truth is a matter of internal harmony. It is easy to illustrate these two views. When I describe a happening correctly, my description is regarded as being true **to** the event; and when I say: "*A* is the best girl in the class, but *B* is also equal to her", my remark is said to be untrue simply because its two parts, which the comma serves to distinguish, contradict each other. The very meaning of the word 'best' is better than everyone else. If *A* is the best of all students **in this sense**, how can *B*, or anyone else, be equal to *A*? In other words, in first calling *A* as the best (girl) student, and then equating *B* with her, I contradict myself; and so commit an untruth.

Let us now see how these theories of truth can be applied to music, so as to suggest some questions of philosophical aesthetics. It is common knowledge that a classical vocalist has to be true **to** the demands of *svara*, *rāga* and *tāla*. So, an obvious philosophical question of truth with regard to a particular bit of music would be: 'Is this music true to the demands of *svara*, *rāga* and *tāla*'? Be it noted, however, that the answer to this question can be provided only through the exercise of percipience, and not through thinking or ordinary listening. That no mere thinking would here suffice is easy to see. Whether a *svara* is being rendered truly or not is obviously not a matter of argument, but is to be judged by actual perception of a trained listener, or, in other words, by percipience. It is common knowledge that, however attentive be the way in which a man presently listens to the music, the truth of a *svara*, or of the rhythmic aspect of singing, cannot be judged by him if he has not trained his ear and imagination through long years of actual listening to music. The judgement as to whether a particular *rāga* is being rendered truly or not is a more complex affair. It may be said to involve a double activity of imagination: positive and negative. To illustrate, the listener may have to judge that the music he is attending to is, positively, an exposition of *rāga* Bhūpālī: and, negatively, that it is not a treatment of *rāga* Deśkār.

Another important form in which a philosophical question of truth may be put about music may be put thus. Is the musician at work true to his own conception of good music, or is he merely trying to be true to the way of a master? This question too, it is clear, can be answered only by a *rasika*, i.e., by one who possesses enough prior experience of musical listening.

Let us now turn to the coherence theory of truth. Here, some obvious questions of philosophical aesthetics, of course, in relation to music, would be as follows:

> Is it consistent or proper to bring an extra measure of easy appeal to *vilambit* singing by incorporating some light-hearted and quick embellishments in the way of a *ṭhumrī*?
>
> Is a morning *rāga* rendered truly if the text of its composition smacks of cheap sensuousness? This question again is to be decided by a *rasika* who can truly judge as to whether a particular musical passage or combination of *svaras* evokes images of dawn, emergence of light, yearning in prayer, or mere light-hearted frolic.

Ordinarily, music is regarded as good only if it tickles the ear. But it would be wrong to believe that this is the only reason of its significance. Music is important also because it gives us some **knowledge**; and it is the task of philosophical aesthetics to bring out — say, as follows — how this end is, in fact, achieved by music:

1. Music enables us to contemplate and realise the nature of quite a few feelings and emotions better than we do in everyday life. In life what happens is this. We only experience, but do not **attend to** the states of suspense, and expectation; and we feel gratified when we are able to get what we have been looking forward to. Now, all such states of the mind can become objects of explicit attention when we listen to music. This happens, for example, when the vocalist, projecting *rāga* Puriyā, tarries at the *niṣād* in a tantalising way; and then touches the *śadaj* in a moment of consumate sweetness after a momentary glimpse of *r̥ṣabha*; or when the drummer attains to the *sama* with split second accuracy and in a well-designed way. In everyday life we only undergo the states of mind referred to, and let them pass without attending to their own character. But in musical listening we come to know how they feel.

   Further, when we experience sadness or tranquillity in everyday life, our experience of how they feel is mixed up with the awareness of a specific objective situation, and with the impulse to deal with that situation in terms of behaviour of a particular kind. But in listening to, say, *ālāp* in Jogiyā, Sohinī, Lalit or Yaman Kalyān, we may get a chance to contemplate the sadness and tranquillity in complete isolation from involvement with any objective situation or with the impulse to behave in a particular way.

2. It is important to note that the musician himself may come to know, through the music which he produces, more about specific mental states than in the light of his personal experience in daily life. This must, however, be brought out.

   It is true that, like an ordinary person, the musician too has his own experiences of sorrow, joy and jealousy. But apart from his own personal experiences of these emotions, we may suppose, he has also come to know something about them, say, as a result of his talking to people and reading books. Now, he may well avail of these extra-individual sources of his knowledge of emotions when he tries to project them in his own music; and when this happens his own felt knowledge of these emotions may be deepened and enlarged. This explains why Susanne K. Langer speaks as follows:

   > Music . . . bespeaks his (the composer's) imagination of feelings

rather than his own emotional state; and expresses what he knows about the so-called 'inner life'; and this may exceed his personal case, because music is a symbolic form to him through which he may learn as well as utter ideas of human sensibility.[1]

3. Today, aestheticians like S.K. Langer and Nelson Goodman insist that art gives us **knowledge**, say, of the ways in which an emotion gets evoked, arrested or expressed. Our own experience of listening to music justifies the view that this art gives us a knowledge of the ways in which *svara*s and rhythmic beats can be combined in ever more beautiful ways. Above all, musical listening gives us the definite knowledge that, though it is, on the one hand, a specific individual form, a *rāga* is, on the other hand, never quite exhausted by its individual expositions. Indeed, *rāga*-music is a clear illustration of the way in which something can be both specific and organised, and yet infinite in significance.

Finally, in so far as it has not been clearly brought out, let us turn again to the truth that the analytic approach in aesthetics today does not slur over the evidence of fact and actual practice. Consider, for instance, the concept of 'empathy' which occurs freely in our talk about attention to art, and is true also to an aspect of our musical listening. What does this word mean? Is it identical with what is called imaginative sympathy? By way of answering questions such as these, and also to make it clearer how philosophical aesthetics concerns itself with questions of meaning, we may here reflect as follows, essentially in the way of C.J. Ducasse as manifest in his well-known work: *The Philosophy of Art*.[2]

Empathy is the more or less intuitive identification with, and perception of, the **dramatic** quality of an **agent** or **patient** who is real or is supposed to be real. We may now explain what we have just said by first considering an illustration of empathetic perception. Suppose, as we enter a room we see a statue which appears to be extending a hand towards us.

Now, the work may be so powerful that the moment we see 'the extended hand' we may feel impelled either to extend our own hand **towards it**, or just to imitate the action, though not in the direction of the statue itself. Here, if we react in the second way, we quickly identify ourselves with the represented 'action'; perceive the statue not as a mere lifeless object, but as an individual; and so imitate 'his' action. This is what is meant by empathetic perception.

This mere illustration is, however, not enough. We have to do a little more thinking by attending to the other words in our definition of empathy, namely, 'agent', 'patient', and 'dramatic'.

An agent is a doer, anyone who initiates and sustains a change or a process. The word 'patient' is here to be taken not in the sense of a sick person, but as anyone who **incurs or suffers** an experience. When **I do** something I am obviously the agent of the action. On the other hand, when something is **done to me** — say, when I am hit — I just have or suffer an experience, and am in that sense a patient. It is obvious that suffering an experience is not action in the same sense in which causing or producing an experience is. If that is so, and if, as is admitted, the word 'dramatic' originally means 'relating to action', how is Ducasse justified in speaking of the dramatic quality of an agent **or** patient? This is obviously a question arising from a consideration of meaning; and is therefore, a philosophical question, specially because it makes us wonder about the accordance of one idea ('dramatic') with another ('patient'). Ducasse's answer is that the present meaning of 'dramatic' or 'drama' is not the same as their derivative meaning; that, **in actual fact**, an actor in a play does not merely deliver speeches, but also appears **to suffer** conflicts and emotions; and that therefore, the meaning of the word 'dramatic' should be enlarged to cover **the having of an experience, or the conscious living through the course of an experience**.

In any case, empathy means that, for a while, we identify ourselves (imaginatively) with the object and perceive its **doing** or **suffering** clearly. This is surely quite different from merely perceiving the design of the object. At the same time, we must remember that, though what is here perceived is a dramatic (not a merely structural) quality, it is necessarily regarded as a quality of the object itself, exactly as the up-and-down movement of a *tāna* appears to be of the pattern itself. To take an example from a visual art, in case I am looking at a landscape painting which shows a path in a forest of trees laden with flowers, if the path is perceived as meandering its way, lazily, through the forest, or if the flowers are perceived as perching gently on the twigs, it would be a case of empathetic perception. If, on the other hand, the path appears to me as an **inviting** walking place, and if the flowers seem to tempt me to smell or pluck them, it would not be a case of empathy, but (according to Ducasse) only a case of **peripathy**.

It may here also be noted that though, on the one hand, empathy is not a matter of reasoning, but is only a kind of perception, it is not a matter of feeling either. Empathy is not the same thing as sympathy. How the two differ is easy to see. First, according to Ducasse, when we sympathise with an object, we, so to say, receive it within the fold of *our* being; it becomes a part of what we are. In a moment of sympathy we experience an enlargement of the self. On the other hand, when we empathise the dramatic quality of an object, we forget for a while what **we** are; identify ourselves with the object, and perceive **its** doing or suffering in utter separateness from self-awareness. Second, whereas sympathy is essentially a matter of feeling — a feeling for others — empathy (we have seen) is in general, a perception of the **action** represented in the object.

AESTHETICS AND THE WAYS OF PHILOSOPHY

The linguistic-analytic approach is one of the two major approaches required for a proper study of philosophical aesthetics. Its main function is to expose the **lack of clarity** in our writing. It also seeks to show how a 'craving for generality' can impel one to make too sweeping statements about art. But it would be wrong to suppose that this approach is confined to mere talk about art; it is by no means indifferent to the fact of art. How, indeed, can a statement be shown to be too sweeping unless we are able to point to some **facts** which are not covered by it? However, to get a clear idea of how the linguistic-analytic approach works in aesthetics, we must discuss some examples.

Take, for instance, the following specimens of some actual writing on music:

1. Music is identifiable with the delight of the Self that realises by conscious attention a beautiful or meaningful tonal matrix out of sound matrix in action, feeling and understanding.[3]

Here, for the sake of simplicity, let us consider only the following opening words of the quotation cited: "Music is . . . of the self". If music is really itself the 'delight of the self', we straightaway ask, can it also be the **cause** or **source** of this delight, as it is generally taken to be? Further, when we say, "Come, let us go to listen to 'his' music, do we mean that we should listen to the delight of 'his' self? It would be absurd if we meant that. Again, if we take the decision that a study of music should be made compulsory in all the teaching institutions, do we resolve to make a study of spiritual delight binding on all? We can hardly say, yes.

2. Music is sometimes identified with the realisation of music, but realisation as the location of music can at best be called the ground of musical process.[4]

Here, again, let us look at the words actually used. What could the writer mean by the **realisation** of music? One can only say: the translation of one's idea of music into audible sound, rhythm and structure; or, quite simply, practical music. But if the realisation of music only means practical music, it would obviously be an understatement to say that music is (only) **sometimes** identified with the realisation of music. The word in question is improper, because it makes for an understatement. Let us turn, next, to **location**. How is it to be taken? As the **act** of localising music — say, on a musical instrument — or the (proper) **place** where music is presented? The trouble is that in neither sense can the realisation of music be said to be its mere 'location'. To be sure, to realise music is to realise its perceptual charm and aesthetic significance; but such 'realisation' is certainly much more than the mere playing of music at some instrument; and, of course, it is not the hall in which the music is presented.

3. Musicology, i.e., theory and history of music, is talk about music. Metamusicology is talk about musical theories.[5]

Here, the author's intention is, of course, to distinguish musicology from metamusicology. But the intention will be carried out only if the words, 'talk about music' are prefaced with scholarly emphasised (or italicised). In its present form, the first sentence is likely to convey the wrong impression that musicology is (just **plain**) talk about music.

4. In every art, the distinction between the good and the bad is made. The good is called beautiful or aesthetic. . . .[6]

Here, the first sentence is all right. But, let us look at the second. It implies that all good works of art are (necessarily) beautiful. This is clearly wrong. Today, there are quite a few works of art which are said to be not merely good, but great; and the reason of their excellence is said to be their expressiveness, *not their beauty.* Two good examples of such art-works are: Picasso's *Guernica*, and Goya's *The Colossus.*

This is how analytic attention to verbal meaning exposes the lack of clarity in our writing on music.

AESTHETICS AND PHENOMENOLOGY

As for the phenomenological way of doing aesthetics, it may be brought out by considering the three key concepts of phenomenology: intentionality, constitution and performance.

1. Consider, to begin with, the concept of intentionality. It is quite different from intention. An intention is a plan. It is fixed in the sense that one is supposed to stick to it, to carry it out, instead of changing it continually. Also, it is an aiming at some future achievement. Intentionality, on the other hand, is immediately involved in every mental act, as much in just being silent as in perceiving a present object and in thinking. As such, intentionality is constantly changing process.

   Now, in thinking about creation in art generally, intentionality — or the mind's immediate involvement with what is done or avoided at the moment — keeps us close to truth. For the making of a work of art is truly not the faithful execution of a **pre**-fixed plan. It may be that the artist sets out to create a work according to some plan. But when creation actually begins, what happens is that he gets deeply involved with the detail of the moment — may be, the line he draws or the tuft of syllables being danced; contemplates and responds to its individual character;[7] makes it fine or sparkling according to his passing fancy; and is then impelled to take the next step accordingly. In other words, the course of creation proceeds not as the artist's independent working out of a pre-fixed plan, but as responsiveness to what the detail being made at present suggests or demands. As a result, the completed work may turn out to be something quite different from what it was initially planned to be. It is indeed intentionality which explains the possibility that the completed work of art may turn out to be quite different from what the artist originally intended it to be. Thus, one important aesthetical view, that a work of art is an 'emergent' — or the appearance of something which was not quite pre-planned[8] — is supported with reason by a distinction that phenomenology makes.

   There is at least one other way in which the concept of intentionality helps us realise a truth about art. It is the artist's involvement with what he is presently doing — or the loving care he lavishes on the detail being created — that partly enables him to stamp the doing with his individual manner of treatment or **style** or, in the case of music, *gāyakī* or *bāj*.

It is, however, a bit too general to say that art creation, at its best, proceeds more on the basis of intentionality than as the execution of a preformed intention. Some details of the matter have to be brought out, because what is directly given to the mind — say, during the course of singing — can change infinitely; and the phenomenological approach must take note of the resulting changes in the artist's experience. Thus, where the vocalist tries to establish the form of a *vilambit sthāyī*, what is directly given to him is the form of a *rāga*, the form of a *tāla*, and the structure of the *bandiśa* itself. Here, the artist's involvement with the immediately given is necessarily an experience of getting attuned with, and so becoming more clearly conscious of the three given elements listed. On the other hand, when the singer sings the *tāra sā* reposefully and tunefully what he experiences is just a feeling of absorption in the sweetness of the note, and not the vivification of any form. Here, of course, in the tuneful utterance of the note the artist completely rises above the idea of a plan, and of a preceding and succeeding context. But, where he is seen to do what is technically called *barhat*, however intense be his involvement with the directly given, the implicit sense of a plan must be said to determine his singing. Thus, *barhat* in *rāga Lalit* is a planned, though of course reverential, ascent to the two *madhyamas*; and in *rāga*-music generally, the artist is nowhere free during the process of music-making to ignore the technical character of the *rāga*. The plan of the melody-type (*rāga*) must be all along adhered to. To conclude, though intentionality is certainly the basis of creative freedom in the forming of our music, the part played by intention and a measure of planning cannot be denied.

2. Turn now to another concept which phenomenology favours: constitution. Here, it means not the act of physical establishment or institutionalisation, as when we speak of constituting a new society or of preparing a 'constitution' for a country that has just won freedom and become a new state, but an interpretative reading, a construing, a making out (not merely making), an 'experiencing-as'. Constitution, thus regarded, is said to go along with 'reduction' which, according to Husserl, means

stripping the object of all its relations and properties that make it significant in life. All this, however, has got to be clarified:

Consider the case of a classical singer. Suppose, after singing the tonic (सा) for a while, he turns to *komala ṛṣabha*. Now, from the common, grammatical point of view, this note has the relational property of falling between the tonic and the *śuddha ṛṣabha*. It may also be thought of as capable of making the trained listener experience some tenderness. But, the singer himself, as engaged in the act of creating music, does not consciously think of the note in these 'before-after' and 'cause-effect' ways,[9] though he certainly does not forget the right location of the note in the scale. He deals with it in his own way. He may choose to invest **the note** with a yearning tenderness or to make it appear steady and luminous, which is all quite different from **aiming at making the listener** experience these effects. This is what is meant by the joint working of 'constitution' and 'reduction'.

It may here be objected that 'reduction' — that is, indifference to a thing's setting in actual life — is possible only where art is non-representational. But take the case of cinematography. Nobody would deny its net effect of representational realism. But even here the initial approach is to ignore the reality of the screen as a mere surface and to regard it as a possible locus of objects that appear to have a 'depth'. So, we cannot easily dismiss the insistence of phenomenology that 'reduction' and 'constitution' are relevant to every art-form and every work of art.

3. The artist, however, does not merely regard or deal with his materials in his own way, but as a rule creates a complete work of art. This takes us to the last of the three concepts we listed at the outset: **performance**.

   It may be taken to be synonymous with 'production'. But why does phenomenology use these words, instead of the established word **creation**? The answer could be that whereas 'creation' can be taken in a merely ideal sense — to be sure, we freely speak of creative ideas, and Croce actually identified creation with mere experience — 'performance' clearly suggests some overt doing, some actual manipulation of materials.

But another protest could here be that whereas the making of art is necessarily the emergence of something new, the word 'performance' is not thus suggestive at all. To this it may be rejoined that if 'performance' is taken along with intentionality, constitution and reduction — which, if taken as one, convey the sense that the material is stripped of its everyday significance *and* is treated quite freely by the artist in his own individual way — the defect in question would at once seem remedied.

Performance is a making, a doing, an artistic production. From the viewpoint of everyday talk the word is eminently applicable to the performing arts. But, phenomenology uses it to describe all artistic making; and, regarded as making or production, the word at once provides for the element of physical manipulation of material in art creation. What is, however, distinctive of the phenomenological approach here is that even art *contemplation* is regarded as 'performance'. If it be contended that this is rather an overstretching of the applicability of the word, the answer would be that, in terms of common aesthetic discourse, even the word 'creation' covers both the constitution of the **aesthetic** object and the production of the work. In any case, the onlooker (or the reader) does not simply passively watch or receive what the 'performance' has to deliver. He makes a collaborative effort — 'collaborative' because he is throughout helped and guided by the work — which begins with a decoding of the work, and succeeds, through repeated acts of attention — in arriving at his own reading of the work of art, a 'secondary noema'.[10] This 'reconstitution' too is done not strictly according to a pre-fixed plan, but under the stress of whatever appears immediately striking in the 'object', partly because of the specific training and orientation of the onlooker. Here too, in the contemplator's attitude, intentionality — as against the mere intention to find this or that meaning — plays a vital part. Ultimately, after the decoding and reconstitution done by him, what remains with the contemplator is a residue of meaning, and eventually a souvenir, a sheer remembrance of his own experience; but in no case is the secondary 'noema' identical with the primary one, or that of the artist. Thus the initial 'intention' is never identically reconstituted and we may ignore for ever what image the artist 'had in mind'. All we can judge, identify ourselves with, read, constitute, decode, interpret is his performance or the result thereof, the (work) before our eyes.[11]

Indeed, Husserl would say that when we attend to a work of art in the right way we do not transport it into any abstract 'space of contemplation' or analyse it in a merely objective way, but react to it in numberless, minute and very personal ways, so that here, in aesthetic experience, "even the purest 'untainted' and self-contained work breaks up into a bundle of intentionalities".[12]

Having seen what philosophical aesthetics generally is, we may pay a little attention also to some such aesthetical concepts as are expected to occur quite freely in our study of form (as aesthetic) in Hindustānī Music. These concepts may be listed as follows:

1. The Aesthetic Attitude
2. Aesthetic Experience
3. The Aesthetic Point of View
4. Aesthetic Judgement
5. Aesthetic Predicates.

The Aesthetic Attitude

Now, to begin with the first of these, we may straightaway cite the following definition put forth by J. Stolnitz:

> The aesthetic attitude is the attitude of disinterested and sympathetic attention to, and contemplation of any object of awareness whatever for its own sake alone.

The important words in this definition may now be explained. To begin with, the aesthetic attitude is one of **disinterested** attention. It is disinterested not in the sense that it does not involve interest, but in the sense that it is without such interest as may prevent us from giving our full attention to the object. It is obvious that when we attend to an object of art in the right way, we often feel captivated by it, we give it all our attention, **and for sometime do not think of anything at all**. So the word 'disinterested' cannot be taken in the negative sense of 'lacking in interest'. What the word in question positively means is that when our attitude to the object is really aesthetic, our attention is full and impartial, like that of the judge who attends to both sides of the case without any bias for any side. If I attend to a dramatic play only because the central character in it is a friend of mine, the attention is plainly not aesthetic for I do **not** attend to the play **for its own sake**. The same may be said when I purchase a painting merely because the possession of it will raise my status in the eyes of others.[13] The disinterested quality of the aesthetic attitude really means that when I adopt such an attitude with regard to an object, I am completely cut away from such practical considerations as to how this thing is going to be useful to me. Such separation of an object from our practical needs and fears has been called "distancing" by Bullough.

This at once gives us a clue to the meaning of the word 'sympathetic'. The aesthetic attitude is sympathetic in the sense that, instead of looking at the object in the light of **our** needs and expectations, we give it enough time to reveal *its own* significance to us. It also means that, instead of remaining confined to the outer aspects of the object, we try to get into its essential spirit. The next word, 'contemplation' means that in the aesthetic attitude we dwell on the object for quite sometime, and are not distracted by what is unrelated to it.

The only idea which now remains to be brought out is the one implicit in the words: "any object of awareness whatever". We may here consider a question. Can the aesthetic attitude be really adopted with regard to **any** object? Now, we may not answer this question with a ready 'yes'. For nobody has in fact tried to adopt this attitude with regard to **everything** that is there. We can only speak negatively, and say that no limit may be drawn to the number of objects to which the aesthetic attitude can be adopted. A new artist may well make us see great significance in an object which has so far appeared quite simple and uninteresting to us.

We may now take an example of the aesthetic attitude to illustrate the points made out above. Consider the case of a man contemplating the beauty of a rainbow. He is not concerned with the question as to whether the rainbow **really** hangs in the sky as it seems to. Nor does he consider the question as to how his attention to the rainbow is going to help him. He may not even try to understand how such an appearance is created in the horizon. So, the attitude of the man is here neither practical nor theoretical. It is simply aesthetic. His concern is neither with the utility nor with the reality or scientific significance of the object, but only with its beauty.

Having understood what the aesthetic attitude is, let us see how a *bandiśa* of Hindustānī classical music may be so looked at. To begin with, we have to attend to the *bandiśa* not merely because it is a composition of the *gharānā* to which ***we*** belong; nor from the viewpoint of its possible saleability if recorded, but for the sake of its own character and charm. Further, our attention to it has to be sympathetic as well; it will not do merely to identify the *rāga-tāla* of the *sthāyī-antarā* twosome. We have also to see if the inner details of the *bandiśa* are in tune and properly interlinked. This is what it means to attend to form in music in a disinterested and sympathetic way. What is more, we have to contemplate the form in question; to notate or even to hum it would be a merely practical, not a contemplative activity. But, be it noted, contemplation is an activity, not a passive state of awareness. Here we purposely attend to what meets the ear and actively follow it and explore its details from the inside, shutting out, at the same time, all those sounds — such as the singer's occasional cough or the drummer's use of his own little hammer for bringing 'the right one' (दायाँ) back to tune (*sur*) — which are not really integral to the music. Likewise, in maintaining the aesthetic attitude in respect of a *bandiśa* we have to attend to it for its own sake alone. This means that, while listening to it we do not allow the physical appearance of the artist — say, his dress and gestures — to distract our attention from the music.

Similarly, in listening to a *sthāyī* (first half of the *bandiśa*), even a little wonder as to what the *antarā* (second half of the *bandiśa*) is going to be may weaken the requisite character of the aesthetic attitude towards the *sthāyī*. But no such risk will be there if a hint about the possible form of the *antarā* is implicit in the terminal phrase of the *sthāyī* itself; because, in this case, *sthāyī* will still remain the focus of our attention.

Further, the aesthetic attitude will also suffer if, at the moment of the vocalist's transition from *vilambit* to *drut khyāl*, the *tablā* player is not at once able to adjust himself to the change in pace, because if it so happens our attention will turn away from the singing to the drumming. It may be added that if our attitude towards the *sthāyī* is to remain aesthetic, we will certainly register the details of *svara*, *rāga*, *tāla* and *sāhitya*, but not too explicitly. If, even for a moment, we begin to admire the poetic quality of the text of the song, our attention will deviate from the musical aspect of the *bandiśa*; and, to that extent, our aesthetic attitude towards the form of the *sthāyī* will weaken.

Aesthetic Experience

Ordinarily, aesthetic experience is taken to mean the delight that we take in the beauties of nature and art. As such, it has a wider appeal than many other kinds of experience, such as moral and intellectual.

It is also important for aesthetics. Indeed, some aestheticians, like Clive Bell and Pepita Haezrahi, maintain that aesthetic experience alone is the true *starting-point* of aesthetics. Others insist that talk about art is meaningful only if it is *somehow based on* aesthetic experience.[14]

To begin with, we may say that aesthetic experience is always an exercise in percipience or perceptiveness or clarity of perception; and that such perception is 'aesthetic' in so far as its clarity arises in part, but necessarily, from indifference to the everyday considerations of usefulness and real existence. Except in the case of literary works, a clear notice of the perceptual details of the objects is a necessary starting-point, if not the whole of an aesthetic experience. Yet, perception as aesthetic cannot be **identified** with aesthetic experience. Even trained and subtle perception does not cover all the features of aesthetic experience: say, its many felt movements; the sense of flowing along with, or of following, the course of the art-work; the exchanges of being, so to say, between self and the object — for instance, the radiation of being with wonder and delight on seeing a resplendent sunrise, a sunset on the river Brahmaputra, or the Tāj for the first time; or the suck of the sweetness of a musical *svara* or phrase that seems to yearn for something far away. Aesthetic experience is indeed pretty often a very rich mass of organised sensations, thought, half-blown impulses to visualise what may come next, and occasional uneasiness at the thought that the aesthetic promise of a detail or segment has not been fully brought out. Reference may here be made to moments when, during the course of musical listening, we feel that a single *svara* — say, the *tāra ṣaḍaj* has not been duly 'fed', or that the *sthāyī* has not been firmly 'established'. What is more, as when we admire the expressiveness of a song, aesthetic experience often includes the recognition — and sometimes the actual experience — of the emotion projected in the work. Therefore, we cannot **identify** aesthetic experience with mere perception, however refined it be. A music critic or musicologist may be able to perceive every detail of the sound of the ongoing music, but his experience will yet not be properly aesthetic if he does not, for a while, lose himself in the emotive expressiveness of the song. To conclude, aesthetic experience is that kind of experience which does not care for the usefulness or reality of the object experienced; it is an experience which is satisfying in itself; and it is not troubled by the thought as to how it is going to further our theoretical or practical interests.

To confine ourselves to music, the following points may be made about aesthetic experience:

(a) It is primarily a clear and correct perception of the perceptual, decorative and emotive character of all the sounds and passages that the music presents.

(b) It is also, if not all along, the perception of the form of the *sthāyī-antarā* twosome and the pattern or *tāna*s. It may here be added that, in so far as the bulk of our music is set to a definite rhythm cycle too, the aesthetic experience of our music is, in a way, generally bifocal. In other words, we experience not only the *rāga*, but the *tāla* which the music builds upon.

(c) Finally, we must remember that, though patience is certainly necessary on the part of the *rasika* to allow the music to unfold its glories, our aesthetic experience of music cannot be said to be wholly passive. We admire the skill with which a vocalist is able to preserve the purity of the *rāga* he has chosen by keeping it distinct all along from the other *rāga*s which may be close to it; and we also at times anticipate, and may be correctly, the tuft of *svara*s which is to follow the one being projected presently. So, our aesthetic experience of music does not simply demand a good deal of past experience and training, but also an active and present exercise of discrimination and imagination.

The Aesthetic Point of View

Another essential factor which influences our perception of form in art is the aesthetic point of view. This is, obviously, not only a point of view, but a **particular** one too. It is also quite different from the aesthetic attitude just discussed. The basic difference between the two is that whereas an attitude is the way in which **the subject** is **disposed towards the object**, a viewpoint is, on the other hand, **the angle from which an object is considered**. To put it differently, whereas a viewpoint is merely **adopted** by a man, an attitude **is his** own orientation towards the object. It is true that a viewpoint and an attitude often go together; yet the distinction remains. An attitude may well be a disposition **to feel**, but a viewpoint is essentially a way of **regarding** a thing. It relates to perception and thinking, not to feeling. A man's **attitude** can be easily sympathetic. But there is nothing like the sympathetic **point of view**.

The word 'point' too is here important. As a **point** of view, a viewpoint is determinate or specific in two senses. First, it is different from the other points of view; and second, it has its own set way of working. In other words, a point of view is also implicitly exclusive; it not only requires us to look for some specific features or qualities in the object, but also to **ignore** the others. Both these considerations apply also to the aesthetic point of view. Thus, in adopting it we get committed to pay attention to some specific features in the object of attention, and to abstain from caring for such matters as its possible usefulness.

Positively, to adopt the aesthetic point of view is to care only for the **aesthetic value** of the object, or for the satisfaction that a work of art can give by **virtue of its formal unity and (or) regional qualities** as revealed to the *trained* attention of a normal person (*rasika*). Two points to be noted here are that value is inseparable from, though not identical with, satisfaction; and second, that however various be the ways in which they may be found in the different arts, formal unity and regional qualities are fairly easy to determine.

Now, to give a little individual attention to the two concepts, formal unity is the **unity of form**. Its full meaning can, however, be had only by reflecting on the two words separately. Now, in aesthetics, 'form' is the unique internal organisation of a work of art, and not the mere shape of an object. Similarly, 'unity' too may be taken in two senses: the quality or state of being a complete unit; or unity as distinct from variety or plurality. But the unity of a work of art is no mere singleness; it is rather a complex unity which incorporates differences in an orderly way. Every work of art is **unity of distinguishable parts** which retain their **individuality**, but this individuality **is not so** assertive as to weaken the unity of the whole. In other words, an art-work is an articulate unity. So, taking both words together, 'formal unity' may be taken to mean the completeness and coherence of a work of art.

Let us now pay some individual attention to 'completeness' and 'coherence'.

COMPLETENESS

To adopt the aesthetic point of view is at once to decide to see whether or not a work, which is presently attended to, is or appears to be complete. But we cannot speak of **completeness** in exactly the same sense of the word in respect of every art. In the region of occurrent arts like music, dance and dramatic presentation, where we see the work being actually made — and are therefore in a position to note its beginning, middle and end — it makes sense to say that the work in question is complete or incomplete. On the other hand, we cannot speak of completeness **in this sense** in respect of non-occurrent arts like painting, sculpture and architecture. Speaking quite generally, a painting is often considered to be complete if it has a clearly marked frame, as standing out against the neutral colour of the wall. To make it appear complete, it is most essential that none of **its** colours should seem to run out into a similar colouring of the wall. This risk is much less in an "assembled painting" than in one of a conventional type using pigments alone. But, in many cases, it is difficult to isolate completeness from coherence. To illustrate, in the case of a dramatic play, to determine its completeness we have to look at its opening and following scenes. However, as in many of Shakespeare's plays, a good opening scene not only comes before the other scenes, but also gives us a glimpse of the spirit of the entire play. In other words, it goes well, **or is coherent with** the other scenes. Thus, when we try to mark the completeness of a play, we naturally give some attention to its coherence as well. What we have said is also applicable to music, and more particularly to rhythm. In any *tāla*, the first beat or *mātrā*, i.e., the *sama*, is of value not only as the immanent goal of the rhythmic movement, but as that which sets the pace of what follows it. In other words, it directly determines the speed of the playing that follows. Thus, if we utter the *sama* of *tāla dhamār* very briefly (or quickly) as a dainty dot — say as क् — the following *bols*, namely धिट धिट will also have to be spoken at the same speed. On the other hand, these will have to be correspondingly decelerated if the *sama* is uttered as a leisurely का. Conversely, that way of completing a recital is not good either which sacrifices the coherence of the *gat* or *sthāyī*. This may be easily explained. Generally, when a recital reaches its final (*ati drut*) stage the pace is so hectic that the inner design of both the *ṭhekā* and the *bandiśa* becomes indistinct and mutilated; in other words, coherence is sacrificed. This is obviously not a good way to complete a recital. So, once again, we see the impossiblity of separating completeness from coherence in music.

It is here also essential to distinguish completeness from self-comple**tion** and self-complete**ness**. A statue with all its limbs intact is a simple case of actual completeness which will not be regarded as a merely external matter of unbroken outline if the work's inner design too is complete. But completeness, as mere termination, may also seem to be merely imposed on a work. Thus, in a duet recital of instrumental music (*jugalbandī*) — or even in a solo exposition of the same accompanied by *tablā* — when, at the *ati drut* stage, and towards the end of the recital, the music loses all its structured appearance, the performers may **have** to bring it to a close, and to even show that they are doing it, by openly banging their instruments to signal the end. On the other hand, when a properly structured *sthāyī* attains to the *sama* in a natural way, it may seem to be **completing** itself.

However, the two suggestions of self-comple**tion** and complete**ness as contributed by the artist**, may also occur as a kind of mutual supplement. Thus, in good *Kathak* dancing, at the completion of a pattern, the dancer too may stop dancing for a while in terms of a still posture, thus actively contribut**ing** to the completeness of the pattern which may also seem to be self-completing because of its shapely inner design. This suggestion, that a work of art is complet**ing** itself, can be more easily had in occurrent arts. That self-completeness is essentially a matter of the dynamics of internal design may be brought out by considering some artistic designs which are not actually, but only virtually, complete. For instance, rhythmic patterns of *anāgat* variety are so organised that they are not actually complete, in the sense that they do not really touch the *sama*; yet their internal design is such that they easily enable the *rasika* to complete the gap between the *bol* that marks the end of the pattern and the *sama*.

COHERENCE

Coherence or consistency is the other important meaning of formal unity. Therefore, that work of art in which the details blend in such a way that they seem to harmonise and heighten each other's significance as they appear in the completed work, even though the work may have been made out of very diverse materials, can be said to be a formal unity. The term is much closer to the aesthetic meaning of form than mere completeness, 'form' in relation to art being simply the unique internal organisation of a work.

But we can speak of coherence in at least two ways: as aesthetic and as theoretical. The former is found in art and it means that two or more details **in fact** make an agreeable unity. The appeal here is to the evidence of facts and not to any accord of meaning which is what theoretical coherence means. Thus, in music a *svara* which **actually** appears pleasing to the ear when played along with, or immediately after, another note is aesthetically concordant (*saṁvādī*). On the other hand, we dismiss the idea of **two best** students in a class as logically incoherent, because the word 'two' clashes with 'best' in respect of meaning. We cannot say that in a particular music concert the item rendered by Kishori Amonkar was the best and that Prabha Atre's was also equally good. By virtue of its very meaning 'the best' can only be **one**.

The difference between these two kinds of consistency can be more clearly understood by considering them both in relation to the same case. Thus 'silence' **means** 'absence of sound', and is therefore **theoretically** inconsistent with sound. But, **aesthetically** the two may not clash at all. In fact, subtly regulated pauses of **silence** only heighten the effect of musical **sounds**.

There is no rigid limit to the kinds of materials which can be agreeably combined in art. For example, in music even *vivādī* notes are sometimes used with great effect by master musicians. In *phirat*, this is better done after evoking an intense musical atmosphere of the *rāga*.

There are many ways in which coherence can be secured in the region of art. But its basic meaning is that the art-work should seem to be internally well-knit or cohesive. One simple way to achieve this end is as follows. A particular part or region of the work may be made to appear aesthetically central. That is, though it may not be mathematically or spatially so, it may yet seem to lend beauty or significance to all the other details; or, to put it differently, everything in the work may seem to contribute meaning or beauty to the focal detail or part. It is easy to see how this is achieved in classical music. Here, the aesthetic centre is rarely a single *svara*, but generally a relation between two specific notes. It is this relation which is known as *saṁvāditva*; and the ideal for actual music really is that this relation should be manifest not only in the *sthāyī* but so far as possible in pattern-weaving, i.e., *barhat* and *tāna*s as well. In rhythm or *tāla* we normally consider the *sama*, i.e., the first beat of the rhythm-cycle, as the focal point; and its centrality is often heightened by the *āmad* (which is a well designed approach of the *sthāyī* towards the *sama*).

Balancing the different parts of the work is yet another effective way of securing coherence in art. This is mainly done in two ways; i.e., symmetrically and and asymmetrically. The former kind of balance is provided by details which seem to be two similar halves of the same object, like the wings of a flying bird; and the latter, by balancing through contrast or opposites, as that of black and white. In the region of music, the *tīna tāla* is balanced symmetrically, and asymmetrical balance is to be seen in *rūpaka tāla*. Sheer similarity of parts is another way by which a work may be made to look balanced. In poetry this is done by employing alliterative sounds such as in "**the soft solace of my solitary hours**", or by using end-rhymes as in the following case:

लाई हयात आये, कज़ा ले चली चले,
अपनी ख़ुशी न आये, न अपनी ख़ुशी चले

In the region of rhythm, a simple example of coherence, achieved by means of similarity of parts, is provided by what is known as *tīyā*, i.e., a pattern divided into three more or less similar sub-sections.

Finally, the consistency or individuality of manner in which its different parts are made also provides coherence to a work of art. For example, the entire recital of a musician may appear single and unified because of the very way in which he all along applies his voice to the different *svara*s or *svara-samūha*s. For instance, a subtly regulated rise and fall of *ākāra* is all along seen to distinguish the music of Ustad Abdul Karim Khan and Pandit Onkar Nath Thakur, making it appear unified because of the sameness of idiom.

REGIONAL QUALITIES

Such qualities provide the other essential feature found in a work of art, apart from the formal unity. A regional quality arises from the putting-together of different parts, and is of two kinds; summative and emergent. The former arises out of mere addition and does not bring about any qualitative change. Here, only the extent of the content increases. For instance, the mere extension of a boundary wall, with a totally indentical shape and design, is a simple case of a summative regional quality. Similarly, in music the steadfast quality of a note that is sung long enough and the repeated playing of the *ṭhekā*, are other examples of this type. On the other hand, an emergent regional quality is one which arises as a result of the creative handling or organisation of details. A clear instance of this kind is the pathetic and far-away look of the *tāra komala r̥ṣabha* of *rāga* Sohnī. This quality is both regional and emergent. It is regional because it arises as we perceive the *r̥ṣabha* in relation to the preceding note *sā*; and it is emergent because it is not merely the result of the sequence of the two notes which can at best give us only the suggestion of 'higher' and 'lower'. A very clear example of how creative organisation produces emergent regional qualities is provided by the linear designs of the different kinds of *tāna*s in Hindustānī classical music.

Aesthetic Judgement

An aesthetic judgement is a report on **how** an object appears to aesthetic contemplation, or on the individual aesthetic **value** of an object. Here is an example:

1. 'This is *dhruvapada ālāpa* at its best.'

If, on the other hand a *rasika* says:

2. 'This is the *ābhoga* of this *dhruvapada* composition',

it would simply be to register the identity of a segment of the *dhruvapada* in question. It would not ascribe any **value** to the piece; it would not be **normative**, and so not an aesthetic judgement. A parallel should make the point clearer. If we say:

3. 'This is his doing',

it would not be a moral judgement. It would become 'moral' only if we say:

4. 'He has behaved nobly'.

Similarly, the first judgement we have cited **is** an aesthetic judgement. It does not simply say 'this is *dhruvapada ālāpa*, but 'this is excellent *ālāpa*'. In other words, **value** is here manifestly ascribed to the *ālāpa* in question. But, it is important to see how a (normative) **aesthetic** judgement differs from other judgements of value. Let us take some examples of the latter:

5. He has acted in the ideal way of a friend.
6. This table seems to be perfectly triangular in shape.

A little attention to these two judgements makes it clear that both of them may be said to involve a reference to a clearly conceived and commonly accepted ideal or norm, say the ideal of self-sacrifice in one case, and the definition of a triangle in the other; and that no such **clearly visualised and commonly accepted** norm is involved when an exposition of *ālāpa* is said to be **the best of its kind**. For, by such *ālāpa* one listener may simply mean that *ālāpa* the fabric of which is reposefully, sweetly and correctly (from the viewpoint of the *rāga* chosen) structured. But another listener may insist, and express his disagreement by saying that the best kind of *ālāpa* is only that which is able to work up an atmosphere of peace and tranquillity, quite **undivided** by the distinct individuality of notes and formal graces. Therefore, we may say that an aesthetic judgement is **not so objective** as a moral or intellectual judgement. This point should become clearer as we turn to some general features of a (normative) aesthetic judgement.

Consider the following judgements which are freely made on the music of the Late Ustad Bade Ghulam Ali Khan:

7. His *tāna*s are perfectly executed.
8. His music is a model of sweetness.

Now, when the judgement number 7 is made by a *rasika* the criterion on which he bases the judgement may simply be the balance of fluency and *dānā* (or discreteness of *svara*s), of which Ghulam Ali's music is indeed a perfect illustration. But another *rasika* may refuse to accept the criterion we have referred to. He may insist that the best kind of *tāna* must also appear imbued with power and elevating quality, and so he may prefer the *tāna*s of the late Pandit Onkar Nath Thakur at his best. Further, when I admire Bade Gulam Ali Khan's music for its 'sweetness' I may take the word to mean simply that quality of *svara* which never grows feeble and never appears strained or creased even at the highest *svaras* (*tāra saptak*). But my friend, while agreeing with my net judgement, may regard sweetness as a matter of emotive tenderness, and may be thinking of the *ṭhumrī*s of the late maestro while acclaiming his sweetness.

To conclude, an aesthetic judgement is not so generally based on commonly accepted criteria as moral or intellectual judgements.

Yet, it would be wrong to believe that an aesthetic judgement is merely subjective. This becomes clear when we compare an aesthetic judgement with a judgement of the merely agreeable, such as:

This is tasty food

When a man makes this judgement, his meaning only is that **he** likes this food. If he is even a little cultured, he will not insist that others also should find it tasty. On the other hand, when I say: 'this is a beautiful picture' I insist, if only implicitly, that the picture in question should appear beautiful **to others** as well. This is why when someone disagrees with my judgement, I would only be too ready to advance arguments in support of my judgement. On the other hand, as Kant pointed out, my insistence does not mean that others **must**, as matter of fact, find the picture beautiful. I only insist that others should, and **can** find the picture beautiful if they look at it properly. Another difference between a judgement of the agreeable and an aesthetic judgement is that whereas the former **is**, the latter **is not** based on a faith in the reality of the object. An apple, at a remote corner of the table, appears pleasant to a hungry man partly because he believes that it is real fruit. If he is told that the apple in question is just an imitation in clay, its pleasantness for the man would forthwith disappear. On the other hand, an interested reader's enjoyment of the Shakespearean play, Hamlet, may not be affected at all if he is told by a researcher that such a character never really lived. An aesthetic judgement is not based on considerations of the abiding reality or usefulness of the object.

References

1. S.K. Langer, *Feeling and Form*, Third Impression, 1963, p. 28.
2. Dover Publications, INC., New York, 1966.
3. Ritwik Sanyal, *Philosophy of Music*, p. 206.
4. *Ibid.*, p. 74.
5. *Ibid.*, p. 34.
6. *Ibid.*, p. 140.
7. This seizing of individual character may be said to be intuition. See, here, the following: "... It would be an abandonment of phenomenological axiology to give up intuition in aesthetic perception". H. Bratu and I. Marculescu, "Aesthetics and Phenomenology" in *The Journal of Aesthetics and Art Criticism* (hereafter referred to as *JAAC*), Spring 1979, p. 335.
8. This is the view of L.A. Reid. See his *Meaning in the Arts*, 1969.

9. This negative concern is 'reduction'.
10. An intentional experience has two aspects: 'noesis' and 'noema'. Suppose I am just wishing to hold a pen in my hand. Here, the act of wishing is 'noesis', and its objective 'meaning-content' — the pen's being held — is 'noema'. Both are different from the sensory content of an experience. In the present case there is no sensory content.
11. Ritwik Sanyal, *Philosophy of Music*, p. 340.
12. *Ibid.*, p. 341.
13. J. Stolnitz's essay, "The Aesthetic Attitude", in *Introductory Readings in Aesthetics*, ed. by J. Hospers.
14. See, here, the essay: "What makes an Experience Aesthetic" by Michael H. Mitias, in *JAAC*, Winter 1982, p. 169.

2

Of Artistic Expression

THE subject of this essay is an aesthetical study of form in music. Here some questions may be readily put. Why have we chosen **form** alone? Is **expression** not equally important in music? But our answer is ready, and may be put thus. First, within the limits of a single essay every aspect of an art cannot be studied. Second, why should we assume that form has nothing to do with expression? May not form itself be expressive in some way? The possibility may not be flatly denied, because some eminent aestheticians like Susanne K. Langer have defined art itself as **expressive form**.[1] But, a mere appeal to authority is hardly enough. We must see how form can in fact be expressive. Now, to answer this question we have to deal with two other ones. First, what is artistic expression? Second, what is form in art?

Now, to begin with the first question, expression in art is not identical with the expression of emotions in daily life. Normally, when a man gets angry the bodily changes which reveal his feeling occur automatically; he does not have to **try to make them happen**. On the other hand, when a musician wishes to put some feeling in his music he has to choose and organise the *svara-samūha*s, the precise tempo, and the modulation of voice with great care. However, in so far as the expression theory of art is not only quite popular even today, but has been the subject of great controversy among aestheticians, the entire question may be discussed at some length, by attending to the theory in question.

The Expression Theory of Art

Art has been regarded as a kind of expression by Veron and Tolstoy in the following ways:

> Art is the manifestation of emotion, obtaining external interpretation, now by expressive arrangement of line, form or colour, now by a series of gestures, sounds, or words governed by a particular rhythmical cadence.[2]

> Art is a human activity consisting in this, that one man consciously, by means of external signs, hands on to others feelings he has lived through . . .[3]

> To evoke in oneself a feeling one has experienced and having evoked it in oneself then by means of movements, lines, colours, sounds or forms expressed in words, so to transmit that feeling that others experience the same feeling — this is the activity of art. Art is not (merely) the expression of man's emotions by external signs but it is a means of union among men joining them together in the same feelings. . . . Thanks to man's capacity to express thoughts by words, we may know all that has been done for him in the realms of thought . . . So thanks to man's capacity to be infected with the feelings of others by means of art . . .[4]

Now, according to the first two views, expression in art is essentially the projection of the artist's own emotions and feelings. But, if this is true — i.e., if a work of art merely gives vent to the artist's own experienced emotions — how is any provision made for the **distinctive** significance of art? That will be done, upon this view, only if the emotions of the artist happen to be of an exceptional quality. But this is not in fact so. Second, if during the course of creation, the artist merely expresses his own emotions and feelings, then he must himself be in the immediate grip of some strong emotion. But if this really happens, he will lose the composure of mind without which the materials of art cannot be carefully chosen and organised into a work of art. The point of the argument may be brought out with the help of an example. Suppose a danseuse sets out to present the number known as *navarasamālikā* which is a string of rapidly successive emotions. If, per **impossibile**, she really comes to experience these emotions one after the other, she will lose her balance of mind, and will not at all be able to take care of the demands of *abhinaya* and *tāla*, and will fail to proceed in the way she should. Thirdly, if the excellence of an art-work lies only in its ability to express the artist's own felt emotions during the process of creation, the critic will have to ascertain from the artist himself as to what this particular emotion was before he (the critic) sets out to write his critical piece. But this is something which is never done. Therefore, the emotion which a work of art may seem to express has nothing to do with the personal emotions of the artist himself, if any, at the moment of creation.

This may also be seen by considering the case of music. Vocalists who have distinguished themselves as exponents of devotional *rāga*s have not always been devout men themselves. Nor is it necessary that a man who specialises in singing *śṛṅgārika rasa rāga*s like Bāgeṣri or Deśa should be an expert in making love. The point is borne out more clearly by the art of rhythm. The *tablā* maestro who gives a solo racital does not express any emotion whatsoever. All that he worries about is the clear and methodical projection of the patterns he chooses to play at the proper pace. Likewise, the basic need in *vilambit* singing is unhurried contemplation, and adherence to the demands of *rāga* and *tāla*, of course along with the right employment of a duly trained voice. Projection of feeling is here certainly possible, but it is only an episodic, not a necessary, feature of this musical form. Moreover, what the projection of feeling in music requires of the performing artist is only an imaginative recall and contemplation not actual experience, of the emotion in question. Yet another important factor which has to be kept in mind is that in artistic expression we just cannot separate the aspect of 'feeling' from its material media. This is so because the latter is the very means by which **it** (the feeling) is produced or created in art. To make the matter clearer, we may take the example of music. *Rasa* or feeling in this particular art is produced by a blend of many factors of which the singer's tonal quality is an important one. These two aspects of music, i.e., feeling and its media, are therefore inseparable. On the other hand, Tolstoy's remark that art enables the artist to **hand on** the feelings he has experienced to others, suggests that a work's 'feeling' is detachable from its materials.

We may now turn to the third view (of Tolstoy) which also makes a mention of the response of the *rasika* towards art. The first point to be noted in this regard is that, like in the case of the artist, the *rasika* too need not get **infected** with the feeling which a work of art expresses. He is only to see or recognise the particular expression of emotion. In other words, he (the *rasika* or the trained contemplator) is only to register the look or semblance of the feeling in the work.

From the other side, as Ducasse points that, it is by no means essential for a work of art to actually transmit feeling to a contemplator; for a work of art may be excellent as art, and yet not be **presented** to any contemplator, in which case the question of 'transmission' will not at all arise. What is more, whether or not a particular person is emotionally stirred by a work of art is no sure index of its excellence as art. A person may be too easily moved to tears by even a slightly 'sad' *ghazal* if it happens to be the one that he has himself freely hummed in his moments of despair, or if it projects an image that reminds him of some unhappy experience of his own; and yet it may not be a very good specimen of *ghazal* singing. To conclude, if the focus of the listener's attention is really on some 'sad' music itself, it would be truer to his actual experience to say that 'the music is or looks sad' to him than to say that 'it is **expressive** of sadness in his view', or that 'it may be taken to be expressive because it makes him sad'.

This is, however, not to deny that a good deal of art seems to express, or is in some other way related to, identifiable feeling or emotion. In order to understand this relation a little better we have, however, to see the distinctness of emotion in art from our everyday experience of emotion. To begin with Clive Bell, aesthetic emotion may be emphasised and characterised as follows:

> The starting-point for all systems of aesthetics must be the personal experience of a peculiar emotion. The objects which provoke this emotion we call works of art . . . . This emotion is called the aesthetic emotion.[5]

Further, in his work, *Art and Enjoying Pictures*, he described the aesthetic emotion as a kind of thrill or shock that is evoked only by the unique organisation of lines and colours. But although this view may be relevant to certain visual arts, in relation to other arts like music, where aesthetic delight takes quite sometime to emerge in its fullness, it sounds inadequate. What is more, as borne out by the following example, not merely the form, but even the very **material** of art as transformed in a work, can produce a sudden and powerful impact. See, here, the following:

> We stood gaping and struck speechless at the sight (of a bronze statue) when we saw the bronze leaving its proper province and accomplishing the works of nature. For though bronze, it blushed; and though hard

> by nature, it melted into softness yielding to the artist's skill; and though devoid of living sensation, it created the impression that sensation dwelt within it.[6]

Even according to the Indian theory of *rasa*, the right aesthetic response is not one of a momentary shock, but a deeply satisfying delight which takes time to establish itself and may last for quite sometime. In music when one listens to a good *ālāpa*, the overall experience is commonly described as one of tranquillity and elevation to a kind of contemplation serene; and only rarely does the singer's impressive use, say, of *gamak*-singing give the *rasika* a gentle shock of wondrous delight. Even in the region of painting, to which Clive Bell so freely refers, critical applause may be elicited by a quality which is quite opposed to the effect of a thrill or shock. See, for instance, the following reaction to the art of Vermeer, the famous Dutch painter.

> Every painting of Vermeer's is bathed in . . . serenity. . . . There is no violence in his work of thought or action. There is an eternal stillness, of music that dies on the echo, of the mind entranced by a message of love, of fingers that gently guide a thread of lace, of a tiny pearl suspended in delicate scales. Even Clio's eyes are downcast, as if embarrassed by the symbols of Fame she is compelled to hold.[7]

Here, an important point may be made. The quality of serenity or repose may be easily perceived by one and all in the art-works of painters like Vermeer and Cezanne. But in the field of music this quality can be perceived by that listener or *rasika* only who is used to the habit of deeply attending to the finer details or aspects of *vilambit* singing. It is very true that to relish the aesthetic emotion or *rasa* in art, the *rasika* has got to be thoroughly trained himself. This is a fact which has been overlooked by Clive Bell, but has been specially emphasised by Bharat Muni, the propounder of *rasa-siddhānta* (*rasa* theory). Even in the musical parlance of today the right kind of response to artistic beauty and significance is said to be a matter of *nigāh* or discriminating attention, and one who lacks the ability to make such responses is dismissed as a *koorh* or an ignoramus, not as a merely impassive person. In listening to music the *rasika* must be capable of subtle perceptions such as the following: the immaculate tuning of the *tānapūrā*; the ongoing invariance of rhythm as marked by the drummer, and felt as the gently supportive matrix of the whole music; the subtlety of a sudden rhythmic turn in the 'unfoldment' of a *quāyedā* on the *tablā*; and a hardly perceptible suggestion of violence to the grammatical identity of a *rāga* arising from just a little longer stay at a *svara* than is permissible.

What is, however, specially relevant to our present purpose is that there is a substantial part of our music which can be very good without being expressive of any feeling — say, for instance, *tarānā*, *trivat*, *drut gatkārī*, and solo expositions of *tablā*-rhythm; that form or *bandiśa* (structural design) is a much more pervasive feature of our music than emotive expressiveness; and that, therefore in deciding to reflect on form, as against expression in our music, we have not chosen the less important concept.

References

1. Thus see: "A work of art is an expressive form created for our perception through sense or imagination, and what it expresses is human feeling." S.K. Langer, *Problems of Art*, p. 15.
2. Eugene Veron, "Art as the Expression of Emotion", in Melvin Rader's *A Modern Book of Esthetics*, p. 51.
3. Leo Tolstoy's essay, "The Communication of Emotion", in *A Modern Book of Esthetics*, *ibid.*, 1973 edition, p. 63.
4. *Ibid.*
5. Clive Bell, *Art*, 1961, pp. 21-22.
6. Osborne, *The Art of Appreciation*, 1970, p. 119.
7. Sir Herbet Read's, "Critical Appreciation", in *Vermeer* (The Masters, 2), p. 6.

3

Form in Art

WE may now discuss what 'form' means in the region of art. In everyday talk the word conveys many meanings. Some of these which are close to, or may even be said to cover — if not to seize — the basic aesthetic meaning of the word may be listed thus: external shape or appearance, considered apart from colour or material; a structural condition, character or mode of existence exhibited by a thing — as water in the form of ice; and, finally, the manner or style of arranging and coordinating parts for a pleasing or effective result, as in the case of a literary composition.

We may now to see which of the above-mentioned meanings of **form** may be said to be its **basic aesthetic sense**. But before doing this we have to see what the word 'aesthetic' itself means. It obviously means related to aesthetics or **the arts**. The more important arts, as we know, are: painting, sculpture, architecture, *saṅgīta* and literature. We may here add that literature is perhaps the most comprehensive art. It includes drama, which itself has been regarded as a very rich art-form in India, in so far as it is often seen to include music and dance, poetry, painting, and sometimes even sculpture.

Let us now take up the first meaning: that is, form as external shape or appearance. The word 'shape' is used in respect of objects of the eye and the ear, the two aesthetic senses, according to Bharata. We may, in passing, understand why he so believes. An aesthetic sense, it is reasonable to say, is that which gives us aesthetic experience. But what is an aesthetic experience? A very simple answer to this would be: an experience which has two features. First, it is shareable; and, secondly, it unravels and revels in the structure of its object. What is more, such experience may well be shareable. When many friends relish the same dish they may be said to share the same experience of **taste**. But what they here enjoy is the taste of the edible contained in the dish, and not the **structure** of anything. In fact, it would here be meaningless to speak of the structure of the delicacy in question, though we can certainly talk about the way of preparing it. On the other hand, when we attend to an art-form like music, it is natural to speak of the beauty of its *bandiśa*, be it a *sthāyī* or a *gat*. This truth may be emphasised by saying that perception of form is a vital part of aesthetic experience. Now, in the sense of shape, the word 'form' can also be used in the context of music. We may indeed say with regard to a particular *bandiśa* that it is tight or flaccid in shape. In the region of rhythm we speak of cycles as being **symmetrical** (*tīna tāla*) or **asymmetrical** (*rūpaka*, *savārī*, etc.). In so talking of rhythm we go by the number of *mātrās*, even or odd. What is, however, important to note here is that the terms emphasised are not merely mathematical; they are partly aesthetic too. The Tāj is a model of **symmetrical** architecture. When we say so, we do not simply mean that the building can be ideally divided, by means of a vertical line, into two equal and similar halves, but also that we **like** this relation between the parts. However, an extra feature is found when we consider form as visible shape. Here we sometimes use terms which are purely mathematical or rather geometrical. Thus, we may say that a table is **oval** or **round**. But terms such as these are clearly not, as a rule, applicable to **works of art**. It would make no sense to say that a poem is square or triangular. In other words, these terms do not apply to **every** work of art. Therefore, shape (as visible) cannot be said to be the **basic aesthetic** meaning of form.

This is, however, not to deny that adjectives signifying geometrical shape **are** sometimes used in the region of particular arts. Thus, it makes perfect sense to speak as follows:

> The Kandariya Mahadeo temple (Khajurāho) is 'one of the finest example of *curvilinear* building construction.[1]
>
> This twin-towered temple (Brihadisvara temple, Tanjore, tenth-eleventh centuries) is perhaps the most imposing example of *pyramidical* form.[2]

Yet it is clear that terms such as these are not usable in respect of every work of art; and that, therefore, they cannot be said to convey the **basic aesthetic** meaning of 'form'.

There is one more point which supports what we have just affirmed. When we talk of the geometrical shape of things, we do not think it necessary to mention their other details. This can be easily illustrated. Suppose I want to buy a lamp-shade and the shopkeeper shows me one. Now if I tell him: "Show me another piece of the same shape, but in a different colour, and of a bigger size", my words will be fully understood by him, though I have not made any mention of the weight and material of the piece he has shown me. In other words, 'form' as **abstractable** shape is a perfectly intelligible use of the word. But this is just not possible in the region of our talk about art. We cannot describe the form of a poem as oval or circular. Now can we understand the form of a poem **without attending to whatever is there in it**. Take, again, the case of music. Can we say that a particular *bandiśa* is good without attending to all its details of *svara, rāga, tāla* and *calan*? Obviously not. So we see, once again, that form in art cannot be taken as mere shape.

Further, 'form' as visible appearance is obviously limited to objects which can be seen. Thus, it is common to speak of the form (or shape) of tables and teapots. But the form of a poem or of a good *bandiśa* cannot be seen, though we, of course, freely use the word 'form' in these contexts. In such regions of art, the work's form is perceived through contemplation. Hence, visible appearance cannot be regarded as the **basic aesthetic** meaning of 'form', as it cannot (in this sense) be applied to all the arts.

'Form' as a thing's distinct mode or state of existence is the word's next meaning which we may take up. This is the meaning of form when we speak thus: water in the form of ice; a mild form of the disease; wood in the form of a table, and so on. We can also talk of music in this way. Thus, we may say that *svara*, in the form of musical utterance (लगाव), is more important than as a mere element of the notational scheme. But in spite of all this, the meaning in question cannot be regarded as the **basic** aesthetic sense of 'form'. We can easily clarify this point by reflecting as to what it is to be aesthetically basic. Strictly speaking, the 'aesthetic' is that which relates to the **contemplation** or experience of a work of art, as against 'artistic' which means relating to the **making** of an art-work. Now, when we speak of *svara* as being 'more important in the form of musical utterance' what we have in mind is only the **making** of music. Therefore, the meaning of form, here, is artistic, and **not aesthetic**. Nor can it be said to be **basic** because it is hardly applicable to those arts which are non-occurrent. While listening to classical music we can certainly say that in the ongoing recital the *vādī* and *saṁvādī* have been used in their proper relational form, or that in good singing the notes of a *saragam* appear in the form of dancing accents, and not as stiff, successive steps. But in the region of other arts we attend to a work only after, not **during** its completion.

It is thus obvious that 'external shape or appearance' and 'a thing's distinct mode or state of existence' cannot be regarded as the basic aesthetic meaning of 'form'. But, as already brought out, it must also be admitted that these senses are quite meaningfully used in the region of **particular** arts in relation to their aesthetic form.

Now, the third and final meaning, which is in fact the required sense, may be put as follows:

> Form is such an arrangement of all that is there in a work of art that the entire work may be able to draw and hold the attention of the *rasika* or knowledgeable contemplator.

The key concepts in this definition are: arrangement, effectiveness of form and artistic content.

Arrangement means proper organisation, or ways of inner integration of the elements, not inoften around a focus. How this is actually done can be seen by considering some actual instances of art. However, before doing this it seems necessary to make two points regarding arrangement in a work of art. First, arrangement in a work of art is not always essentially conscious or voluntary. It may be largely determined by a working of the unconscious. This is borne out by the following remarks of Sir Herbet Read on Picasso:

> He does not know in advance what he is going to put on the canvas, nor does he decide what colours to use. He does not will to do anything.... He allows his sensibilities a free rein, paints in a trance. . . . The later pictures of Picasso (which so emerge) differ from his pure abstractions in that they do definitely represent 'something' . . . a strangely distorted female form, heads incomprehensively interlocked or dislocated, swollen forms in which one can still distinguish a stretched mouth, an occluded eye; vague rhythmical shapes which can be identified as a monstrous bust, a branch of leaves, a bowl of fruit, a

> guitar. . . . Such works of art cannot be rationally explained without some theory of the unconscious origin of imagery . . . such paintings (have) . . . a very haunting quality. . . .[3]

Secondly, whereas in many art-works all the details are so arranged that they gain an extra manifestness, in others what is projected is the whole form, not the details of the work. A good example of the latter is provided by Impressionistic painting, as for instance, "The Meadows" by Paramjit Singh.[4]

Form and Content

Turning, again, to our definition of form, we may point out that to speak of form as arrangement of all that is there in a work is at once to suggest that the concept of form is related to that of content. Indeed, as Ducasse puts it,

> by form is meant simply **arrangement** or order; and by content . . ., whatever it happens to be that is arranged, ordered.[5]

But, we may add, the content of a work of art is whatever is found in the work when it is (properly) contemplated. And, in so far as whatever is here found, — say, in contemplating a painting — is not mere colours, but colours **as organised in a particular way**, and as invested with a specific significance, content in the aesthetic sense is very different from the mere material of art. Materials like bronze, marble and paints are merely given to the artist. It is only when these materials have been creatively used in the work of art — so that what we now see is not mere colours, but (say) coloured lines suggesting tension or a relaxed quality — that artistic content comes into being. Here we may also see the distinction which Dewey draws between material, medium and content. 'A material element becomes a medium when employed with other materials in some order, so that it becomes part of an inclusive whole'.

The subject-matter of art is another distinct aspect of a work. It is that to which a work of representational art refers. The (artistic) **content** of a poem written about a village scene is the scene which is the subject-matter, plus words and metre, which are the materials — all blended into a significant form.

It here becomes clear that the aesthetic meaning of 'content' cannot be had without making some reference to 'form'. Content, we repeat, is everything that we find in a work of art (as organised in a particular way). Here, because we are trying to understand **content**, the emphasis is on the first part of the sentence, but the (bracketed) reference to form is also necessary, if subsidiary.

What is more, the content of a work of art is **inseparable** from its form. It is not like the content of a box — the clothes it contains — which can be easily taken out of the box without causing any damage to it.

Turning to music, the (artistic) content of a *khyāl* being sung is its text, obviously, if weakly, representational; and the *svaras* and the rhythm cycle it builds upon. Here, the present **text** may well be replaced by a different complex of words; but if we take out the musical elements and replace them with different *svaras* and *tāla*, the present *bandiśa* would forthwith disappear. As for the form of a musical piece, when we are actively **contemplating** the music and want to **see** its form, we have in fact to attend to every detail of it; and when we merely **speak** of the form of art quite generally, we **mean** by it the inner organisation of all its details. In neither case is the content left out.

It may, however, be pointed out that artists themselves sometimes speak of a musical form or *bandiśa* in a more or less abstract way. This happens, for instance, when they characterise a *bandiśa* as taut (कसी हुई) or as swinging (झूलती हुई). It is obvious that in such talk **every** detail of the composition is neither pointed out nor thought of.

The actual contemplation of a *bandiśa* is different experientally. When a *rasika*, who (we may suppose) is actually listening to the music, characterises the *bandiśa* as swinging, what happens is pretty complex. First, the structure of the *bandiśa* is registered. Second, the *bandiśa* is also, at the same time, seen to wear or project its swinging or taut character. And thirdly, no gap is at all felt between the *bandiśa* and the quality it appears to project. This is why aestheticians like Susanne Langer speak of the significance of a work of art as its **import**, rather than as its **meaning**. It is indeed true that whatever is expressed by a musical form cannot be abstracted from, because it is not merely conjoined with the form.

Another point may here be made, from the phenomenological point of view. It would be quite proper to speak of a *bandiśa* (or a musical form) as the unique integration of all that it comprises. But this should not make us think that a good composition is literally complete in the manner of a circle. The fact, on the other hand, is that the singing of a *vilambit sthāyī* is interspersed with intervals of silence, without however appearing broken into fragments. In other words, though the *sthāyī* is literally interrupted, virtually or in respect of appearance it may seem undivided. Now, it is important to distinguish the various factors which make for this **aesthetic suggestion** of completeness. They relate to the *rasika*, the manner of singing, and also to the quality of the rhythmic accompaniment. Thus, where there is a pause in singing, the *rasika* keeps himself busy either in dwelling imaginatively on what has just been sung or on the notes that may be expected to follow in accordance with the scheme of the *rāga*. In either case he does not experience any vacancy; and so, because of his own imaginative engagement, does not see any gap in the singing either. Further, the singing itself may be marked by such a flowing quality that the literal gaps may be, more or less, bridged over by a suggestion of continuity. Finally, if the *ṭhekā* has been well established, its ongoing rhythm keeps the listener supplied with such an unbroken sense of continuity that — partly because the *sthāyī* is expected to move along with the pace of the *ṭhekā* — the awareness of the literal gaps in singing is utterly lost in this ideal and unbroken contemplation of rhythm. To conclude, not merely the making of a *khyāl-bandiśa*, but even its **contemplation** is a fairly complex process. In *dhruvapadas*, on the other hand, where there are very few literal gaps in singing, the listener's imaginative attunement with the singing is much less than in the case of a *vilambit khyāl*; say in *ektāla* or *jhūmrā*.

Apotheosis of Form — Formalism

Mention may here be, in passing, of an old aesthetic problem in respect of form and content. Which of the two is more important for a work of art, or a greater determinant of its value — form or content? Does excellence in music depend (more) on what *rāga* you choose, or **how** you treat its constituent notes? Here, if we vote for the 'how', we would be subscribing to aesthetic formalism. It is the theory which maintains that, in our concern with art as art, it is form that really matters, and that this is so whether we consider the appreciation or the creation of art, or even the basic question of the very nature of art.

It is easy to see that if, as indeed (we have seen) is the proper view, form means organisation or arrangement, formalism must emphasise qualities like design and harmony. 'Form' has been stressed by Plato, Kant and Clive Bell. In *Philebus* Plato speaks of the intrinsic appeal of geometrical designs. He may even be said to have anticipated the theory of pure form associated, in our day, with artists like Cezanne. We may also here refer to Cubism, a geometric type of art, practised by Gris, Braque, Ozenfant, Picasso, and Kandinsky.

Theoretical defence of aesthetic formalism, in the last one hundred years (or more), has been attempted not only by Clive Bell and Rogery Fry, but also by the German school represented by Herbert and Zimmerman. Here, we may confine ourselves to the first two, Bell and Fry; for the concepts they developed, the rejections they cultivated, and the issues they inspired, make these two aestheticians extremely valuable models for our aesthetic analysis.

BELL

1. What is a work of art? Bell answers: it is a **significant form**. So, his emphasis on form is at once manifest. He must, however, explain what he means by form of this kind; and he does it, as follows:

   "Lines and colours combined in a particular way, certain forms and relations and combinations of lines and colours, these aesthetically moving forms, I call 'significant form' ".[6]

   Be it noted that significant form is here regarded as being both objective and subjective. It is, first, an objective feature, specific combination of lines and colours that are in fact there **in the work itself**. And second, the presence of this property is known directly by **experiencing the unique (aesthetic) emotion** it evokes. The critic can, of course, invite our attention to the objective combination of lines and colours. But we truly come to see that the object is a work **of art** only when the combination is able to **move us aesthetically**. We have no other means of recognising a work of art than our feeling for it.[7] So, if, as here seems warranted, 'form' be taken to mean the knitwork of line and colour, 'significant' may be interpreted as 'tending to move us aesthetically'. But, here at once two further comments seem needful:

   (a) In Bell's view, a painting is **not** singificant because it is **about**, **or represents** something. He is convinced that the value of art does not depend on its representational elements, that is, those that make the work resemble things, events and states of daily life. This is borne out by his following emphatic words:

"If a representative form has value, it is as form, not as representation. The representative element in a work of art may or may not be harmful; always it is irrelevant. For, to appreciate a work of art, we need bring with us nothing from life, no knowledge of its ideas and affairs, no familiarity with its emotions . . . nothing but a sense of form and colour and knowledge of three-dimensional space."[8]

Bell suggests that representation is harmless when it is dissolved into the plastic elements of lines and colours. But there is one emphasis in the passage just cited which is certainly questionable. If representation is always to be a subordinate element in painting, why should it at all be there? However, Bell's ready answer, here, is that representation is demanded by the concrete character of art. A painting is not an abstract universal, but something specific, **this** or **that** combination of lines and colours. (We may here argue that the fact that something is specific becomes manifest if it is identifiable; and that representation helps identifiability). In brief, representations are necessary as foci of significant form.

(b) Further, and this is allied to the point first made, the way significant form moves us, or the aesthetic emotion, is different from the non-aesthetic emotions evoked by the use of line and colour in descriptive art which sacrifices significant form for representation.

"Art transports us from the world of man's activity to a world of aesthetic exaltation. For a moment we are shut off from human interests; our anticipations and memories are arrested; we are lifted above the stream of life."[9]

"The contemplation of pure form leads to a state of extraordinary exaltation and complete detachment from the concerns of life."[10]

2. This at once gives us the essence of Bell's theory of **art appreciation**. The right way to appreciate art is not to ask how it is useful in life or helpful to morals, but simply to respond to its form. The mathematician too is **as such** concerned only with the (structure of) proofs. He too, in enjoying mathematics, brings nothing from life, no knowledge of its affairs or emotion. In the context of art appreciation it is meaningless to speak of

the attitudes of belief, disbelief and make-believe; for they are all responses to representative elements which are not the essence of art. To respond to a work properly, we have to regard it as isolated from everyday life. The experience is here exalted, rapturous and contemplative or disinterested and non-practical. It is these characteristics which are meant when Bell speaks of the 'unique aesthetic emotion'.[11]

3. True **artistic creation** too is, in Bell's view, tied to significant form. The superior artist, we are told, sees reality **in a particular way**, without caring for what it means to us in life; and it is this unique vision of reality that he transforms into his art object. Descriptive art, which is essentially art in which representations have **not** been dissolved into line and colour, is the product of those artists who are unable to achieve significant form and who consequently aim at something else. The aesthetic way of looking at things is truer as vision than the practical; for it sees things purely as they are, not as overlaid with any thoughts of what they mean to us in life. **The essence of music too, Bell believes, is significant form**.
4. But literature, he realises, is different. It is basically informative and cognitive in its content, the embodiment of ordinary emotions. Here, formal excellence is not an essential quality. Even Shakespeare's sonnets, Bell alleges, are impure because the form is burdened with an intellectual content, and that content is a mood that mingles with, and reposes on, the emotions of life.

FRY

By and large, Fry shares and supports Bell's views outlined above. But some differences too are manifest as we set out to see the details of Fry's aesthetics:

1. His final view in respect of **the art object** is indeed a little different. He agrees with Bell in regarding it as the embodiment of **significant form**, but he interprets the latter as compositional space structure rather than as combination of lines and colours. Art, upon this view, is severely pure. It is thought to transcend even the decorative qualities of line. Generally, however, in *Vision and Design*, Fry cites with approval the view of Bell and Cezanne that 'a work of art has the peculiar property of conveying the aesthetic emotion . . . in virtue of its having significant form'. And in

Transformations he says, with emphasis, that a picture in which representations work for dramatic ends — instead of being dissolved into the plastic elements — are not pure painting, but mixtures of this art and narrations, — **hybrid, like song (with a text) in the region of music**.

As for the art of **music**, Fry merely echoes Bell's view that it is, in essence, pure form — that is, a significant combination of sounds that move us in an aesthetically unique way. But his view of literature is again distinctive. Quite unlike Bell, Fry does not here hesitate to use significant form as an interpretative principle. Thus, he maintains that the essence of dramatic art is not single figures (characters), or collection of events (that is, plot), but the relation of inevitability. A tragedy, we are told, owes its greatness to 'the vivid sense of the inevitability of . . . (the) unfolding' of events.

2. In respect of **art appreciation**, Fry again subscribes to the basic view of Bell. So, we may here mention only the essence of the matter. Ordinary responses, in Fry's view, relate to objects, sensations and events; but the true aesthetic response is to **relations**, the sum of which constitutes 'significant form'.

3. Fry's theory of **art creation** too is largely similar to that of Bell. But it is grounded in a distinctive emphasis on the bipolarity of man. Fry holds that man is eminently capable of a double life, — the instinctive and the imaginative. The former serves the ends of survival. The latter, on the other hand, makes for enrichment of experience. When our reaction to an object is instinctive — say, like flying away from something dangerous — we prepare for the response, instead of noticing in detail the object's own nature. But, in the imaginative mode we can contemplate everything at length.

Now it is **this** mode, Fry says, which rules not only the spectator, but the creator of art, — 'the contemplation of formal relations'. The view he develops finally, largely on the basis of his study of post-impressionism, is that true artistic vision springs from a function of vision, of seeing the world as a spatial, relational, compositional structure, or as significant form.

Characterisations of Form

In aesthetics we commonly speak of form as **significant** or as **expressive**. But, the two words are not exactly synonymous. For, when we speak of a thing's being **significant**, we mean merely that it **means**, is **related to, or can stand for** something else. The relation here meant does not work up any in-out image. On the other hand, when we speak of something as being **expressive**, our meaning necessarily is that the thing in question makes some content **explicit**. The word 'table' merely signifies objects of a particular kind; it cannot be said to express them. Poetic language, on the other hand, is often said to be expressive of some feeling-content. To signify is merely to **mean**; to express is to make **manifest**.

Yet, we may note, in relation to the present-day arts, the word 'significant' too is of great value. Today we prefer to speak of the significance, rather than of the beauty of a work of art. However, as we have seen, the concept of 'significant form' does not merely mean 'meaningful form', but form which is 'aesthetically moving'.

'Significant' is, however, only one of the many predicates that have been ascribed to form. Others are: **expressive**, **organic**, **abstract**, **dynamic**, and **static**. Some comments may be made on each one of these.

Aestheticians who emphasise the concept of expressive form — and Mrs. Langer is easily the most important of them — take care to emphasise that, though it certainly expresses something **to the beholder**, what is expressed is not just (loosely or distantly) meant by the work, but seems to be **directly in** the latter, exactly as sorrow writ large on a grief-stricken face is seen to be there in the face itself.

We may now attend to the question as to how artistic form is known. Some philosophers, like Leibnitz and Gilson, have held that the consonances in music please because the mind unconsciously recognises the ratios on which they are based. In so far as this view relates to **music**, it may not be dismissed. But it can hardly be stretched to cover arts other than music. It would be more proper to say, with Gestalt psychology, that the formed quality of works of painting, sculpture and architecture is known by **perception**. But, of course, in the context of literary arts the word has to be taken in a special sense: that is, as awareness of a 'form' which is not visual or auditory, but ideal-imaginative.

Their Relative Importance

Though the ideal, as Walter Pater points out, is such a relation of form and content that neither of these may be easily distinguished, we can divide philosophers into two classes — one which gives more importance to form, the other, to content. Thus, those who attach exaggerated importance to content — say, men like Longinus, Hegel and Hartmann — seem to reduce it to mere theme or subject-matter. On the other hand, Plato and Kant emphasise form. Plato, in *Philebus*, is said to have anticipated the thesis of the modern geometric types of art. But both Plato and Kant seem to regard form as merely abstract shape or measure. Even some literary critics have succumbed to this error in overemphasising 'form'.

It is, we may note, not only philosophers and literary critics, but even artists who have tended to regard form and content as separate entities. Thus, in the region of English literature, poetry which is called 'classical' seeks to fit 'content' into predetermined and conventional forms.

Their Ideal Inter-relation

If it be asked as to how we are to conceive the ideal inter-relation of form and content, the answer could be that in a work of art the two should seem fused inextricably as one. In other words, whatever is found **in** the work should at once **seem to gain in significance or charm from its relatedness to content**. The work's unity should be intense, and permeate all its details. About form and content it would indeed be right to say, with Pater, that though 'the **understanding** can always make this distinction, yet it is the constant effort of **art** to obliterate it'.

Where and how is such ideal inter-relation manifest? Music has often been cited as the answer. Even generally, a work of art does not express what it does in the way a telegram communicates a message. In the latter case, once the message is seized by the receiver, the telegram becomes useless; and is, in fact, generally put aside as such. But in our concern with a poem or painting, however successful be our attempt to distil its significance, the work as a visible, (observable or intelligible) artefact still remains of basic value; and we continue to feel the need to repair to the work for the sake of verifying or enlarging our interpretation. This is so because what an art-work expresses is inseparable from what is there in it. This why Langer chooses to speak of art as an express**ive** form rather than as a mere vehicle that express**es** something:

> A work of art is a composition of tensions and resolutions, balance and unbalance, rhythmic coherence. . . . 'Music sounds as feelings feel.' And likewise, in good painting, sculpture or building, balanced shapes and colours, lines and masses look as emotions, vital tensions and their resolutions feel.[12]

She also takes care to emphasise the idea of form as the integrated totality of **all** that is there in the work:

> To the total effect that is an artistic form, the colour matters, the thickness of lines matters, and the appearance of texture and weight . . . Form, in the sense in which artists speak of 'significant form' or 'expressive form', is not an abstracted structure . . . (and what) a good work expresses seem(s) to the beholder to be directly contained in it.[13]

As for the distinction between 'organic and abstract' form, it has been put succinctly by Sir Herbert Read as follows:

> When a work of art has its own inherent laws, originating with its very invention and fusing in one vital unity both structure and content, then the resulting form may be described as organic. . . . (But) when an organic form is stabilised and repeated as a pattern, and the intention of the artist is no longer related to the inherent dynamism of an inventive act, but seeks **to adapt content to predetermined structure**, then the resulting form may be described as abstract . . . .[14]

The distinction can be easily brought out by considering a detail of our vocal music. Some of the *sthāyī*s of our *vilambit* singing are merely an attempt to adapt the text to the rhythm-cycle chosen, say, *ekatāla*, *tilavāḍā* or *jhūmrā*. Neither the extent nor the pace of the rhythm seems to be demanded by the character of the text itself. This is why it is very difficult to sing such *sthāyī*s in a rhythmically proper way **without the explicit assistance of a** *tablā*-**player**. Their form is obviously 'abstract', that is, deficient in respect of an inwardly affirmed accord of text and rhythm. On the other hand, the text of *drut ekatāla*, *jhaptāla* and *madhya laya tritāla sthāyī*s seems itself to demand the cycles to which it is set. Their form may, therefore, be said to be **organic**.

Finally, the distinction, as also the relation, between dynamic and static forms may be made out as follows:

> A waterfall seems to hang from the cliff, waving streamers of foam. Actually, of course, nothing stays there in mid-air; the water is always passing; but there is more and more water taking the same paths, so we have a lasting shape made and maintained by its passage — a permanent dynamic form. A quiet river, too, has dynamic form, if it stopped flowing it would either go dry or become a lake . . . [but it is important to note that] when a river ceases to flow because the water is deflected or dried up, there remains the river bed, sometimes cut deeply in solid stone. That bed is shaped by the flow, and records as graven lines the currents that have ceased to exist. **Its shape is static, but it expresses the dynamic form of the river.**[15]

A complete work of art, however, as distinguished from its form, is spoken of not as abstract or dynamic, but as beautiful or pretty. A music composition is freely so characterised. So, our next task is to give a little thought to some aesthetic predicates.

References

1. *The Oriental World* (Landmarks of the World's Art), p. 65. Italics added.
2. *Ibid.*, p. 59, Italics added.
3. W.A. Archer, *India and Modern Art*, pp. 60-1.
4. *Indian Painting Today*, 1981, facing p. 51.
5. C.J. Ducasse, *The Philosophy of Art*, p. 202.
6. Clive Bell, *Art*, p. 23.
7. *Ibid*, p. 23.
8. *Ibid.*, pp. 36-7.
9. *Ibid.*, p. 36.
10. *Ibid.*, p. 71.
11. To the question, why we are at all moved by (a specific) combination of lines and colours, Bell's simple answer is that the artist's way of looking at things — which the combination in question expresses — is really natural to the onlooker as well, though he is of course not able to project it on the canvas.
12. S.K. Langer, *Problems of Art*, pp. 8, 26.

13. *Ibid*, pp. 25-6.
14. Cited by F.E. Sparshott in his *The Structure of Aesthetics*, p. 339.
15. Langer, *Problems of Art*, pp. 18-19.

4

Aesthetic Predicates

SOME aesthetic predicates which occur in our talk about music, if not with equal frequency, are: the beautiful, graceful, pretty and sublime. Of these, **the beautiful** is the most commonly used. So let us begin by discussing the question: what is beauty? To help understanding, however, this question may be divided into two subsidiary ones. First, what is the **meaning** of 'beauty', when we talk about it in relative abstraction from art contemplation? And what is it to actually **experience** beauty? The two questions cannot, however, be kept utterly apart; for the word 'beauty' has in fact been used in relation to all the arts, even in respect of literature where sensuous charm is not so obvious as in the case of, say, painting and music. Further, the meaning of 'beauty' has also been marked off from that of words like 'pretty' and 'sublime'. When we make **such** distinctions, the transition to facts of experience will be easy and unavoidable. Finally, though our concern has to be mainly aesthetic, it seems desirable that the ordinary meaning of 'beauty' — that is, fascination of sense — is not merely left out.

With an eye on all these requirements, we may begin by positing the following total view of beauty:

> The word 'beauty' means that a 'form' is accessible and acceptable to perception and (/or) imagination; and that it is (or can be) the object of contemplation and disinterested delight, as distinguished from mere amusement, gratification of need or desire, and sublime feeling.

It is not here said, we may note, that beauty is just an objective property that one has only to find by a simple act of attention. Training of the contemplator's sensibility is here absolutely necessary. To be sure, not everyone can perceive the beauty of a Shakespearean play; and the traditional Indian aestheticians are, in this context, quite right in emphasising that the *rasika* has to fulfil many conditions of eligibility for contemplating art. Nor is our approach here merely subjective. We propose no such view as the one which says that beauty goes with the slant of the beholder. We seek rather to reckon **both** kinds of factors, objective and subjective. This is, however, yet to be brought out by attending to the key ideas of our formulation, one by one:

I. To begin with, wherever we speak of beauty, there is a 'form' which is (in principle) acceptable to perception and (/or) imagination, and of course accessible to these mental powers, **without making them feel overwhelmed**. 'Form' is here to be taken not in the sense of mere shape, but in that of a **distinct whole of agreeably related parts**. Why we put precisely this interpretation on 'form' may be clarified in terms of the following remarks:

(a) Where the object is a **physical figure**, not a work of art, our chosen meaning would appear acceptable because **proportion** — as mutual agreeableness of parts — **is** one of the qualitites of a good figure. So, our refusal to take 'form' as shape **alone** is to be warranted by cases of shape itself where it seems charming.

(b) What is said to have 'form' (and to be beautiful) may well be a literary work, say, a poem. But nobody speaks of the **shape** of a poem. And if, as is freely the case, we admire its 'form' — and not merely **identify** it as a *dohā* or *caupāī*, or as a lyric or a sonnet, or as a *dhruvapada* or *khyāl* — we mean to refer to **the excellence of its inner organisation**.

(c) Finally, in interpreting 'form' we have chosen to speak of a **distinct** whole. This is done with a view to providing for the truth, pointed out by Kant, that 'form' suggests limitation, and that it is this which (along with other factors) distinguishes the beautiful which always has a 'form', from the sublime which seems limitless and may be said to be, in a way, formless.

But then, it may be asked, why do we not speak of 'form' quite simply as 'a limited whole. . . '? To this, our ready answer would be that the 'limited' character **of a work of art** is quite different from the given finiteness of, say, trees and stones. Here, in the region of art,limitedness is the distinguishability of the work (from things and other works) that follows from the unique manner of its inner organisation by virtue of which it not merely invites, but **holds** our attention. Surely, we say nothing about the form of a work **as art** if we merely remark that it is limited. **We** have sought to speak of limitedness that is but a reflex of individual character;[1] hence, the word 'distinct'.

Now, we may turn to consider what is meant by saying that 'form' is acceptable to perception and (/or) imagination. One reason why we here speak of **both** perception and imagination is that — though it is more pronounced in the case of arts like painting, music, and sculpture — the role of perception cannot be ignored even in the case of, say, poetry, where the mere sound of the words is a vital constituent of total significance. Again, we have to speak thus also because in the case of the literary arts it is mainly imagination which gives us access to the form of the work. Imagination is in fact needed even for the proper awareness of musical form. **The form of a melody is occurrent and successive, and when one is actually listening to the terminal notes, he must hold on ideally also to the preceding ones, if he is at all to see how they are all organised as one**.

The mere thought of the 'acceptability' of form is, however, not enough for distinguishing the beautiful from, say, the pretty, the graceful and the sublime; and we must also give heed to **how** the 'form' **affects** us.

The beautiful means a 'form' that is acceptable uniquely. It not only invites, but holds attention; and it makes us happy wholly because of what it itself is, **and not because it answers a question or fulfils an everyday need**. It is the object of the contemplative attitude, and is interesting in itself. The delight it gives us is wholly disinterested. In other words, the feeling is quite independent of the questions as to whether the object in fact exists, and whether it is in some way useful. It is this contemplation of the object's own form alone which makes for *tādātmya*. We may here note that desire and the thought of existence go together. We desire only that which exists or which can be brought into existence. Sartre rightly says that desire is a plunge into the heart of existence. To contemplate a human figure and to find it **beautiful**, we have not merely to attend to its 'form', which here means shapeliness or proportionate quality, but must be free from the desire to appropriate it to our appetites.

It may also be marked that disinterested delight does not by itself constitute an experience of beauty. For, we find such delight also in an act of selfless service, or even in the contemplation of such service. Beauty means, in addition, that such delight is produced **by the contemplation of a form**. What here deserves emphasis is, however, the idea that if the 'form' is found likeable **at once**, without any effort, the object may only seem pretty and amusing rather than beautiful; and that if, on the other hand, our apprehending powers are almost **stretched to a breaking-point** before we are able to see and admire its form, the object would tend to appear **sublime, and not merely beautiful**.

This is, however, only a clearing of the ground, as it were, for a more definite indication of the nature of beauty by distinguishing it from allied concepts such as the pretty, graceful and the sublime.

The word 'pretty' may be said to mean that which pleases in a moderate way, without affecting us deeply. A **pretty** object can be perceived as such quite easily, that is, without causing any strain on our apprehending powers. It is generally a small object possessing superficial charm and mere sensuous appeal, and so cannot be said to be dignified or impressive. However, we cannot say that an object which is small and likeable can only be characterised as pretty and not otherwise. A baby or a kitten playing with a ball of wool may well be said to be pretty or a pretty sight. But a **small** poem with an intense theme, calling for deep thinking, may have to be said to be closer to the sublime. Consider, for instance, the following well-known lines of saint poet, Kabīr:

कबीरा हम जब आये थे जग हँसे हम रोये
ऐसी करनी कर चलो हम हँसे जग रोये

The beautiful is not so closely related to smallness as the pretty. To contemplate beauty one has often to strain the mind; and where this is not necessary, the object's impact on the onlooker, as in opening one's eyes to the beauty of the Tāj, may be one of wondrous delight, not one of an amusing titillation of sense. The marvellous worksmanship, perfect symmetry and overall grandeur of the structure prevent us from calling it merely pretty or graceful.

Yet there are features that the pretty may be said to share with the beautiful. Of these, one is sensuous appeal, and the other is the disinterested quality of the likeable feeling. Neither object appeals to us because it provides gratification of an everyday want or desire.

The **graceful** is another aesthetic predicate which we use for things that we like. But it is used, we may note, for objects which possess actual or virtual movement. Indeed, in the region of art, this feature is commonly seen to distinguish singing and dancing. But the word is by no means inapplicable to play. Thus, the batting of a seasoned cricketer is freely called graceful because it is without jerky, discontinuous movements and also because it appears quite effortless. Similarly, a dancer who seems to float and glide while dancing is also rightly admired for her grace. Even in the region of rhythm, patterns which seem to move effortlessly, and of course in a shapely way, are acclaimed as graceful. But, apart from fluency and effortlessness, it is also important that the movement should not be too rapid. It will appear graceful only if it is not so quick that one may find it difficult to follow its flow. That is why, in the region of music, the extra fluent *tānas* of the late Ustad Bade Ghulam Ali Khan — though admirable for their blend of sweetness, pace and articulateness — cannot be described as graceful. On the other hand, the relaxed little flourishes present in the singing of Pt. Jasraj, right from the beginning of the recital, can certainly be so termed. Further, since it appears to describe an easy-to-follow meander, the musical passage known as *dagar* in *ālāpa* (of the *dhruvapada* manner) may also be called graceful.

In the literary arts, we may find grace in the lightness of movement with easy winsome meaning, as in the following couplets of the Urdu poet, Jigar:

हम दुआ दें और तुम कोसो
अपनी अपनी ज़ुबान है प्यारे
हम तो तुमको ख़ुदा समझते हैं
अपना अपना ख़्याल है प्यारे

On the other hand, if, as in the following couplet from the same poem, some deep meaning is embodied in lines of similar extent and flow, the impression on the reader will not be that of grace, but of a high seriousness:

तुझमें मुझमें तो कोई फ़र्क नहीं
इश्क़ क्यों दरम्यान है प्यारे

Be it noted, however, that the term 'graceful' is applicable not only to cases of real movement, but also to what **suggests** movement. For instance, the curvaceous quality of a slim and shapely human figure may be said to be graceful simply because the figural curves **appear** to move.

The predicate 'beautiful', on the other hand, is as applicable to a wholly moveless form, such as a rain-washed landscape, as to a well-designed *madhya laya* musical composition. Dance, we may add, covers both the aspects of actual and virtual or suggested movements, the former in the form of patterns danced, and the latter in that of postures of shapely *aṅga*. Unlike prettiness and grace, the beautiful does not positively exclude 'greatness'. A beautiful landscape, we know, may be extensive and impressive; and to refer to the Tāj again, it is by no means a puny or flitting structure. Beauty may also be found in represented situations of a tragic character; but of course nobody would call them graceful. However, although the delight of beauty is more serious and contemplative than the relatively easy charm of the visibly graceful, it is not as great a strain on our apprehending powers as the sublime, a predicate we shall now briefly discuss.

The sublime signifies things and experiences of exceptional depth, quality and seriousness. Not being dependent on — though it may well go with — a measure of sensuous charm, the sublime is also not inseparable from **form** in the sense of a limited shape.

The commonest feature of what seems sublime is, in fact, its greatness, which may be taken to mean bigness of size, or surpassing excellence of quality, or both. Some easy ways to experience sublimity are provided by: standing at the foot of a lofty and snow-clad mountain range; contemplating the wide expanse of a big, flooded river wanly alight with the last few rays of the setting sun; or listening to the leisurely, expansive *ālāpa* of the *dhruvapada* singer.

Subjectively, a clear element in the experience of sublimity is the feeling of one's own smallness as compared to the immensity of the object. The onlooker feels, in the beginning, a little subdued; but, on the whole and ultimately, he is profoundly satisfied and even feels elevated. So deep is the impact of sublimity that one feels as if the very bounds of one's being are stretched in having the experience. The experience is by no means unfamiliar to lovers of good music, though what they most commonly admire is fluency and range of *tāna*s or the form of a good *bandiśa*.

Reference

1. Cf. Croce, "What intuition reveals in a work of art is . . . character, individual physiognomy". Croce, *Aesthetic*, p. 20.

5

The Knitwork of Musical Form

HAVING understood the concept of form in the context of art taken generally, we now turn to consider it in the specific context of Hindustānī music. At the very outset, however, we may make two remarks by way of supplementing our discussion so far. One of these relates to what our attitude has to be in an aesthetical study of music; and the other aims at adding something essential to what has been said in the earlier chapters about form and its conceptual allies.

A. Now, to begin with, our study cannot obviously confine itself to the linguistic-analysis and phenomenological approaches as they relate to the *rasika* and the critic. The person who is nearest to this art is the maker of music, i.e., the musician himself. And because in our aesthetical study of this art we cannot afford to ignore its subtle **creative** details, we have also to consider the musician's own point of view in this regard. But is the musician's point of view different from that of the listener? If yes, how? Questions such as these may be answered as follows:

(a) It is true that language about music is used also by the listener, and not by the musician alone. But the musician's language has its own distinct character. It is more insightful and imaginative than discursive. For example, if the impact of a particular *svara* has been feeble, the listener would perhaps remark "the note should have been prolonged a little". On the other hand, a traditional musician may like to speak thus. "मियाँ सुर का पेट तो भरा ही नहीं". Language of the latter kind may seem to be awkward. But it is in fact insightful. It complains that the aesthetic demands of the *svara* in question have not been fully met.

(b) Similarly, though the experience of music is of course had by both the listener and the musician, the latter's reaction is here a little different from that of the former. Take, for instance, a phrase of *svara*s which has just been sweetly rendered. The listener will only relish it, but the musician may also be inspired to create another melodic pattern on the basis of the present one. In other words, the musician's experience of music-making is forward-looking in a **creative** way. On the other hand, the listener only **gets set** to receive the melodic riches that are yet to come. Another instance of the difference between the experience of the listener and that of the musician is that when, at the end of an inspired recital, we admire the latter for his brilliant performance, we obviously regard **him as the conscious creator** of the music in question. But if we say so to him **he** may disagree and insist that it was in fact the power of music itself that led him on to sing so well. In other words, we forget that when the musician experiences the inspired moments of his musical creation he ceases to be self-conscious as the agent of an effort.

However, in spite of these differences, there are certain factors which are common to both the listener and the musician. One of these is that, to both, the form of music appears dynamic — which is indeed a distinct feature of this particular art — whereas in the other fine arts, like painting, sculpture and architecture the form is literally static. But the occurrent form of music is different from the same kind of form as found in nature. For example, a waterfall is not merely a torrential, but a **ceaseless** flow. The form of music, on the other hand, is studded with **pauses**.

But, be it noted, these pauses are of a particular kind. They are moments **of silence**, not the visible marks of punctuation which only signify a relative suspension or slowing of the flow **of thought**. Here, in passing, we may note a point of difference between the inconsistent in meaning or thought and the inconsistent in fact. In respect of meaning 'silence' and 'sound' are opposed to each other, for whereas the former **means** absence of sound, the latter means privation of silence. But pauses in the fabric of music enable the listener — that is, both the singer himself and the *rasika* — to suck the impact of *svara*s or musical sounds. In other words, we may say that what is logically inconsistent can be aesthetically quite consistent.

The pauses further generate tension by creating in the mind of the *rasika* an eager waiting for what is to come, as he follows the flowing form of music. His feeling of anticipation makes the music appear tightly structured in many ways. For instance, during a recital when an artist moves towards the *sama* and purposely gives a pause of silence, instead of coming straight to the focal beat, he creates an aesthetic tension which also includes psychological tension. But the difference between the two kinds of tension is that whereas in the former the *rasika* does not feel unhappy — but is only a little keyed up — as he awaits the advent of the *sama*, in the latter case the person who has to suffer the waiting, is very likely to grow impatient **and fretful**. Further, when an aesthetic tension, as that of looking forward to the *sama*, is released, the creator of this semblance — namely the artist — is applauded. In psychological tension, on the other hand, the eventual release is an occasion for a mere greeting — or maybe for fretting with — the other, not for showering praise on him.

If, however, we confine our attention to music, a little more thinking on the point seems necessary, by way of amplifying the remark that as mere moments of silence, **pauses in music** are clearly not the same as pauses or **marks of punctuation in writing**. The former, it is clear, relate only to the listeners' **imagination**, not to his ear. The latter (or pauses in writing) affect, in the main, the reader's **understanding**. Nor can we confuse pauses **in** music with the silence that **encompasses** it. The latter is merely the abiding context of the music; the former, though momentary, are integral to the very form of the music as contemplated. These pauses (within music) are judged and determined aesthetically. On the other hand, the passage of the context of silence around music is measured by clocks or watches. What is more, whereas the silence around the music only helps listening; the pauses in it enable the music itself to bloom, as an art-work. But it would be wrong to assume that pauses in music occur only as moments of silence **between** the notes. A pause is also given, where the need arises, at some select individual *svaras*. This is done by letting the music tarry at the note. Mostly these *svaras* are *ṣaḍaj*, *pañcam* and the *vādī-saṁvādī* of the *rāga* chosen. The guiding consideration here is the proper and effective projection of the grammatical character **and** the aesthetic personality of the *rāga*.

The two kinds just distinguished are different from one another also in the sense that, unlike a pause **at** an individual note, the ones **between** the notes (it is obvious) are only contemplated, not heard by the listener. Yet, though unheard, these intra-*svara* pauses are important, for they give the mind a greater scope to get attuned with the form of the music, as a result of which listening to this art is as much an exercise of the mind as that of the ear. In other words, whereas pauses **at** individual *svara*s often bring out the distinctive nature of the *rāga*, the ones **between** the notes make for the unbroken semblance of the music contemplated. But in spite of these differences, the two kinds of pauses are in some ways similar too. Both are regulated aesthetically, Further, the element of aesthetic duration or *laya* is alike present in both. *Laya*, incidentally, is an essential feature of all the three aspects of *saṅgīta*, i.e., *gāyana*, *vādana* and *nṛtya*. It is also, we may note, a vital element of musical form. As pace, it is in fact an obvious component by means of which we easily distinguish the form of a *vilambit* composition from that of a *drut* one.

Laya, incidentally, is also a determinant of formal graces and effects in music. For instance, *dagar* which is supposed to have the look of a winding passage, can be effectively used only at a somewhat **leisurely** pace. The same may be said about *mīṇḍ* or glide. But the latter admits of a diversity of effect. If the reposeful glide, embracing a few adjacent notes, is an ascending one, it will perhaps seem to be a little concave; and somewhat converse, if it is seen to describe a descent. And as for the effects which are seen to beautify music variously, whereas those of sparkle and liveliness are commonly seen to occur at a **nimble** pace, the opposite effects of inwardness, depth and yearning tenderness call for a pace that is a little unhurried. However, though the effects and formal graces, referred to above, are all alike important for the beauty and charm of music, they are but its individual features and are not so deeply satisfying as immaculate sweetness, steadiness of pace, and an intense, yet articulate form. In music such a form appears in terms of a good *bandiśa* or a *sthāyī-antarā* twosome. Here, every individual note is distinct or clearly perceivable. Further, the nature of the *rāga*, the idiom of the *tāla* and the centrality of the *sama* are also clearly manifest. What is more, the composition of music is (in principle) made to accord with the meaning of the text or words of the song. But we should not underestimate the other essentials of good music. With all its beauty, musical structure would fail to move us if there is any weakening of *svara* or unsteadiness of *laya*.

B. We just said something, if without notice, about some of the **elements** and material of music. But a good deal more may be said at this point, primarily with the intent of bringing out the **distinctively creative** nature of the art of music:

A work of art is not any kind of form. It is a **created** form, created by the artist. Now, whatever is created is shaped out of something and in a particular way. That out of which, or by manipulating which, a work of art is made, is its **material**; and the created units which go to make the work of art are its **elements**. But the distinction between the material and elements of art has to be brought out at some length, of course, with special reference to music.

Speaking quite generally, the material of music may be said to be 'notes' or *svaras*. We may leave out beats or *mātrās* because *ālāpa*, which is an important form of our music, does not employ them. But, if we confine ourselves to Indian music, we find that its material, or the plurality of *svaras*, is not only determined by arrangement in a scale but by their unique ordering in a melody or *rāga*. When a painter sets out to make a painting, his material, i.e., pigments, has no order about it. It is he, the artist, who has to invest it with an order, as he sets out to create his work. In the case of our music, on the other hand, however creative the artist may be, he has to deal with the *svaras* in the determinate order of the *rāga* chosen. In other words, the **material** of our music is never as raw or unformed as the material of the other arts. To turn, now, to the **elements** of music, we may say that the most important of these are those which indicate the nature of the *rāga* clearly, if not fully. Other elements will be provided by **individual** *svaras* or *svara-samūhas*, which are permitted by the *rāga*, and which have a certain wholeness of appeal about them. What is more, though they may not all indicate the nature of the *rāga* equally clearly, they will all be elements, and not mere material, because everyone of them will be possessed of some character which is not to be found in the *svaras* arranged in notation as the mere material of the *rāga*. For, in actual music they will all appear to be tender or steadfast, slender or ample in volume, **and** the beginning, the middle or the terminus of a passage. In other words, an element of music is its material as invested with some extra character, and as identifiable in terms of something unitary or relatively complete, or satisfying in itself.

It may be added that, in so far as in actual music the notes used do not remain separate but are inter-connected, the ways in which, or the formal graces in terms of which, the notes are inter-related are as much elements as the constituent notes of the *rāga*. Further, a distinction must be made between the elements of a number and the numbers themselves which go to make a whole recital. A complete recital may comprise a *vilambit khyāl*, a *drut khyāl* and a *ṭhumrī*, *bhajan* or *tarānā*. These are all numbers, not mere elements, though they are certainly distinguishable **parts** of the complete recital.

The distinction between an element and a complete number may now be brought out. One clear difference is this. In a complete recital any one of the three numbers we have distinguished as components of a complete recital may be left out, without necessarily incurring the charge of impropriety. Thus, an Ameer Khan may not sing a *ṭhumrī* or a *tarānā* at all, and may even devote much more time to the *vilambit* than to the *drut* composition. On the other hand, a vocalist like Ustad Aman Ali Khan may begin the very first composition at a pace which is clearly a little quicker than the standard *vilambit* pace. The elements of music, on the other hand — i.e. the constituent notes of the *rāga*, and the basic *vādī-saṁvādī* relation — are all alike necessary. No one of them can be left out without incurring the charge of grammatical outrage. From the same point of view, though they are clearly included in the complete recital, the little pleasing effects that may be produced by adroitness of the way in which the next number is begun can**not** be regarded as an **element** of the recital. For, though if such subtle marks of skill are not there the complete recital may well lose some of its overall appeal, the omission would yet not be regarded as a clear error.

To turn now to 'form' in the context of our vocal music, the word is used in two senses. First, we speak of the form of a composition or *bandiśa*, in which case the word signifies the unique internal structure of the composition; and second, we also speak of the various forms of Hindustānī music like *khyāl*, *dhruvapada*, *dhamār*, *tarānā*, *ṭhumrī*, etc., in which case 'form' means simply a **sub-type** of the art of music. But forms such as these, admirable though they all be, cannot be said to be fundamental, in so far as they are all themselves set in the forms of *rāga* and *tāla*, and therefore, can only be said to be "**forms within forms**". It is hence essential to give due thought to the truly basic forms of *rāga* and *tāla*.

Of these two, however, *rāga* may be said to be the more fundamental because, though some classical music — such as *ālāpa* — may well be possible without *tāla*, *rāga* cannot be avoided by any form of our classical music. This concept may, therefore, be taken for elaborate discussion last of all, so as to provide a kind of a fitting climax. Presently we may pay some attention to the concept of *tāla*.

Here, however, some sceptical questions may be put at once. Is it proper to give **separate** attention to rhythm? Is rhythm an **independent** art at all? Now, questions such as these may be readily answered by pointing to a fact of our musical practice. Today, it is obviously possible that a *solo tablā* or *mṛdaṅgam* recital may turn out to be one of the more important items of a whole session of music in a big music conference. But, even from the viewpoint of aesthetic theory it is possible to argue for the view that rhythm is an independent art. The argument may be put thus:

As Susanne Langer says, an art which claims to be independent much have its own unique material; its distinctive primary creation; and some criteria of evaluation which are **uniquely** relevant to it. Luckily, rhythm **is** able to meet all these conditions. This may be brought out as follows:

(a) For its unique material rhythm employs *bol*s or mnemonic syllables which are meaningless letters like *tā*, *dhā*, *tin*, *dhin*, *dir dir*, etc. These *bol*s perform a positive function in the region of this particular art. They identify the *mātrā*s of a *tāla*, and also aim at seizing the manner of sounds produced by striking the drums at particular points in specific ways. The beauty of these *bol*s arises from their clear execution and methodical grouping. But these *bol*s are used for the purpose of rhythmic creation only, and **not** for any non-aesthetic purpose. It is partly because of this reason that rhythm is regarded as a distinct art.

(b) Rhythm also fulfills the second condition because there is something in it which may well be said to be its primary or fundamental creation. This basic something is here the shapely, evenly moving, self-regulating, and internally articulate character of a *ṭhekā* or rhythm cycle. How a *ṭhekā* really shows all these features, may be explained as follows:

A *ṭhekā* is **shapely** in the sense that it begins from and returns to the very first beat, i.e., the *sama*, after completing a round (*āvṛtti*), and keeps repeating this process. Consequently, the shape or form assumed is that of a self-completing whole. We call it evenly moving because its pace is always required to be steady and unfaltering. In other words, the *laya* never slackens or quickens **involuntarily**. Further, a *ṭhekā* is said to be self-regulating in the sense that it is the length or brevity of the very first beat (i.e., *sama*) itself which directly determines the pace at which the entire subsequent drumming is to proceed. This is a unique instance of the determination of the whole-form by the manner of a single part, which clearly indicates the automotive or self-determining character of rhythm. By the internally articulate character of the *ṭhekā* is meant the requisite clarity of the *bol*s as executed, whatever be the pace of playing. The *ṭhekā* is called the fundamental creation of rhythm because the excellence of every rhythmic pattern is judged not only from the viewpoint of its own inner design, but from that of its relation to the flow of the *ṭhekā*. What is more, this *ṭhekā* (as played) may be called a creation, and not a mere making, because its self-completing or self-regulating character is an emergent quality which is not to be found in the mere notation of the cycle.

(c) Finally, there **are** some criteria which are used for evaluating the excellence of rhythm alone, and not of any other art. The more important of these are: perfectly timed advent at the *sama* or focal beat, and an unfaltering steadiness of pace.

To conclude: rhythm **is** an independent art, and it is therefore, proper to consider it separately from the melodic aspect of music.

Now, to begin an independent discussion of rhythm, our word for it is *tāla*. Yet, the two words are by no means identical in meaning and character. For *tāla* as practised in the region of our music *bol*s are essential. In Western music, on the other hand, rhythm is subject to no such necessity. Our present concern, however, is a little different. We have to see how rhythm is a **basic form**. This question itself may be broken up into two. First, how is rhythm a **form** at all? Second, how is it **basic** as a form? The second of these questions is easy to answer. Barring *ālāpa* which precedes music accompanied by drumming, — or of the *dhruvapada* kind, and also in instrumental music — **every** form of our classical music is, in respect of its basic composition, set in a particular *tāla*; and, what is more, when this basic composition is presented as a part of a whole recital, it is invariably accompanied by drumming.

But the first question, how rhythm is a form, cannot be so summarily dealt with. We can, of course, readily say that a *tāla* is a form in so far as it is an identifiable **organisation** of some beats or *mātrā*s and *bol*s. But what these elements or constituents of a *tāla* really are, and how exactly they are organised to produce various rhythms, — questions such as these require analytic attention to the concepts of *laya*, *mātrā*, *ẓarab*, *bol* and *sama*. It is to this task that we presently turn.

Laya: Better known in the West as aesthetic pace, *laya* is one of the basic concepts of Hindustānī rhythm. Its meaning or aesthetic character may be put thus:

> *Laya* in rhythm means a flow which is (when established) even and one and continuous so long as the music lasts; has distinct ways of movement and its own orbit or extent; permits, as their ground and controller, a variety of effects and arrangements; and which — by virtue of its organisation around, and shapely access to, the central beat — can look well-oriented and complete, without being cut short, as it wheels without faltering its flowing rhythmic rounds.[1]

Mātrā: A *mātrā* is a measure or a measured quantity or extent. Here, in rhythm, it is a beat which marks a basic and equal sub-division of *laya*. With the help of *bol*s, *mātrā*s make *laya* articulate, and also enable us to organise it (*laya*) into cycles of different extent and character.

Zarab: In actual rhythm, the impact of a *mātrā* or *bol* on the flow of *laya* is *ẓarab*. Ordinarily, a *ẓarab* occurs at the normal (or fixed) location of the *mātrā*. But, to create novel effects of beauty it is sometimes put even **between** two adjacent *mātrā*s.

Bol: A *bol* identifies the *mātrā*. As already discussed, *bol*s are mnemonic or meaningless syllables like *tā*, *dhā*, *tir kit*, *dhin*, etc., which are used exclusively for rhythmic creation.

Sama: A *sama* is generally regarded as the first beat of a *tāla*. But, it would be truer to call it the focal beat because it not only starts but also completes a cycle or *ṭhekā* in a *tāla*. It is focal also in the sense that after executing various patterns, melodic or rhythmic, the musician is required to return to **it** with split second accuracy. Its centrality may be further heightened by showing how the flow of the patterns in question moves towards it designedly, and by the sharp and definite way in which it itself is required to be marked on the drums. Finally, as already discussed, it is this very beat which fixes the pace of the entire subsequent drumming.

We may now turn to analyse some patterns the character of which is generally meant to be understood mainly in relation to the *sama*. But before so doing, it is essential to remember that our task now is not so much to **name** the diverse look of the various patterns as **to unravel their inner organisation**, for this is how we have understood form as aesthetic. Our attempt will indeed be to bring out how the aesthetic character of a pattern depends upon a careful selection and organisation of its constituent materials. The first two arrangements that we pick for such analysis are both patterns of the *viṣama* kind, that is, their last syllable does **not** coincide with the prefixed occurrence of the *sama*. Here is the first of these, a pattern of the *anāgat* variety:

1	2	3	4	5	6	7	8	9	10	11	12	13	14	15	16
								घिन	नन	नागे	तिट	क्ड़धि	तधा	तिट	घेघे
तिट	घेघे	ना	तिट	गद	दी	घड़ा	ऽन	नागे	तिट	किड़ा	ऽन	तकि	टधि	किट	धा
तिट	घिन	तरा	ऽन	ऽ	धा	तिट	घिन	तरा	ऽन	ऽ	धा	तिट	घिन	तरा	ऽन
×				२				०				३			

Before, however, we subject this pattern to aesthetic analysis it seems necessary to explain why it is made to arise from the off-beat (i.e., *khālī*), primarily because most of such *viṣama* patterns take off from the first beat itself. **Our** argument is here simple. As we have already brought out, the *sama* is not merely the first, but the focal beat of the cycle; it marks both the opening and close of the rhythmic round. If this is so, a pattern that is **truly and wholly** *viṣama* should avoid coinciding with the *sama* at **both** its terminii, that is, not only where it consummates the *āvṛtti*, but also where it begins the pattern. Otherwise, if it avoids the *sama* only where it ends as a pattern, it would be *viṣama* only half-heartedly, so to say.

Consider, next, the audile character of the syllables which this pattern builds upon. The relatively heavy sound of syllables like *ghi* and *dhā* here dominates, partly because of its intrinsic character, and partly because it occurs at points of explicit emphasis, the reference here being mainly to the three individual locations of *dhā* in the concluding part of the pattern. This partly explains **the impressive character** or the seeming depth of the whole pattern. Some contribution to this effect is also made by the insistent quality of the opening syllable: घिननन which just cannot be recited at too leisurely a pace without appearing odd, and by the rather emphatic suddenness of the syllable क्ड़धित.

But it would be wrong to suppose that the 'look' of this pattern is one of unrelieved heaviness. The 'relief' we have here in mind is provided by some details of unquestionable symmetry, alacrity and directed pace. Some attention may be given to each one of these features. Elements of shapeliness or similarity are here easy to point out. This, each of the two opening syllables घिननन नागेतिट comprises four letters, so that their temporal extent is equal. Further, the syllabic complex नागेतिट किड़ान is a clear parallel of गद्दीघिड़ान which precedes it. Finally, the closing triple occurrence of धा तिटघिन तरान the triplicity of which is made quite manifest by the intervening pauses, lends a clear look of order to the way in which the pattern attains to its climax at the *sama*.

As for the effect of alacrity — or चमक, as we call it in Hindustānī — the details which conduce to it are provided not only by the syllable क्ड़धित, but by two other syllables as well: first, the *dhā* which follows the syllable क्ड़धित at once and emphatically; and second, by everyone of the three *dhā*s which punctuate the closing segment of the flow, and which gain a little nimbleness from the fact that they all alike deviate from the marks (or claps) of the basic sub-divisions of the cycle with split-second accuracy.

Finally, the suggestion of not a mere flow, but of a **directed** flow — that is, of a flow that seems **to make for the** *sama* — is worked up by the closing *tiyā*, the unit of which is धा तिटघिन तरान and the last two *dhā*s of which gain a clear measure of spiritedness from the impatience, so to say, with which they come after the fifth and the twelfth beat respectively. On the whole, we repeat, the aesthetic form of this rhythmic pattern wears the look of an impressive, spirited, and well-directed flow towards the *sama*, which, however, is not directly marked, but is only, yet clearly indicated to contemplation by the very wilful, yet orderly withholding of itself from literal contact with the *sama*. It may here be pointed out that **form in rhythm is no mere syllabic collocation as such, but how or what it appears to a trained and imaginative grasp**. This does not, however, mean that the *bol*s' own character is here unimportant. The truth rather is that the overall form of any rhythmic pattern depends, quite importantly, on the audile character of its constituent *bol*s. In the present pattern too, if we replace the *bol*s तिटघिन with तिनगिन the requisite weightiness of the form of the pattern will suffer. Generally, however, one or two details of lighter hue may **not** give rise to this risk; they may even add to the requisite overall effect. To take a parallel from literature, in the Shakespearean tragedies the comic relief provided by the speeches of the Fool heightens the overall effect of depth, suffering and seriousness which is necessary for a tragedy. But here, in the pattern being discussed, the तरान upon which the closing threesome is built is already a *bol* without much depth. So, the **substitution** visualised will be definitely harmful to the requisite aesthetic form of the pattern.

We may now analyse a pattern of the other kind of *viṣama* compositions, or an *atīta torhā* . Unlike the *anāgat* patterns, such a *torhā* completes itself just **after** the *sama*-instant. The specimen that we set out to analyse presently is, however, distinguished by an additional feature. As demanded by our norm of full or two-way displacement, it also takes off from the *khālī*, that is, not from the *sama*; and is, moreover, *cakradāra*. It runs thus:

1	2	3	4	5	6	7	8	9	10	11	12	13	14	15	16
								तक्	थरि	तक्	थरि	कुकु	थरि	कुकु	थरि
तक्	धलां	ग	तक्	धलां	ग	धुम	किट	धाधि	गिन	धाधि	गिन	ता	धा	धाधि	गिन
धाधि	गिन	ता	धा	धाधि	गिन	धाधि	गिन	ता	धा	ऽ	ऽ	तक्	थरि	तक्	थारि
कुकु	थारि	कुकु	थरि	तक	धलां	ग	तक	धलां	ग	धुम	किट	धाधि	गिन	धाधि	गिन
ता	धा	धाधि	गिन	धाधि	गिन	ता	धा	धाधि	गिन	धाधि	गिन	ता	धा	ऽ	ऽ
तक्	थरि	तक	थरि	कुकु	थरि	कुकु	थरि	तक्	धलां	ग	तक्	धलां	ग	धुम	किट
धाधि	गिन	धाधि	गिन	ता	धा	धाधि	गिन	धाधि	गिन	ता	धा	धाधि	गिन	धाधि	गिन
ता	धा														
×				२				०				३			

Now, the aesthetic form of this pattern, or how it "looks" if properly presented, is that of an orderly **ebullient** flow. How this is so may be explained thus. The suggestion of **ebullience** arises because of some distinct features. First, as if because of its own inner filling, design and amplitude, the pattern seems to spill over the focal beat. Second, some syllables here are so arranged, in an order of increasing extent, that the pattern appears to swell. Thus, whereas the first few syllables up to the second धलांग are all twosomes, the *bol*s that follow — that is धाधिगिन धाधिगिन ता धा, — appear as a threesome. This device of arranging elements in terms of growing or mounting extent is, of course, not confined to rhythm. It is seen to work in the region of poetry as well. For example, in the following lines of Wordsworth the suggestion of growing depth is evoked by means of a sequence of words of increasing length (*see* the last four words of the second line):

. . . . A sense sublime
of something far more deeply interfused

As for the pattern under review, how its ebullient flow appears **orderly** or inwardly organised may be brought out as follows:

To begin with, the very opening syllables from तक्थरि to the second धलांग appear organised because of the operation of the Gestalt laws of contiguity and similarity. Here the first three pairs of *bol*s are obviously similars; and, just as clearly, they are close to, or contiguous with, each other. A closer look even reveals a subtle detail of sameness. The second letter of the first syllable, i.e., क् is to be presented as a light or tangential *bol* and a similar effect is demanded by the *laghu mātrā*s of रि and कु. On the other hand, a very clear measure of orderliness is provided by the big *tiyā* which embraces, in the way of a circle, three occurrences of the same syllabic complex "तक्थरि (2) . . . ता धा". What is more, the ता धा, which provides the close of the complex just referred to, is to be recited in the manner of a leisurely and somewhat elongated flow which at once provides a requisite measure of inner continuity by linking the three segments.

Finally, through the operation of the Gestalt law of contrast, the single *pakhāvaj bol* धुमकिट, which punctuates the long and flowing string of dance syllables, provides a relief which heightens its own distinctness as well as the mutual affinity of the dance *bol*s.

Likewise, considering a dance *torhā* of the (Benāras?) School

1	2	3	4	5	6	7	8	9	10	11	12	13	14	15	16
तिक	धा	दिग	दिग	दिग	थो	दिग	दिग	थे	ई	ऽ	त	अ	त	थे	ई
ता	ऽ	थे	ई	कु	कु	धा	ऽ	तिक	धा	दिग	दिग	दिग	थो	दिग	दिग
थे	ई	त्रा	म	थे	ई	तिक	धा	दिग	दिग	दिग	थो	दिग	दिग	थे	ई
त्रा	म	थे	ई	तिक	धा	दिग	दिग	दिग	थो	दिग	दिग	थे	ई	त्रा	म
थे	ई														
×				२				०				३			

we find here the unmistakable suggestion of an **undulating** flow relieved by a few moments, provided by the syllable त्राम, that seem to stay and sparkle for a while. But, what is dominating here is the rapid and repeated string of closed *bol*s provided by the passage: दिग दिग दिग

Now, an analysis of this *torhā* requires us to look at it from both the literal and the aesthetic points of view. It is therefore, important to first understand how the two viewpoints differ. The literal point of view looks at syllables in their own individual character. The aesthetic point of view, on the other hand, considers the *bol*s **as they appear to a rasika in the setting of the pattern which embraces them**. Now, to consider the pattern first literally, we may focus on धा and त्रा. Their individual audile character is similar in one respect, and different in another. It is similar insofar as both the syllables are **open** because they use the sound आ, and different because in the syllable त्रा alone do we find some inherent quickness and sparkle. But what we have just said will have to be revised if we look at these *bol*s aesthetically, that is, how they appear in the knitwork of the pattern. Here we find that whereas the openness of धा is in no way heightened by the preceding क, because the difference between the two is not one of contrast, the openness and sparkle of the other *bol* त्रा is readily thrown into bolder relief by the expressly closed sound of the immediately preceding ई (in थेई).

As for the suggestion of an undulating flow that the pattern being attended to evokes, it may be explained as follows. First, it is the rapid, yet somewhat relaxed string of the *bol*s दिग दिग दिग which are often repeated here, and are put along with each other in such a way that their utterance at a lively, measured tempo, right from the first syllable तिकधा up to थो दिग दिग थेई, gives the pattern a look of the suggestion in question. Moreover, except perhaps on the first occasion, the *bol* थो always occurs as a kind of emphasis, so relieving and heightening the generally galloping character of the pattern. Further, if we look at the phrase तअतथेई its correct utterance also conduces to the same up-and-down suggestion, because were this syllable presented as a stiff and compressed *bol*, it would appear sharp, **and would seem to detract from the undulating flow of the pattern**. Moreover, by applying the Gestalt law of contrast, we may see how the effect of the undulating flow in this *torhā* is heightened. To begin with, the contrast of the quick pace of syllables from तिकधा दिग दिग to थो दिग दिग with the steady movement of the syllabic link ताथेई कुकुधा heightens the galloping character of the segments which precede and follow it. An important point to be noted here is that this adjudgment of the pace of the segments as quick or steady takes place not only through mutual comparison of the segments in question, but also by looking at them all **against the basic** *laya* **of the** *ṭhekā*. So we may say that the perception of the aesthetic form of this *torhā* involves the awareness of multiple relations. It may also be pointed out, in passing, that the **perception** of the **aesthetic form** of a *torhā* and its **analysis for understanding** are two different things. Mere analysis of a pattern or *torhā* may not require us to all along bear in mind the basic *laya* of the *ṭhekā*; that is, we may confine our attention to the character and inner disposition of syllables in the pattern itself. But when the same pattern is presented in an actual recital, and we contemplate it, the *laya* of the *ṭhekā* is all along borne in the mind; and it works as an implicit determinant of how the syllables look: fleeting or steadfast, emphatic or unassuming.

Having analysed a few *torhā*s we may now give some attention to a couple of *ṭhekā*s with a view to bringing out their **form**. The **aesthetic function** of a *ṭhekā* in music is to establish and reveal the requisite pace at once, and to keep it as such, that is, steady and manifest, throughout the recital. It **is** also to indicate the measured cross-section of *mātrā*s within which the basic composition is to be sung or played. Therefore, it is essential for a *ṭhekā* to have an identifiable **form**, and this is indeed so. Every *ṭhekā* is an integration of some specific *bol*s and a fixed number of beats in a particular way because of which it can be easily distinguished from the other *ṭhekā*s, and readily identified by the main performer.

Further, it is indeed the **form** of a *ṭhekā* which enables a musician to manage compositions that may even cover an extensive stretch of *mātrās*. How a *ṭhekā* does all this may be seen by analysing the following rhythm-cycle:

1	2	3	4	5	6	7	8	8½	9	10	11	12
धिन	ऽधा	ऽगे	तिरकिट	धिन	धिन	धातिर	किट	तिन	ऽता	तिरकिट	धागे	तिरकिट
×				२				०				

13	14	14½	15
धिन	क	धा	तिरकिट

The first noteworthy thing about this *savārī ṭhekā* is that the very opening twosome of syllable, धिन ऽ, covering two *mātrās* indicates and fixes the pace which the whole rhythmic matrix (*ṭhekā*) has to follow. Besides, it is interesting to see how this cycle is inwardly organised. All organisation builds itself around a focal point by employing elements some of which are similar to, and others quite different from, each other. Here the element of similarity is provided by the repeated occurrence of the syllables तिरकिट and धिन as well as धागेतिरकिट. As for difference or contrast, we have to refer, first, to the *bol*s धागेतिरकिट and धातिरकिट. Here we find that the धा which precedes the second तिरकिट appears more open than the धा which initiates the syllable धागे. Thus, though literally similar, the two *dhā*s **appear** to be, or are **aesthetically**, different. Only the second धा seems to proclaim itself, and this difference is traceable to two factors. First, the single धा in question consumes the temporal length that is occupied by the two-in-one धागे. Second, whereas the ongoing character of धागे is shared, and so diluted, by the more flowing character of तिरकिट, the other धा seems to stand for a while against the easy roll of तिरकिट. But it would be wrong to suppose that this *ṭhekā* is **divided** between the similar and different elements. On the other hand, it remains a manifest unity or singleness because the similar elements appear to bracket, or to provide a kind of frame to the *bol*s which make an other to them. Thus, in the opening passage, the syllabic tuft धागेतिरकिट is framed on either side by somewhat flowing (or gentle) employment of the syllable धिन.

Yet, another *bol* that immediately captures our attention in this *ṭhekā* is the syllable तिन. It **appears** flighty, **though it is not so in itself**. Now why does it so **appear**? To answer this question we have to see how it is related to the adjacent *mātrās*. It occurs **between** the eighth and the ninth beat, or **at** the 8½ beat; and this is why it seems to be a spurt. In other words, the form or organisation of a *ṭhekā* does not mean that the *bol*s in it are merely put together, but that the *bol* and its setting determine each other in respect of appearance. Thus, whereas the *bol* in question acquires the look of a nimble wedge from its precise location in the *ṭhekā*, the *ṭhekā* itself appears segmented into two balanced halves because of the accent of abandon provided by the तिन. In sum, the form of the *ṭhekā* is a dynamic inter-relatedness of *bol*s, beats and aesthetic pace.

It would thus be wrong to suppose that the form of a rhythm-cycle depends merely on the fixed number of beats it employs. *Ektāla* uses 12 beats to complete its *āvṛtti* and so does a *cautāla*; a *tritāla* and a *tilavāḍā* both employ 16 beats each; and *āḍā cautāla*, *jhūmrā*, *dhamār* and *dīpachand* are all cycles of 14 *mātrās*. Yet, every one of them is different from its temporal colleagues in terms of the following characteristics: the nature and number of *bol*s, the location of the offbeat, and the focal beat (*sama*) which sometimes occurs on the left one; and, in certain cases, on the pace required for adequate effect. How such differentiating features may produce diverse cycles out of the same number of beats may be brought out by analysing four asymmetrical rhythms namely, *teorā*, *rūpaka*, *pashto* and *mughlai*. These are all seven-beat cycles with the *sama-bol* तिन occurring at the left one or the *khālī*. To begin with *teorā*, its syllabic form is as follows:

1	2	3	4	5	6	7
तिन	नाऽ	तिरकिट	धिन	धिन	धाऽ	धाऽ
०			२		३	

The operation of the Gestalt principles of contrast, contiguity and similarity is apparent in the organisation of this particular rhythm. Excessive repetitiveness tends to bore us, and so a measure of contrast is necessary for the maintenance of interest; it provides moments of relief. Contiguity and similarity, on the other hand, lessen the difficulty of holding the many details of an art-work as one. They make for unified perception. Now, in the cycle under review the *sama-bol* तिन is a closed sound which is immediately followed by the open syllable ना. This provides a closed-open contrast. Further, although the bol धिन धिन and धा घा are pairs of similars, yet, in relation to each other, they show a similar closed-open contrast akin to the opening तिन ना.

The element of continuity is here provided by the slightly elongated way in which the two *dhin*-s are visualised during recitation or contemplation. But the most noteworthy detail in this *teorā* rhythm, is the तिरकिट which here occurs at double the speed of any other *bol*. Projecting a sparkling effect, this syllable appears as a distinct figure against the setting of other *bol*s. Hence its perceptual character and pace are both responsible for making it appear quite different from the other *bol*s of the pattern.

This particular beauty or liveliness provided by the तिरकिट to the *teorā-cycle* is not found in *rūpaka-tāla ṭhekā* which has the following, syllabic rhythmic form:

1	2	3	4	5	6	7
तिन	तिन	ना	धिन	नाऽ	धिन	नाऽ
०			२		३	

Here, we can easily notice the elements of similarity, contiguity and contrast. Similarity is here provided by the dual occurrence of the bol तिन in the opening passage and of धिन ना in the closing part. The open and steadfast utterance of नाऽ after the second तिन, and the धिन of the 4th *mātrā*, followed forthwith by नाऽ, provide the requisite element of contrast in the same closed-open relation as is to be found in the previous *ṭhekā*. This cycle, *rūpaka*, does not however incorporate a single *bol* that could be regarded as a distinct figure against the occurrent context of other *bol*s.

Consider, next, *pashto* having the following syllables and form:

1	2	3	4	5	6	7
तिन	ऽ	तक	धिन	ऽ	धा	धा
०			२		३	

Here, the bol तिन, which marks the focal beat, occurs only once, just as in *teorā*. But, here the empty second *mātrā* after तिन invests this *bol*, if properly recited, with an elongated quality which is not there in the तिन of *teorā*. Further, the filling of *bol*s in this cycle is sparse as compared to that of *teorā*. This indeed is why *pashto* can have the requisite measure of continuity *only* **if it is played at a quick speed**. Further, within a single *āvṛtti*, or in the basic fabric of the *ṭhekā*, there is here nothing to heighten by contrast the तिन as a distinct *bol* in the cycle. However, if the *āvṛtti* is repeated, as is indeed the usual practice, the openness of the terminal *bol*s, धा धा will certainly provide a palpable measure of otherness to the closed *sama-bol* तिन. Yet, the element of similarity is here more pronounced, for the opening syllables तिन ऽ तक धिन ऽ are all (more or less) closed *bol*s and the last 2 *bol*s धाऽ धाऽ are **both** open. A suggestion of inner undividedness is here provided by the slightly lengthened way in which the *bol*s तिन, धिन and धा धा are here recited or visualised.

Finally, the *mughlai thekā,* which incorporates more *bol*s than *pashto* has the following form:

1	2 2½	3	4	5	6	7
तिन	ऽ ता	तिरकिट	धिन	ऽ	धागे	तिरकिट
०			२		३	

This cycle is easily distinguishable from the above-mentioned rhythm-cycles because, first, the *sama-bol* तिन here appears steadfastly single, and not merely closed. But the तिरकिट which precedes this *bol* **during the continued playing of the rhythm as a cycle** appears entirely different; it is marked by succession and is relaxed, yet lively. This contrast of the one with the diverse, and of the steady and firm with the lively, helps to bring out the distinctive effect of the focal beat (तिन). The point may be brought out by imagining a change. If an element of successiveness is introduced in the *sama*-bol itself — say, if the तिन is converted into a quicker 2-in-1 तिन तिन — the contrast as well as the distinctive effect of the same bol तिन will both suffer or utterly disappear. As for the needed measure of continuity, it is here provided by the elongated quality of तिनऽ and धिनऽ. The element of similarity arises because of the dual occurrence of तिरकिट at the third and seventh beats, and by virtue of the similar perceptual quality of the syllables तिन and धिन. To some extent, we also here notice an element of contrast in the closed-open manner of the bols तिन-ता and धिन-धा in this *ṭhekā*.

But the syllable which here cannot fail to catch our attention is ता. It influences the same-bol तिन in two ways. It occurs between the second and the third beats with such flightiness that it appears to be a close rival to the focal beat — and in a way shares — and so somewhat bedims the essential centrality of the focal bol तिन.

And now we may turn to see how, as Dewey rightly points out, the consummatory phase in aesthetic form is recurring and not merely final. The needful may be done by analysing a *paran-āmad* relating to *Kathak* dance of the Lucknow Gharānā.

The beauty of such an intra-form lies in the way it blends *aṅga* (i.e., bodily configuration in dance) with (the formal character of) *bol*s and in its handling of rhythm. In other words, the form or look of a *paran-āmad* depends upon the character and knitting of the syllables it employs, and — according to this syllabic content — determines bodily configuration. Now, the art-elements involved in the process are: the basic rhythm (as marked by the *lehrā-ṭhekā* matrix); the individual character (both rhythmic and audile) of the *bol*s; their order; the intervals that hold the segments apart; changes of pace and demands of syllables in respect of bodily aptness.

The *āmad* to be analysed, on the basis of these art-elements, has the following syllabic and rhythmic form:

1	2	3	4	5	6	7	8	9	10	11	12	13	14	15	16
धा	त	क	थुं	गा	ऽ	धा	गे	दिं	ग	ता	ऽ	धा	तिं	ता	ऽ
धि	त्ता	कुड़	धा	तकु	का	थुं	गा	तकि	टत	का	ऽ	तिट	कत	गदि	गिन
ता	थेई	ततु	थेई	आ	थेई	तत	थेई	थेई	तथे	ईत	थेई	थेई	थेई	ततु	ततु
ता															
×				२				०				३			

To begin with, the most apparent and appealing feature in this intra-form is its **terminal definiteness**, provided by the open syllables धा — as the initial note, and ता as the concluding one. This makes the *āmad* appear **self**-complete — a requirement which every good pattern is supposed to meet. Indefinite terminal endings spoil the overall look of any recital or performance because they tend to make the presentation somewhat loose and flowing as well as deficient in inner clarity. It is therefore important to give due attention to the intrinsic character of the opening and the closing *bol*s of an intra-form.

Furhter, a pattern is considered to have an articulate form if it reveals clear segments, each having its own clear beginning and end. These segments provide inner intervals to an intra-form which give enough space to the *aṅga* to unfold itself that gets restricted if long stretches of लड़ीबन्द syllables are incorporated in the pattern. However, such a device is highly appreciated if it is able to provide a contrast which heightens the held-apart look or identity of the *bol*s that come before and after it. We may see how this beauty of form is projected in the present *āmad*. It opens with three clear segments (from the first to the twelfth beats), having धा, ता गा and का as distinct end-side *bol*s and they provide enough space for bodily configuration. The tuft of rapid syllables (लड़ीबन्द) occurs once in the form of "तकिट तका तिटकत गदिगिन". Now the *bol*s which come before or after this syllablic link are slower in pace. This spurt helps to heighten by contrast the *āmad*'s overall impressiveness — a quality revealed in the very way the intra-form opens, its first three segments all beginning with धा. It also goes very well with both the preceding *pakhāvaj bol*s and the gentler ones of dance that follow it because, though it is impressive due to its filling and pace, it does not appear heavy or bold since the *bol*s in it are neither open nor assertive. It therefore, serves as a link that does not jut out but leaves the pattern phenomenally one.

In this pattern, the ता that follows गिन immediately appears aesthetically apt for two reasons. First, the adjacence of a closed and an open sound provides a likeable contrast; and second, this *bol* also serves as a needed moment where the lively spurt can return to the basic pace which is here decided, by the very deliberateness (unhurried movement) of the first *bol's* utterance. The धा which opens this intra-form is of necessity steady. Any attempt to utter it quickly would only cramp its *mātrā* and thus spoil its literal character. Similarly, the immediately following तक is also quite steady here. Its correct utterance is exactly identical with the way we articulate the word तक in the following sentence "चलो ज़रा वहाँ तक घूम आऐं". Here too, a change in its apt utterance — say, as तक् or तका — would make it seem inconsistent pace-wise with the steadiness of the opening धा as well as with the intra-form's overall look of dignity projected by the pattern.

Finally, keeping in mind the norm of *aṅga-bol* accordance, which is a cardinal requirement in dance, we notice how, in this intra-form, the formal character of some *bol*s like थुं and धिं demands a measure of depth in *aṅga*. The थुं coupled with गा demands a suggestion of depth or inwardness in *aṅga* just as धिंता here demands a fuller *aṅga* than धित्ता. It is indeed the clear need of the liberal use here of धा and of *bindī*s in थुंगा, दिंगता, धिंता which demand a measure of depth in *aṅga* and of the very intervals between the segments distinguished which permit and call for an opening of *aṅga*. But here we also see how the formal character of *bol*s, where it does not expressly demand a bold and open *aṅga*, at least goes well with such a disposition of the body. Syllables like धा and ता do not permit figural compression. But many of the syllablic pairs here seem to open because, though the first letter is subdued or closed, the immediately following one is open, as seen in the following *bol*s थुंगा दिंगता धिंता धित्ता कड़धा तक्का and तकिटतका. Dominance of *bol*s like दिग दिग थेई would here destroy the very essential character of an *āmad* which is a kind of formal openness or flowering.

The Rāga-form

Another concept which is as important for Indian music as *tāla* is *rāga*. We all know that every *rāga* has a distinct sensible character, and some internal order too. So, it seems natural to assume that a *rāga* is a form in the aesthetical sense. But, insofar as *rāga* has been defined in various ways in our traditional musicology, — and also because, in the view of great musicians, the creative range of a *rāga* is inexhaustible — the matter demands a little closer look. This is so even because the concept of *rāga* is but one of the many concepts embraced in our philosophy of music, and also because, like every other art, music is related to its creator — that is, the musician — as well, and to the *rasika* who can partly facilitate the proper continuance of a particular music recital. What is more, our discussion of *rāga* cannot be kept apart from the question of etymology which has always been important in our traditional scholarship.

Now, to begin etymologically, the word *rāga* — because it comes from the root *rañj* — may be said to mean that which charms or colours the mind. Here, however, it may at once be doubted if it is quite proper to speak of *rāga* as something which (merely) attracts or suffuses the mind. A beautiful landscape may have the same effect on us, but obviously no one would speak of it as a *rāga*. What is more, the interpretation of a *rāga* as something which merely bewitches the mind is not quite consistent with our traditional philosophical conception of the aim of the art of music. The difficulty may be put thus:

All our classical music must build upon a *rāga*.

> But, the final goal of our music has been said to be not mere entertainment for the mind, but liberation for the individual self (मुक्तिदायकं न तु रञ्जकं).
>
> How, then, can it be held that a *rāga* is essentially something which only pleases the mind? Would not such a conception of *rāga* collide with our view of the final goal of music, a view which we profess even today, though it may be difficult to square it with our contemporary musical practice?

The difficulty we have just now posed is by no means imaginary, for there are definitions which seem to regard interestingness as the key characteristic of a *rāga*. See, for example, the following:

> इत्येवं राग शब्दस्य व्युत्पत्तिरभिधीयते ।
> रञ्जनाज्जायते रागो व्युत्पत्तिः समुदाहृतः ।।[2]

The difficulty may, however, by resolved by suggesting that the definition just cited only provides a necessary, but not a distinguishing feature of a *rāga*. Indeed, whatever be the individual nature of the *rāga* that a musician sets out to project, it must somehow manage to please the listeners, if it is to rightfully claim to be music at all. But here, again, a difficulty arises. Must a *rāga* please **one and all**? If we say 'yes', would it not clash with the evidence of practice that it is only a *rasika*, or a trained contemplator, who can taste the delight of a *rāga* in the proper way? The answer to this question may be allowed to emerge later, after we have reflected on the following well-known definitions of *rāga*:

> योऽसौ ध्वनिविशेषस्तु स्वरवर्ण विभूषितः
> रञ्जको जन चित्तानां स च राग उदाहृतः ।। [3]
>
> स्वरवर्ण विशेषण ध्वनि भेदेन वा पुनः ।
> रञ्जयते येन यः कश्चित् स रागः समतः सताम् ।। [4]
>
> ग्रहांशो तारमन्द्रौ च न्यासोपन्यास एव च ।
> अल्पत्वं च बहुत्वं च षाडवौडविते तथा ।। [5]

It is easy to see that between the first two definitions there is hardly any difference of meaning. They alike speak of a *rāga* as an aggregate of some specific notes which charms people. The third definition, on the other hand, speaks of the details which go to make the whole fabric of a *rāga*. The distinctive character of this view need not surprise us, for how a thing appears as a wholeness to those who attend to it, is something quite different from the way, or as a result of the integration of what elements, it comes into being; and the difference between the two must be kept in mind. This is certainly done by our ancient texts in their writings on *rasa* too. Thus, whereas, as a matter of experience, *rasa* has been spoken of as: 'स्वातम् परामर्श स्वातम् विश्रान्ति:' from the creative or genetic point of view *rasa* is said to arise from a proper integration of the three *bhāva*s known as *vibhāva*, *anubhāva* and *vyabhicārī bhāva*.

Because of their relative simplicity only the first two definitions may be considered presently, without quite forgetting the overall philosophy of our music. It is well-known that our music has been regarded as नाद-साधना which means such a disciplined and intelligent communion with the world of sound that one may become better fitted to realise the ultimate end of life which is spiritual exaltation or liberation of the individual. But, it is obvious that if it is at all to command and hold our attention, the world of sound must comprise differences in a way which is appealing because of its designed character. This is the truth embodied in the first two definitions. They tell us that a *rāga* is not merely a distinct, but an attractive unity of some specific notes; and that it can, therefore, invite and grip the attention of listeners as surely as a beautiful physical object. In other words, *dhvani* and *rañjan* are important words in our definition.

Here, incidentally, because of their relevance to the point we are trying to make, mention may be made of the following from George Santayana's work: *The Sense of Beauty*:

> . . . Sounds are also measurable in their own category; they have comparable pitches and durations, and definite and recognisable combinations of those sensuous elements are as truly objects as chairs and tables. Not that a musical composition exists in any mystical way, as a portion of the music of the spheres, which no one is hearing; but that, for a critical philosophy, visible objects are also nothing but possibilities of sensation. The real world is merely the shadow of that assurance of eventual experience which accompanies sanity. This objectivity can accrue to any mental figment that has enough cohesion,

> content, and individuality to be describable and recognisable, and these qualities belong no less to audible than to spatial ideas.[6]

Our essential concern at the moment is, however, with the two words we have picked for attention. It is obvious that the basic material of a *rāga* is *dhvani*. But, the meaning embodied in the second word, *rañjan*, has to be brought out. It is true that if it is properly rendered a *rāgā* may come to pervade or suffuse the minds of the *rasika*s. But, a pervasive or sustained fascination is not the same thing as a mere instant of appeal. The charm of a *rāga* may even outlive the actual duration of the total recital. This is possible not only because the various notes, in case they conform to the definition of a *svara*, are sweet to the ear, but because they make an organised unity of distinct elements. How, otherwise, could they succeed in holding our attention? It is also here implied that, however unremitting be the appeal of the treatment of a *rāga*, our enjoyment is never undiscriminating.

This is true, we may insist, also of the **musician** as engaged in the act of performance. He is, of course, quite well aware of the grammatical character of the *rāga* as he sets out to sing or play; and, what is more, as the music works up its spell, his mind may come to be steeped in the form of the *rāga* being rendered; but this too is a fact that, however intense be his enjoyment of the music, he can never grow indifferent to the need for saving the character of the *rāga* from disturbance by suggestions of other *rāga*s which may be grammatically close to it. It other words, the experience of the charm of the form of a *rāga* is always partly intellectual as much for the musician himself as for the *rasika*s. A *rasika*, indeed, is no mere attentive listener. He is a trained contemplator. What he enjoys is not merely the *rāga*'s sweetness to the ear, but its cleverly planned arrangements, specially those which present the various notes as organised around, or as contributing to, the importance of the *vādī-saṁvādī* relation and the catch-phrase (पकड़).

At this point it can, of course, be objected that space, which is the field of the eye, also directly permits perception of differences and relations, both within a single object and between different objects and that such a locale is just not there in the region of sound. But to this our ready reply would be that the medium of sound, as built upon by music, is possessed of an important additional element, that is, not mere sound, but the **passage** of sound over different notes, and at a regulated pace. The sound of music is at once a rhythmic advance; and because movement or change appears to be the distinctive feature of life as lived, the regulated passage of music easily comes to acquire a lifelike appeal. Things in space attract attention only if they are quite new or big, or in some other way striking; but, in the world of music, even a gentle and short-lived glide may compel and hold attention. Further, in so far as the different notes are easily perceived as distinct, the rhythmic advance of a *rāga* is more a matter of **our** following it than of **its** moving us into sympathetic confluence. Indeed, the charm of the flowing form of a *rāga* is not the coercive appeal of a single isolated note, nor even the aggregative result of different notes, but the emergent appeal of individual *svaras* as they interact in respect of perceptual quality and temporal arrangements. This is why it is easy for a *rāga* to become an object of aesthetic contemplation.

At the same time we have to remember that the charm of a *rāga* is due not only to its unity and internal differences, but also to the inherent beauty of its constituent *svaras*. A *rāga* embraces quite a few *svaras*; and a *svara* is, in principle, something which is beautiful-in-itself (स्वयमेव राजते). A *svara* has got to sound sweet to the ear. This is, indeed, a basic requirement. However, in the definitions which we seek to explain, what is spoken of is not mere *svaras*, but स्वरवर्ण विभूषितः. And this seems necessary. We just cannot stop at the idea that a *rāga* is a distinct sound (ध्वनि विशेषस्तु). It is, of course, true that to the trained ear every *rāga* seems to be distinct. But, even two noises can appear quite different from each other. The *śloka*, therefore, rightly adds that a *rāga* is only such a distinct sound as is decorated with *svara-varṇa*.

The word, *varṇa*, however, calls for some reflection. What could it possibly mean? It has commonly been taken to signify *sthāyī, ārohī, avarohī* and *sañcārī*. But, it is important to note, in the present context the word *varṇa* qualifies *svara*, and not *rāga*. The second and third definitions speak of *svara-varṇa* not of *rāga-varṇa*. The complete treatment of a *rāga* may well be said to comprise a *sthāyī, ārohī, avarohī* and *sañcārī*. But, how can one speak of the *āroha* and *avaroha* or *sañcārī* or a *svara*? So, we suggest, the word *varṇa* has to be understood differently.

Now, some accepted meanings of the word in question which here seem relevant may be put thus:

(a) A musical sound or note;

(b) sound, vowel, syllables;

(c) class, sort, kind;

(d) external appearance, form, shape;

(e) beauty or complexion, lustre; and

(f) character or quality.

But, if our word, *varṇa*, is taken to mean (a), it would make for a senseless repetition, because the word *svara* already signifies sound. Nor would (b) make any meaningful addition to the meaning of *svara*. So far as (c) and (d) are concerned, they tell us nothing at all about the aesthetic character of musical notes. These may indeed be separated as *komala* and *śuddha*. But such classification does not at all provide for the possibility that a note may come to acquire a distinctly aesthetic look; it may seem to yearn for something remote or simply proclaim itself majestically. And if we accept (d), that is, outward appearance, as the correct meaning, an unanswerable question would arise. If *svara-varṇa* is the external appearance of a *svara*, what could be the inside of a *svara*? Nor does it seem proper to speak of the shape or form of a *svara*. An individual note may well be said to be sweet, tender, expressive or luminuous; but nobody would speak of it as being shapely or well-formed. So we are left with only one choice; we have to interpret *varṇa* as **character or quality**. And this only seems proper, because if the word *varṇa* is taken to mean character or quality, it would cover all the necessary features of a *rāga* listed in the third definition. What is more, if so interpreted, the word would not create any obstacle to our conception of the final goal of music. But this must be explained at some length.

A *svara*'s quality or character at once distinguishes it from other notes; and what serves as a ground of such distinction may be anyone of the following details; its being a focal point of melody, and an instant of repose (*vādī* or *aṁśa*); its placement in the lower (middle) or higher *saptak* (तारमन्द्रौ); its appearing as the close or destiny of a passage (न्यास), or as the start of a musical movement (ग्रह); its being brief or prolonged (अल्पत्व बहुत्व); and, above all, its assumption of an emotive, pictorial, or sensuous look. This means that if the hyphenated *svara-varṇa* is interpreted as the quality or character of *svara*, it would cover not only the grammatical character and aesthetic suggestiveness of *svara*s, and so of music, but even the spiritual effects of musical notes and passages, and so justify our exalted conception of the ultimate end of music. Some warrant would be provided even for the pictorial representation of a *rāga*, because colour, line and volume are also **qualities** of things.

But, even if it be agreed that *svara-varṇa* means qualities of *svara*, one question remains. Are these qualities accessible to every listener? If not, how can we justify the use of the words: रञ्जको जनचित्तानाम्? This question may be answered as follows:

It seems proper to distinguish the qualities of *svara* as immediate and mediate. Sweetness may be regarded as the immediate, **or** primary quality of a note, primary because it is demanded by the very definition of a *svara*, and immediate because it can be easily perceived even by those who are not trained in the grammatical niceties of music. Mediate qualities, on the other hand, are those the perception of which is mediated by a cultivated taste. These qualities are the various kinds of appearance or suggestiveness which a musical note may come to assume by virtue of its relatedness to other notes or to the beats of the rhythm-cycle. Of course, we **can** all perceive even these mediate qualities, but this is possible only after a suitable training of our sensibilities. As a matter of fact, however, everybody is not so trained, and is therefore unable to perceive such qualities of a *svara* as are not merely sensuous. Perhaps even the sensuous sweetness of a note can be perceived only by those who have some prior idea of the specific musical system to which the note in question belongs. Thus, those who have so far heard Hindustānī music only may not be able to perceive the sensuous sweetness of quite a few notes in a Carnatic vocal recital. Therefore, the words, 'जन चित्तानाम्' cannot be taken to mean, literally 'the mind of every individual'. We suggest that the word 'जन' may here be taken to mean 'people collectively'[7] which is an accepted meaning of the word. If we accept this interpretation, a quite sensible suggestion would emerge, and it may be put as follows. The delight which is provided by the complex of some *svara*s of specific qualities which we call a *rāga* is a shareable experience, not a private one. This would go well with the well-known view of Bharata that, like the eye, the ear is an aesthetic sense. Be that as it may, one thing is clear; as against works of literature, music can appeal to vast masses of man, including even those who are quite unlettered. Music may indeed be regarded as an art of the masses.

Incidentally, there is another reason because of which our *rāga*s can appeal readily, if not discriminatingly, to the common man. Many general features of the life of feeling or sentience — such as the droop of grief, the upsurge of hope and vitality, and nimble lightheartedness can all be quite easily manifest in our *rāga*-**music** which builds upon both melody and rhythm; and the average man be easily touched by such expressiveness, though he may not be able to see how it comes into being.

All this must be borne in mind in determining what a *rāga* really is. We must also provide for: (a) the key ideas contained in the definitions we have cited, (b) individual differences in responding to music; and finally, for (c) our traditional conception of the ultimate end of music.

The following definition may, therefore, be proposed:

> A *rāga* is a specific melodic form which serves to permit and determine, as a matrix, the creation and contemplation of music on the basis of the quality, emphases, and relatedness of tones and rhythmic abidance or passage, with an eye to evoking the appropriate *rasa*, and inevitably in accordance with one's individual capacities for technical grasp and aesthetic sensitiveness.[8]

What this definition means may now be brought out:

A *rāga* is a distinct melodic form. This conveys two ideas: (a) that *rāga* is a form, or an integration of the *svara*s that go to make it; and (b) that a *rāga* is essentially a matter of melody, not of rhythm. Both these ideas call for some individual explanation. A *rāga* is internally integrated, and no mere jumble of notes. All organisation must have a centre or some focal point. So, a *rāga* too is an **organised** complex because the notes that it embraces, though all of them must appear clear and sweet, have to be so utilised that they may preserve and project the required importance of the *vādī-saṁvādī* relation. The integrated character of a *rāga* certainly does not mean that all its notes receive equal prominence; the *rāga*-form is rather a unity of regulated emphases. As for the idea that a *rāga* is a matter of melody, the net suggestion obviously is that the *svara*s of a *rāga* follow a before-after order. This order, however, is not horizontal, it may rather be said to be vertical, so that *āroha* and *avaroha* are the two essential movements of a *rāga*.

Some attention has also to be given to the idea that a *rāga* is a **specific** melodic form. The general meaning, of course, here is that every *rāga* appears something distinct to the ear. But this distinctness of appearance means two things: first, that a *rāga* is interesting in itself, because of which it takes and keeps us away from the everyday world, if only for sometime; and, second, that it is perceived as being different from the *rāga*s which may be grammatically close to it. To put it differently, when a *rāga* is rightly contemplated, it is not merely received, but is often **understood** as being different from other *rāga*s. In the region of classical music listening is indeed a discriminating exercise of attention.

Further, it is noteworthy that we have spoken of a *rāga* not as a melodic **type**, but as a **matrix** of melody. A type is only the concept of a class. To illustrate, the type of lemon which is called कागज़ी covers all lemons of a particular kind, but it cannot be said to **make** the fruits which it covers in meaning. A matrix, on the other hand, is the mould **within** which, and the ground-mass **of** which, things are made; and insofar as a *rāga* does not only cover, but is the substance or material of the many compositions created within its bounds, it is better to speak of a *rāga* as a melodic matrix than as a melodic type.

How does this melodic matrix or *rāga* make for the creative work that it does? The answer provided by our definition is: by building upon 'the quality, emphases, and relatedness of tones and rhythmic abidance or passage'. Here, however, many ideas are implicit, and they must be brought out for the sake of understanding. To begin with, a *svara*'s quality may be taken to mean its location in one of the three *saptaks*; its brevity or steadfastness, which is a question of how long the voice is allowed to tarry at a particular *svara*; and its expressiveness, say, its sad or lively look. As for variations of pace, they too can vitally affect the look of a note; but they may also work up the effects of free play, flowing-together and sheer decorativeness.

Some comments are also called for by the words: 'relatedness of tones'. In music the relatedness in question may be taken to cover not only the fact **that** different *svara*s are related, but also **how** they are related; and so to mean the various formal graces as well, such as *sūta*, *mīṇḍa*, *gamak* and *lahak*. So, our definition of *rāga* provides for such features of *rāga*-rendering as, in fact, distinguish actual music, but are not explicitly accommodated by the definitions we have picked for attention.

It is by keeping in mind all the qualities of *svara* we have distinguished that a musician is able to evoke by means of a *rāga* the appropriate *rasa*. But it would be wrong to suppose that this *rasa*, or the net emotive colour of the music, is only expressed **through** the *rāga*-form. So to think would be to suppose that the *rāga* is a mere channel for the expression of the *rasa*. The truth rather is that the *rasa* in question is inseparable from the overall atmosphere worked up by the treatment of the *rāga*; it is, so to say, the look of the full-blown personality of the *rāga* itself. The language used in the *bandiśa* is, of course, no essential part of the *rāga-rūpa*; but there is no doubt that it can facilitate or check the emergence of the required *rasa*. This indeed is why it is important to put such words in a composition as may seem to go well with the *rasa* commonly associated with the *rāga* chosen; and, what is more, to be duly careful about the **proper musical utterance** of these words, so that they may conduce, by virtue of their meaning, to the evocation of the required *rasa*. Another important point here is that the ornamental flourishes and regular patterns that a recital ordinarily includes should neither be so profuse nor so independently emphasised that they may detract from the unity of the form of the *rāga*. This would demand, in the case of a *khyāl*-**recital**, that the *sthāyī* which normally clearly embodies the *rāga*-**form** in its distinct individuality, be projected after every two or three *tāna*s; and that, so far as possible, the prominence of the *vādī* and the *saṁvādī* be preserved even during the course of fluent pattern-weaving. In the case of *dhruvapada*-singing, the parallel requirement would be that neither the use of a particular formal grace, like *gamak*, nor *layakārī* be allowed to detract from the seeming undividedness and dignity of the *rāga-rūpa* evoked by the preceding *ālāpa*.

It is interesting to see how the different forms of our classical vocal music project with inequal emphasis the different aspects of the form of a *rāga*. The *ālāpa* of a good *dhruvapada*-singer brings out the repose and extensiveness implicit in the form of a *rāga*. Where the singer gets inspired, or if he is intrinsically a great artist, the *ālāpa* may even succeed in appearing to raise us into a rarefied atmosphere, so to say, of the very essence of a *rāga* as somewhat freed from the sheer plurality of notes which help us identify it. On the other hand, a good *bandiśa*, be it from the region of *khyāl* or from that of *dhruvapada*, is a visible embodiment of the *rāga* as a collected and easily identifiable wholeness. The *tāna*s of the *khyāl*-singer bring out the infinite room which a *rāga* has for decorative patterns of varying range and emphasis, as against the tranquil and leisurely stretches of *ālāpa*. The key features of the form of a *rāga* may therefore, be put as follows:

As the basic **form** to which all our music must conform, a *rāga* is also the **material** of the numberless compositions that it permits. What enables us to identify it is its *āroha-avaroha* and *vādī-saṁvādī*; but what enables it to generate *rasa* and **us** to fall under its spell is its aesthetic potential, that is, the depth, roominess, animation and expressiveness that are implicit in it, so that whereas its grammatical character is given to the musician, its aesthetic personality has to be brought out by, and so is a challenge to him. It may indeed be held that, though

> in its broadest sense (*rāga*) could be defined as a melodic mode having a rigid and apparently circumscribed form in view of the several conditions laid down for its elaboration, . . . (it is) nevertheless . . . capable of infinite improvisation.[9]

Form and Ālāpa

In so far as *ālāpa* of the *dhruvapada*-manner is the oldest existing and aesthetically quite important form (or sub-type) of our music,[10] we may begin our discussion of form with some remarks on *ālāpa*.

Does *ālāpa* have a form? If yes, what would be the meaning of form in this context. Now, as we have seen, two common meanings of the word 'form' are, outline and shape. In these senses of the word, it is obvious, an exposition of *ālāpa* cannot be credited with form. Whatever has a shape or an outline is limited; and, what is more, in most cases it can be encompassed in attention as a distinct object with fair ease. The distinctive effects of *ālāpa*, on the other hand, are those of serenity, seamless quality, and an intense and enveloping, yet identifiable *rāga-rūpa*. It is true that, when it is consummate, *ālāpa* can seem to be quite self-complete; but, we may note, **it** appears so not in the sense of appearing rounded like a circle — for, to be sure, we do not see its outline — but in that of being wholly satisfying.

So we have to turn to the other meaning of form, to see how it may be said to be there in *ālāpa*. Now, this second sense is what we have chosen to regard as the basic aesthetic meaning of the word, that is, form as the skilful and intense inner integration of the elements of a work of art. But what are the elements of *ālāpa*? The following, we answer: the *svara*s that go to make the *rāga* chosen, *laya* or aesthetic pace, and formal graces like *gamak, lahak, sūta, mīṇḍa, āndola* (आन्दोल), *anuranātmaka*, and

> the *mātrās* that distinguish or are implicit in our first ten Hindi alphabets. The *mātrās* that give us *tāla* are equidistant marks in a temporal sequence. But the ones that form the material of *ālāpa* are regulated variations of *ākāra*. The former measure and figurate *laya*; the latter provide distinctive threads in the warp and woof of *ālāpa*. The *mātrās* are included in *ālāpa*, be it noted, not merely as they appear in their parent alphabets such as इ, ई but as conjoined with other letters, so as to give rise to the singer's basic syllables like ते, रे री, नोम.[11]

Mention may here also be made of the traditional view that the syllables of *ālāpa* 'preceding the *dhruvapada* . . . have been lifted from (the following) invocative *mantra* in Sanskrit:

> . . . *auṁ, ananta hari nārāyaṇa tāraṇa tāraṇi tvam*[12]

Our next question is obvious. How are the elements we have distinguished inter-related? Here, our answer has to be three-fold: first, by keeping an unrelenting eye on the grammar and the aesthetic character of the *rāga*, so that the prominence of the *vādī-saṁvādī* relation, as also the requisite affect — say, of devotion of valour — are duly brought out, if not at the very outset; second, through a careful regulation of the pace of singing; and, thirdly, by means of a skilful employment of the various formal graces which enable the singer to not merely conjoin the various *svara*s, but to work up such effects as those of depth and inwardness (*gamak*), twinkling accents, (*dyut, vedāṅga*), upgoing meander (*ḍagar*) and oscillation (*āndola*). The formal graces cannot be properly explained in words; they call for demonstration in terms of actual singing. But an itelligible account can surely be given of the way in which

> aesthetic pace or duration, as handled with an eye to effect, conduces to the variform look of *ālāpa*. If the singer tarries (or spends more time) on a *svara* with the requisite tunefulness, one may 'see' a line or fount of incandescence, according as the *ākāra* is slender or ample. A

> leisurely (or slow) passage across three or even two adjacent *svaras* often engenders the look of a concave curve. In the higher register a return to the tonic after a steadfast (or enduring) but fine and tuneful articulation of *komala ṛṣabha* may project yearning tenderness, as in a '*Sohnī*' *ālāpa*.[13]

Yet all this knitting of the inner fabric of *ālāpa* takes quite sometime. So, considering the way *ālāpa* develops, as also its final appearance as a distinct *rāga*-atmosphere, the form of *ālāpa* may be said to be the dynamic and full-blown unfoldment of a melody along determinate lines, in roughly the way in which a man's present personality is to be understood in terms of the specific talents and ideals that have determined his growth. What is more, just as the growth of the personalities of different individuals proceeds in terms of varying emphases in different directions, and relative neglect of some other dimensions, so it is proper to suggest the identical note-by-note elaboration is not alike suited to every *rāga*.[14] If, for instance, a sweeping descent from *dhaivat* to *ṛṣabha* is supposed to project the quintessence of a *rāga*, it would surely not be proper for the *ālāpīya* to treat the two *svaras* in leisurely isolation.

Form in Dhamār

After *ālāpa*, we may turn to a *dhamār*, to see how form (in the basic aesthetic sense) may be said to be present even here. We propose to do this by analysing a particular *dhamār* in *rāga Hindol*, the *sthāyī* and *antarā* of which may be put as follows:

1	2	3	4	5	6	7	8	9	10	11	12	13	14
सां	सांध	[ध]सांम॑	-म॑	गग	ग	—	सा	सा[ध]सा	म॑म॑	गग	[ध]म॑	-ध	सांध
खे	लऽ	तऽ	ऽहो	ऽरी	श्या	ऽ	म	चऽ	ऽप	ऽल	ऽम	ऽद	माती
×					२		०			३			

अन्तरा

1	2	3	4	5	6	7	8	9	10	11	12	13	14
								गग	—[ध]म॑	[ध]धम॑	धसां	—	सां
								अबी	ऽर	ऽगु	लाऽ	ऽ	ऽल
सां	—	सांगं	-गं	-म॑	गं	—	सा	सांध	—ध	म॑म॑	गग	गम॑	गसा
की	ऽ	धूऽ	ऽम	ऽम	ची	ऽ	है	नाऽ	ऽच	ऽत	ऽदे	ऽदे	तारी
×					२		०			३			

स्थायी

Before, however, we set out to do so, it is essential to distinguish the various elements of a *dhamār*, for, as we have repeatedly said, the form of an art-work is nothing but an integration of its various elements. Now, these elements, as in the case of any vocal composition, are tones, rhythm, formal graces, and linguistic content or the text of the composition. In the case of *dhamār* songs, we may note, the text relates, by and large, to the *holī* festival. In so far as a rhythm and a tonal type (*rāga*) are both here present, the composition is free to explore creative possibilities in two main directions, i.e., the melodic and the rhythmic. The words of the song can also be creatively handled so as to heighten their meaning musically, or to change the flowing form of a musical phrase itself. But, in so far as classical vocal music is neither rhythm alone nor mere poetry, in a good vocal composition the rhythmic and the semantic elements — though they are, of course, not to be ignored — must ever remain subservient to the melodic aspect.

Where this requisite dominance of the melodic is not present — that is, where the composition proceeds in slavish correspondence with the impact of the various rhythmic beats — and where no formal grace is used, the composition will not acquire a distinct melodic individuality. How such non-aesthetic singing is possible, though surely not desirable, may be brought out by changing (for the

1	2	3	4	5	6	7	8	9	10	11	12	13	14
सां	ध	मं	ग	मं	ग	सा	सा	सा	ग	मं	ध	सां	ध
खे	ल	त	हो	री	श्या	म	च	प	ल	म	द	मा	ती
×					२		०			३			

स्थाई

सां	ध	मं	ग	मं	ग	सा	सा	सा	ग	मं	ध	सां	ध
खे	ल	त	हो	री	श्या	म	च	प	ल	म	द	मा	ती
×					२		०			३			

अन्तरा

							ग	ग	म॑	ध	सां	सां	सां
							अ	बी	र	गु	ला	ल	की
							०			३			
गं	गं	गं	म॑ं	गं	गं	सां	सां	ध	म॑	ग	म॑	ग	सा
धू	ऽ	म	म	ची	ऽ	है	ना	च	त	दे	दे	ता	री
×					२		०			३			

Here, be it noted, the singing shows a rigid one-one correspondence of the emphases of tones and beats; no formal grace is employed; and the entire singing seems to be merely an effort to mark the rhythm correctly, though in terms of singing and not by clapping. Some other details or defects of such (unaesthetic) singing will be indicated later, by way of comparative reference, during our analysis of the proper form of the composition.

Before, however, we begin this analysis, two important remarks may be made. First, we have to bear in mind a basic distinction. The *mātrā* of a letter as written is obviously different from a *mātrā* as the unit of a rhythmic measurement; and both are alike different from the time which may be taken in the musical utterance of the *mātrā* as related to a letter or word. Second, if not primarily, our purpose is also to discover some principles of music composition. We expect to discover at least three basic principles: the principles of creative abandon, sound-sense harmony, and similarity or contrast. With these two considerations in mind, we may now address ourselves to the task of analysing the *dhamār* in question in its proper form. It would be easy to make illustrative comparisons if the first, or the aesthetic way of singing the *dhamār* is referred to as *ae*, and the second or the unaesthetic way, as *an*. Now, the first point to be noted is that in *an* the approach to the *sama*, which begins with the word चपल bestirs itself at the eighth *mātrā*; and that, though the *sama* is of course duly reached, the phrase which precedes the advent of the *sama* — i.e., चपल मदमाती — does not itself seem to be heading towards the focal beat. Nor do these words, here, themselves appear to be what they mean, that is, 'lively' and 'tipsy'. In other words, the principle of the mutual accordance of sound and sense (or meaning) is not here observed. We say so also because (in *an*) the word नाचत in the *antarā* only means, but does not itself wear a dancing look.

Now, as we turn to the *ae* form of the composition, the first thing that strikes us is the abandonment of the constraint of one-one correspondence and the free use of formal graces. Thus, the last letter of the word खेलत — that is, त — is made to merge itself into the following word होरी by means of a brief descending sweep; and the first and the last letters of the word श्याम are similarly linked with the help of an intervening and descending flowing curve, making this word (श्याम) — now stretched out on the inside — end at the eighth beat, so that the approach to the *sama* is compelled to begin at the ninth beat with the utterance of the word चपल.

Further, this word, चपल, is itself amplified into चऽऽपऽलऽ which, in turn lends a certain buoyancy to the *sama*-ward approach; and heightens by contrast — and so justifies in terms of effect — a relatively compressed utterance of माती, the second half the word, which detail of manner, incidentally, makes the word मदमाती itself appear to be a little tipsy.

With regard to the express elongation of the word चपल in musical utterance, however, a question may be put. How is it proper to distort the way in which a word is normally required to be pronounced? To this, our ready answer would be that **good singing** is not the same thing as **correct reading**; that, as we have said earlier, in singing it is the musical values that should be given greater importance; and, that if the lengthening in question brings out, by virtue of the change of pace it entails, the proper meaning of the word, it cannot be condemned as categorical indifference to the demands of language. Above all, the fact here is that the stretching in question, as it occurs in singing, does not look awkward, but only provides a touch of added animation to the whole utterance.

Turning to the *antarā*, of which the opening words are 'अबीर गुलाल की', we find that it begins from the ninth beat, and not from the eighth one as in the case of its *an* form. What is, however, here aesthetically important to note, is some details of the way in which the first part of the *antarā* — that is, अबीर गुलाल की unfolds and completes itself at the *sama*. The intervening ला of गुलाल does not straightway touch the सां as a quick vertical, — as in the case of *an* singing — but moves as an upward and gently expanding upward curve which, so to say, relaxes itself as it ends at the *sama-bol* की. Further, the letter की, which rounds off the word 'गुलाल' occurs so daintily, yet quite perceptibly, at the *sama* that, on the one hand, it provides a kind of a sparkle to the *sama*, and, on the other hand, continues to possess the listener's imagination securely enough to prevent the moment of quiet between की and धू from making the form of the *antarā* look divided. The quiet moment, in turn, lends some extra impact to the utterance of the word धूम, and so reinforces its meaning of 'a self-proclamatory quality'.

Finally, the predominantly closed quality of *ākāra* from 'की' to 'है' heightens by contrast the openness of the letter 'ना' which begins the word नाचत. Happily, this word itself is uttered as such a gentle descending and vibrant release of voice that the word itself appears to do what it means, **or** to dance.

After this analysis of the *sthāyī-antarā* twosome of a *dhamār* we may now see how form, in the sense of design and inner shapeliness, may be observed in what is called *layakārī*. But, what is *layakārī*? A simple answer would here be that *layakārī* is the effort to explore the creative possibilities inherent in *laya* (or aesthetic pace) with the help of some identifiable devices. But, one may further ask, is *laya* a matter of pace alone? Here, we cannot say, yes; in fact, *laya*, as movement or *gati*, is as much a matter of manner as of pace. So, *layakārī* should show variations not in pace alone, but in the very manner of its movement. Further, all these variations of pace and manner must follow some design. Let there be no bias against **preconceived** design in *layakārī*, specially when the *sthāyī antarā* twosome is often acclaimed for the beauty of its design. Design in *layakārī*, however, may either be merely mathematical — as in *duguṇa*, *chauguṇa* and *āḍa-kuvāḍa*; or aesthetic, that is, a beautiful mutual disposition of parts which employs not only the customary ways of double or fourfold acceleration of pace, but a winsome grouping of *bol*s and some formal graces as well. Then alone would *layakārī* have form in the aesthetic sense. Where the design is merely mathematical, the charm, we may note, lies partly in the ability to attain to the final *sama* with split-second accuracy, and partly in the relation of the particular bout of *layakārī* to the basic rhythm, but not, in any appreciable manner, in the inner disposition of its contents, nor even in the use of formal graces. But, whether the design of *layakārī* is mathematical or aesthetic, it should not be so abundant that it may eclipse for long or rupture, but should only appear to create patterns that flit variously against, the basic design of the *sthāyī*, highlighting it as their basic ground. Nor should *layakārī* give us the impression of a random fragmentation of the text of the song or of the singer's somehow trying to attain to the *sama* after a random and jerky spell of singing. *Layakārī* should never appear pell-mell or a kind of हाय-तौबा. Further, where the spell of *layakārī* does not directly end at the *sama*, the terminal phrase — of the rhythmic variation — should so complete itself that the design of the approach to the *sama* may be duly preserved and projected.

Positively, we have been able to discover, through analysis of actual music, the following creative devices which make for the proper preservation of form during *layakārī*: initiating the rhythmic variation with a formal grace; segmentation of *bol*s in terms of equal sub-divisions; displacement of the *ẓarab* of the first *bol* from its normal location to some other beat; division of a line into two halves that differ in the manner of their flow; interspersion of bits of reposeful melodic flow, and reinforcing accelerated pace with the subtlety of beginning at a point between two adjacent *mātrā*s. All these devices will now be borne out by the illustrations of *layakārī* which are, by and large, not confined to simple and unremitting adherence to *duguṇa* or *chauguṇa* alone.

Illustration No. 1

1	2	3	4	5	6	7	8	9	10	11	12	13	14
धसां	धध	मंमं	गग	गमं	ग	सा	सा	सा^ध^सा	मंमं	गग	^घ^-मं	-ध	सांध
खेऽ	ऽ,ल	ऽ,त	ऽ,हो	ऽरी	श्या	ऽ	म	चऽ	ऽप	ऽल	ऽम	ऽद	माती
×					२		०			३			

The first device, of employing a formal grace at the utterance of the very first *bol*, can bring about a change in the manner of the melodic flow, and so may be said to be a bit of *layakārī*, provided we remember that *laya* is not merely the speed but also the manner of movement. This is brought out by our very first illustration where the opening letter of the *sthāyī* does not come directly at the first beat, but gains access to it by means of a brief upward passage from ध to सां.

1. Here, be it noted, there is no segmentation of the *bol*s of the *sthāyī*.

Illustration No. 2

From 3½ *mātrā* (5½ *mātrā*)

1	2	3	4	5	6	7	8	9	10	11	12	13	14
सां	सांध	ध,सां	धमं	गमं	ग-	सासा	साग	मंध	सांसां	धसां	धमं	गमं	ग-
खे	लऽ	त,खे	लत	होरी	श्याऽ	मच	पल	मद	माती	ऽ,खे	लत	होरी	श्याऽ
सासा	साग	मंध	सांसां	धसां	धमं	गमं	ग-	सासा	मंमं	गग	ध-मं	-ध	सांध
मच	पल	मद	माती	ऽ,खे	लत	होरी	श्याऽ	मच	ऽप	ऽल	ऽम	ऽद	माती
×					२		०			३			

2. Here, a segmentation of *bol*s, in three equal subdivisions, is so done that the design of the approach to the *sama* is clearly preserved.

Illustration No. 3

From 14th *mātrā* (4 *mātrā*)

1	2	3	4	5	6	7	8	9	10	11	12	13	14
													सां सां
													खे ल
धसां	धमं	गमं	ग-	सासा	साग	मंध	सांसां	सांसां	धसां	धमं	गमं	ग-	सासा
तखे	लत	होरी	श्याऽ	मच	पल	मद	माती	खेल	तखे	लत	होरी	श्याऽ	मच
×					२		०			३			
साग	मंध	सांसां	सांसां	धसां	धमं	गमं	ग-	सासा	मंमं	गग	-धमं	-ध	सांध
पल	मद	माती	खेल	तखे	लत	होरी	श्याऽ	मच	ऽप	ऽल	ऽम	ऽद	माती
×					२		०			३			

3. In the third illustration, given above, the first *bol* of the *sthāyī* is displaced from the *sama* to the preceding or the fourteenth beat, and a triple segmentation of *bol*s is so employed that it does not allow any pause between the 3 segments, and may therefore be said to be बेदम. It is

important to note that, as in the case of number (2), here also the shape of the *āmad* is duly preserved.

Illustration No. 4

From 2nd *mātrā* (6 *mātrā*)

1	2	3	4	5	6	7	8	9	10	11	12	13	14
	मंध	मंध	सांसां	सांसां	सांसां	ध,ध	मं,मं	ग,मं	गसा	मंध	मंध	सांसां	सांसां
	खेल	तहो	ऽरी	स्याम	चप	ऽ,ल	ऽ,म	ऽ,द	माती	खेल	तहो	ऽरी	श्याम
×					२		०			३			
सांसां	ध,ध	मं,मं	ग,मं	गसा	मंध	मंध	सांसां	सांसां	सांसां	ध,ध	मं,मं	ग,मं	गसा
चप	ऽ,ल	ऽ,म	ऽ,द	माती	खेल	तहो	ऽरी	श्याम	चप	ऽ,ल	ऽ,म	ऽ,द	माती
×					२		०			३			

4. This rhythmic variation divides the *sthāyī* into two halves, — one in the form of an *āroha*-movement, and the other in that of an *avaroha*-passage — in such a way that the melodic manner of the two halves is clearly different.

Here, however, the *layakārī* ends directly at the beat preceding the *sama*, that is, without projecting the original design of the approach to the *sama*.

We think it necessary to point out that such *layakārī* may be said to be distinctly aesthetic in the sense that the melodic flow in the two halves is not merely different, but is heightened through mutual contrast, illustrating the point that in artistic form the details are not merely put together but conjoined to heighten each other's character. Thus, whereas the first half, here, takes the form of a gentle upward and undifferentiated swing, the other half seems to release itself in terms of clear and descending accents.

Illustration No. 5

From 9th *mātrā* (13 मात्रा से)

1	2	3	4	5	6	7	8	9	10	11	12	13	14
								सांसां	धसां	धमं	गमं	ग	—
								खेल	तखे	लत	होरी	श्या ऽ	
×					२		०			३			
सा	—	गग	गग	मंमं	ध,मंध	धसां	—	[सां]धसां	मंध	सांसां	धसां	धमं	गमं
म	ऽ	चप	लच	पल	म,दऽ	माऽ	ऽ	तीऽ	ऽऽ	खेल	तखे	लत	होरी
×					२		०			३			
ग	—	सा	—	गग	गग	मंमं	ध,मंध	धसां	—	[सां]धसां	मंध	सांसां	धसां
श्या	ऽ	म	ऽ	चप	लच	पल	म,दऽ	माऽ	ऽ	तीऽ	ऽऽ	खेल	तखे
×					२		०			३			
धमं	गमं	ग	—	सा	—	गग	गग	मंमं	ध,मंध	धसां	—	[सां]धसां	मंध
लत	होरी	श्या	ऽ	म	ऽ	चप	लच	पल	मदऽ	माऽ	ऽ	तीऽ	ऽऽ
×					२		०			३			

5. In the above illustration the *bol*s are so sub-divided into segments that a quick and successive articulation of *bol*s (words) is interspersed with brief but winsome stretches of reposeful melodic flow. Such *layakārī*, we may note, is clearly opposed to that fragmentation of the text of a song in *layakārī* which often appears as a kind of frantic pell-mell.

6. The point we have just made will be clearly borne out if we compare the *layakārī* just presented with the following one which comprises only one reposeful stretch, that is, in the utterance of the word श्याम, not in that of माती

7. Finally, an extra measure of animation may be lent to *layakārī* by coupling quickened pace with the adroitness of beginning at point between two adjacent *mātrā*s. Thus, in the illustration which follows,

Illustration No. 6

From 4th *mātrā* (2 *mātrā*)

1	2	3	4	5	6	7	8	9	10	11	12	13	14
			सांसां	धसां	धमं	गमं	ग	—	सा	—	गग	गग	मंमं
			खेल	तखे	लत	होरी	श्या	ऽ	म	ऽ	चप	लच	पल
×					२		०			३			
धध	सांध	सांसां	धसां	धमं	गमं	ग	—	सा	—	गग	गग	मंमं	धध
मद	माती	खेल	तखे	लत	होरी	श्या	ऽ	म	ऽ	चप	लच	पल	मद
×					२	•	०				३		
सांध	सांसां	धसां	धमं	गमं	ग	—	सा	—	गग	गग	मंमं	धध	सांध
माती	खेल	तखे	लत	होरी	श्या	ऽ	म	ऽ	चप	लच	पल	मद	माती
×					२		०				३		

Illustration No. 7

						14
						--गग
						ऽऽ अबी
1	2	3	4	5	6	7
मंधसांसां	सांसांसांगं	गंमंगंगं	सांसांसांसां	सांधधध	मंमंमंग	-मंगसा
रंगुलाऽ	लकीधूऽ	ममचीऽ	हैऽनाच	तनाचत	नाचतदे	ऽदेतारी
×					२	
8	9	10	11	12	13	14
×				३		
सांसांसांध	धधमंमं	मंग-मं	गसासांसां	सांधधध	मंमंमग	-मंगसा
नाचतना	चतनाच	तदे ऽदे	तारी नाच	तनाचत	नाचतदे	ऽदेतारी
×				३		

From a gay and lively *dhamār* we may now turn to the high seriousness of a devotional *dhruvapada*, but with the same purpose, that is, analysis of artistic form. Such a song, it is obvious, demands images and ideas of a religious colour, a demand which is, in fact, duly met by the text of the song which is as follows:

ध्रुवपदः राग भैरव, सूल ताल

स्थायी

1	2	3	4	5	6	7	8	9	10
									नि़
									प्र
रे॒	—	सा	(ग)रे॒	ग	म	(ग)रे॒	—	सा	—
थ	ऽ	म	ना	ऽ	म	ले	ऽ	त	ऽ
×		०		२		३		०	
म	—	म	प	—	ध॒	(ध)नि	—	—	(सां)नि
शि	ऽ	व	शि	ऽ	व	शि	ऽ	ऽ	ऽ
×		०		२		३		०	
ध॒	—	प	—	(सा)ध॒	—	—	ध॒प	प	—
व	ऽ	ऽ	ऽ	शि	ऽ	ऽ	ऽऽ	व	ऽ
×		०		२		३		०	
म	—	रे॒म	—	—	मग	रे॒	—	सा	नि़
ऽ	ऽ	शिऽ	ऽ	ऽ	ऽऽ	व	ऽ	ऽ	प्र
×		०		२		३		०	

अन्तरा

1	2	3	4	5	6	7	8	9	10
				म	म	प	प	(नि)ध॒	—
				वि	ष	य	न	को	ऽ

(नि)ध॒	(नि)ध॒	(नि)ध॒	ध॒सां	—	सां	सां	रें॒	रें॒	रें॒
ग	र	ल	साऽ	ऽ	धो	नी	ऽ	ल	क
—	रें॒	सां	रें॒मं	-गं॒	रें॒	—	सां	नि	—
ण	ठ	म	हाऽ	ऽऽ	दे	ऽ	व	ता	ऽ
सां	रें॒	नि	सां	नि	ध॒	नि	ध॒	प	प
प	त्रि	वि	ध	गु	णा	ऽ	ती	ऽ	त
म		प	प	(ध)रें॒	—	सां	—	सां	नि़
दे	ऽ	व	न	को	ऽ	दे	ऽ	व	प्रं
×		०		२		३		०	

आभोग

								म	प
								ड	म
ध॒	सां	—	(नि)ध॒	—	म	—	म	(ग)रे॒	(म)रे॒
ऽ	रु	ऽ	से	ऽ	ना	ऽ	द	प्र	ग
सा	रें॒	रें॒	—	रें॒	रें॒	—	रें॒	रें॒	मंगं॒
टे	ऽ	आ	ऽ	दी	रु	ऽ	प	सू	ऽऽ
गं॒रें॒	रें॒सां	सां	सां	सां	—	सां	सां	नि	सां
त्रऽ	निऽ	क	से	ता	ऽ	ल	अ	र	थ
ध॒	—	प	प	प	प	म	—	म	म
भे	ऽ	द	उ	प	जे	शी	ऽ	श	ध
प	ध॒	ध॒	सां	—	—	सां	सांनि	ध॒	—
री	ऽ	गं	ऽ	ऽ	ऽ	गे	ऽऽ	गं	ऽ
—	—	म	मग॒	रे॒	—	—	—	सा	नि़
ऽ	ऽ	गे	ऽऽ	गं	ऽ	ऽ	ऽ	गे	प्र
×		०		२		३		०	

Probably because its purpose is only to steep the singer's mind in contemplation of the Lord's glories, and not to exhibit his own performing ability, this composition has an easy up-and-down, but fairly pleasing *ābhoga* segment, and no *sañcārī*. (The word, *ābhoga*, we may note, means completion or satiety, besides, of course beauty; and, therefore, an *ābhoga tāna* should cover at least one complete *saptak* in a pleasing way). Be that as it may, the important point for us, here, is that the images are evoked not only by the meaning of the words, but by some details of the very manner of singing. But let us first list these images and ideas.

(a) The dawn of the day or sunrise

(b) A sweet and tranquil recitation of His Name.

(c) The thought of the exalted nature of and Śiva which yet has a deep inner appeal for the devotee.

(d) The glories of Śiva distinguished. His absolute subdual of the venom of passion (विषयन को गरल साधो); transcendence of threefold suffering and determination by the three *guṇa*s (ताप त्रिविध गुणातीत); Śiva as the Overlord (देवन को देव, महादेव).

(e) Finally, the descent of the Ganges as attaining to a haven in the tresses of Śiva.

Our task is now laid out. We have to show how, in accordance with the key requirement of artistic form, the meaning and sound of the words of the text are blended as one with the very manner of singing, thus projecting a clear operation of the principle of sound-sense harmony. If it be wondered as to why it is necessary make an effort to adapt the manner of singing to the meaning of words, the answer could be that, though the adaptation in question can well be an exacting process during the process of composition, during actual singing the prefixed accordance is bound to help, effortlessly, the singer's attunement with the song by making his heart and understanding work jointly in the seizure of a single significance.

A. To begin with, the effect of a sudden emergence which is directly evoked by the very sound of the first letter प्र — which has an obvious sparkle about it — is reinforced by the placement of the *sama*, the beat of focal emphasis, at *komala ṛṣabha* (रे) which itself seems to rise from within its immediate neighbour, the *sā* (or *ṣaḍaj*).

B. Further, the compact rhythmic extent of the *sthāyī*, set to the nimble *sūla tāla*, the easy manner in which the word नाम winds its way up like a waft of incense afloat, and its gentle return to the *sā* — all these features coupled, of course, with the overall softness of utterance, provide to the mind a kind of self-completing movement for devout indwelling.

C. The exaltation, and yet the inner appeal, of Śiva are brought out by the triple utterance of the word which first touches the *niṣād* and then gradually lapses back to the *sā* in the way of threefold, yet virtually undivided flow.

D. As far the various glories of the Lord, the wonder that He, the Lord Śiva, has been able to subdue the venom of the various passions (विषयन को गरल साधो) is suggested in terms of an *āroha tāna* which is tinged with a little *gamak*, so as to add to the requisite seriousness of effect. What is more, the word नीलकण्ठ is sung at the *tāra ṛṣabha* (रें); and the high placement of the word is likely to suggest to a sensitive mind the blue of the sky, and so also evoke the image of a transcendent quality, specially because it is quickly followed by an even higher utterance of the word महादेव. Further, in accordance with the principle of sound-sense harmony, whereas the word त्रिविध is so sung as to project three clear emphases (or *ẓarab*s), the word गुणातीत, which means beyond the three *guṇa*s (of *sattva, rajas* and *tamas*) is so set to song in terms of a seamless descending flow that no constituent *svara* appears to be distinct. What is more, in conformity with the same aesthetic principle of accordant sound and meaning, the surpassing quality of शिव as a god is projected by putting the words 'को देव' at the *tāra ṛṣabha* and *ṣaḍaj*.

E. Finally, the musical utterance of the word 'गंगे' is so shaped in terms of an *avaroha-tāna* that the idea of the descent of the Ganges is duly projected. This particular musical passage has two striking features. First, it tapers so gently as a passage from *re* to *sa* that the singing quite agrees with the idea that the life-giving torrent has been gently and comprehensively received by Lord Śiva. Second, the triple utterance of 'गंगे' blends melody and rhythm as one. The triple quality has the semblence of a *tiyā*; but, at the same time, the utterance in question goes to make a single melodic downward flow.

Incidentally, the same may be said to the triple singing of शिव in the second part of the *sthāyī*, with this one subtle difference that though most of the constituent *svaras* are identical in the two cases, the word 'गंगे', essentially because of the elongated, and so manifest, use of the nasal (or *anunāsika*) गं, projects the idea of a flow, the word Śiva, partly because of the absence of the same sonant element, evokes the quite different effect of *nāma-japa* in a state of absorption, and not of the seamless unity of a flow.

In the end, some merely formal or structural excellences of the composition may be noted. One of these relates to the investment of the advent of the *sama* with a measure of extra sharpness. Generally, this is done by making the *sama* occur as the target of a well-designed pattern. But here, at one point of the composition, the same effect is achieved by a sudden descent from the *tāra* to the *madhya sā*, a descent which, in spite of the big gap which it embraces, does not appear abrupt or awkward, for the two sides of the descent, its beginning and its end, are identical in character and manner, though not, of course, in location. The reference, here is to the descent from को देव in *tāra* to प्रथम in the *madya saptak*.

Our analysis of the *dhruvapada* that we have just now discussed will, however, remain incomplete if we do not focus on a point relating to actual singing of the composition in question, or of any *khyāl-bandiśa*. Every composition is meant to be sung to the 'accompaniment' of a *ṭhekā*; and this confluence can at once make for some effects which cannot be produced by the *sthāyī-antarā* twosome alone. First, when it is sung along with a *ṭhekā*, a *bandiśa* necessarily appears somewhat framed, more or less in the same way in which a sentence looks more determinate in form when it is duly punctuated, or, say, when a full stop is put on its either side, and a comma or a semi-colon between its segments which appear to be distinct, though related. Second, where the *sthāyī* does not itself actively seem to make for the *sama* — say, because its approach to the focal beat lacks a dynamic filling — the defect may be made good by the *ṭhekā*'s attainment of the *sama* **by means of a passage of close-banded** *bols*. Sometimes, as indeed in the case of the present composition, **this** is an important consideration in choosing the right *ṭhekā*. Thus, in the case of the *dhruvapada* in question, attainment of the *sama* of the *sthāyī* will appear quite anaemic if the *ṭhekā* chosen as its rhythmic support is *jhaptāla*, though both *sūla* and *jhaptāla* comprise ten *mātrās* each; relatively insipid (or ठंडा) if the *sūla* rhythm chosen is of the *tablā* variety, that is, the following:

1	2	3	4	5	6	7	8	9	10
धिन	धिन	धा	धा	धिन	ना	तिन	तिन	ता	ता
×				२		३			

and positively winsome, because fluent, if the *pakhāvaj* variety of *sūla ṭhekā*, which runs as follows, is made use of:

1	2	3	4	5	6	7	8	9	10
धा	धा	धिन्	ता	किट	धा	तिट	कत	गदि	गिन
×				२		३			

for here the close succession of the terminal phrase, तिटकत गदि गिन provides to the *sthāyī* what it does not itself possess, that is, a nimble, rolling ascent to the *sama*. In brief, as experienced during the course of normal singing, the form of a *sthāyī* emerges from, and is modified by its interplay with the *ṭhekā*.

From *dhruvapada*, we now may turn to a *tarānā*, set in *rāga Sohnī* and in a rhythm-cycle of 11 beats. Our task, however, remains unchanged; that is, analysis of artistic form.

Now, the elements of a *tarānā*, as we know, are a *rāga-tāla* twosome, mnemonic syllables and a sprinkling of language. Mnemonic syllables are also used in *ālāpa*; but here, in a *tarānā*, they are rhythmically organised and may be seen to alternate with meaningful words. *Khyāl*, *dhruvapada* and *dhamār* do not use mnemonic syllables. So, *tarānā* is undeniably a distinct form of our classical vocal music.

But, how exactly is a *tarānā* commonly appreciated by *rasika*s and critics? The view that it has a mystical significance is not verifiable today, though this form of singing might have originated with some religious end in view. What is definitely known to us today is that a *tarānā* teems with mnemonic syllables; that it does not make a pronounced use of formal graces; and that modern exponents of the *tarāna*-form have been freely admired for the extra-fluent articulation of meaningless syllables like *dir dir*.

Our view, however, is that, though like every other form of our vocal music, a *tarānā* too has to be a good integration of rhythm and melody, what distinguishes a *tarānā* is its ability to so avail of mnemonic syllables that their manner or look of feeling may come to add to the meaning or distinctive effect of meaningful words within the confines of a rhythm-cycle. It is mainly from this point of view, in addition to that of a proper integration of all the elements, that we propose to analyse the *tarānā* we have chosen to. It may be added that, insofar as every *tarānā* conforms to a *rāga*, and also because every *rāga* is supposed to evoke a particular *rasa*, to admire a specimen of *tarānā*-singing merely because of the hectic speed at which a particular mnemonic syllable is articulated, dissipating all *rasa* — and relegating the basic form of the *tarānā-sthāyī* to the background — is to adopt a wholly non-aesthetic point of view.

Now, here is the *tarānā* we propose to analyse by way of revealing its artistic form:

1	2	3	4	5	6	7	8	9	10	11
						मं-	मं,मंध	गग	धमंध	निसां
						ताऽ	दा,रेऽ	ऽत	दारे	दानी
रेंनि,सां-	निध	निध	मंग	मंग	रेसा	मं-	मं,मंध	गग	धमंध	निसां
दीऽ,ऽम	तदा	ऽरे	तद	रेदा	ऽनी	ताऽ	दा,रेऽ	ऽत	दारे	दानी
×			२		०		३			
	मंग	गधमं	-मं	ध,मंध	ध सां	सां,मंध	धसां	सां-	सांसां	गंमं
	याऽ	ली,आ	ऽली	आ,लीऽ	अल	ला,ऽऽ	मौऽ	लाऽ	सब	कोऽ
गरें	सां—	नि--सां	ध--नि	मं-मंध	गग	रेमंग	रेसा	-ग	ध मंध	निसां
सांऽ	इ ऽ	दाऽऽऽ	ताऽऽऽ	कऽरीऽ	ऽम	ताऽ	दारे	ऽत	दारे	दानी
×			२		०		३			

The *rāga*, it is clear, is *Sohnī*; so its pathetic, yearning quality is also an element to be properly integrated.

(a) Now, to begin with the very opening part of the *sthāyī*, the approach to the *sama* — that is, the complex of *bols*: ता दारे तदारे दानी दीम — it is so designed that it not only projects the character of the *sama* as the target, but gives a clear indication of the specific nature of the *rāga*, partly by emphasising the *uttarāṅga* of the scale, so that an integration of melody and rhythm is at once, in part, achieved.

(b) What is more, the *avaroha tāna* (त दा ऽरे तदरे दा ऽ नी) which forms the second half of, and so completes, the *sthāyī* in noticeably relaxed in its flow, and so goes well with the emotive character of the *rāga* on the one hand, and with the thoughts of humility and self-surrender which the meaningful words of the *antarā* to follow may evoke, on the other.

But let us first look at the form and flow of the *sthāyī* itself, to bear out the truth of the way we have analysed it:

1	2	3	4	5	6	7	8	9	10	11
						मं-	मं,मंध	गग	धमंध	निसां
						ताऽ	दा,रेऽ	ऽत	दारे	दानी
रेंनिसां-	निध	निध	मंग	मंग	रेसा	मं-	मं,मंध	गग	धमंध	निसां
दीऽ,ऽम	तदा	ऽरे	तद	रेदा	ऽनी	ताऽ	दा,रेऽ	ऽत	दारे	दानी
×			२		०		३			

(c) Now, as for the *antarā*, the meaning of the words it comprises is clear. It is an **appeal** to the Lord who is the sire of all, and the Giver supreme and the Merciful:

या ऽ ली आली आली अल्ला मौला सबको साई दाता करीम.

Here it may be noted, the words अल्ला मौला are so sung, in terms of a gradual waxing of the volume of *ākāra* as it moves to the *tāra sa*, that the effect of a पुकार is evoked by the very manner. What is more, the words सब को साई take the form of an encompassing circle. The utterance of दाता rightly takes the form of a descending passage, so as to accord with the meaning of giving — as against usurping; and also with the attitudes of humility and surrender which the utterance of the words in question is likely to produce in the heart of the singer-devotee.

(d) What is more, and this brings us to a really subtle detail of the *tarānā*, the little complex of *bol*s, तादारे which follows the last word करीम is such in its easy and descending flow that, though meaningless, it serves to add to the pathetic feeling (दीन भाव) generated by the words:

This little complex of mnemonic syllables could have been avoided, and the *sama* yet duly attained, as follows, but then the heightening of the pathetic feeling we just spoke of would have been absent:

1	2	3	4	5	6	7	8	9	10	11
गरें	सां-	नि--सां	ध--नि	मं-मंध	गग	मं-	मं^गध	गग	^धमंध	निसां
साँऽ	ईऽ	दाऽऽऽ	ताऽऽऽ	कुऽरीऽ	ऽम	ताऽ	दारे	ऽत	दारे	दानी

×

For a better appreciation of the point we are seeking to make, see a successive presentation of the two ways of singing the close of *antarā*, one **without** the phrase तादारे as shown above and the other with this phrase:

1	2	3	4	5	6	7	8	9	10	11
गरें	सां-	नि--सां	ध--नि	मं-मंध	गग	मंग	रेसा	-ग	^धमंध	निसां
साँऽ	ईऽ	दाऽऽऽ	ताऽऽऽ	कुऽरीऽ	ऽम	ताऽ	दारे	ऽत	दारे	दानी

×

In the composition we have just analysed, we have tried to show how a string of mnemonic (or meaningless) syllables can be made to add to the emotive character of the meaning of the worded part of a *tarānā*. Next, we proceed to argue for a subtler possibility in the region of the same form of singing, the possibility that, as opposed to those elaborate *tarānā*s which embrace meaningful Persian couplets, a simple *tarānā* may use just one or two invocatory words — say, याली, आली — and yet come to acquire a fairly rich and internally consistent meaning from the musical manner and disposition of its mnemonic syllables which virtually make the entire composition, and against which the two meaningful words appear as a mere relief.

Before, however, we outline this composition, which is a simple *Deśkāra tarānā* in *tīna tāla*, we think it necessary to make some general remarks.

According to the view of the Late Ustad Amir Khan, *tarānā*s were originally possessed of some mystical significance. But, because of limitations of knowledge, we do not find it possible to relate this vocal form to **mystical experience**. Yet, this is surely demonstrable that a *tarānā* may be composed and sung in such a way that, though almost non-verbal in character, it may go well — and so saturate the **singer's own mind** — with determinate thoughts of a prayerful nature, though this devotional significance may not be seen by the listener unless he is told about it. Here, we think it necessary to point out that artistic significance is not merely that which is directly projected for the sake of the listeners, but also the quality of being conducive to a orderly objectification of some thoughts and feelings of the singer himself.

Yet, in so far as a *tarānā* is not prayer as such — and also because by virtue of its setting in a rhythmic cycle, it is closer to the *khyāl* form than to *ālāpa* of the *dhruvapada* kind. The *antarā* of a *tarānā*, as against its *sthāyī* — the aesthetic purpose of which is just to **settle** the singer in a particular frame of mind, may be allowed to avail of a little fluent *tāna* consistently, of course, with the grammatical character of the *rāga*, a device which is, in fact, employed in the composition which we have been able to hit upon and which we now set out to analyse; and the ideal content of which — that is, what it could be taken to mean **for the singer himself** — may be put as follows, in terms of individual points:

(A) Thou alone art my only support.

(B) Apart from thee I am wholly powerless.

(C) I feel unsettled in this deeply troubled world.

(D) Hence my yearning for thee is intenser.

(E) I can only pray to be uplifted with Thy help.

(F) O my Exalted One (या आली)

Now, every one of these feeling thoughts may be seem to correspond, in a parallel order, with the bracketed portions of the *sthāyī* of the *tarānā* in question which we now set down as follows, indicating both the text and its musical notation.

राग देशकार — तराना

स्थायी

1	2	3	4	5	6	7	8	9	10	11	12	13	14	15	16
											ध	—	ध	सां	सां
											A(ता	ऽ	न्ना	दे	रे
सां	[सां]ध	प	प	ग	[प]ग	ध	प	ग	—	सा	सा	—	सा-	सासा	[सा]-रे
न्ना	ऽ	ऽ)	B(त	ऽ	दा	ऽ	रे	दा	ऽ	नी)	C(त	ऽ	दाऽ	रेदा	ऽनी
×				२				०				३			
[सा]ध़	[सा]ध़	[सा]ध़	सा	गं	—	रें	गं	सां	सां	[सां]ध	सा	सा	रे	ग	प
दे	रे	ना	ऽ)	D(त	ऽ	दा	रे	दा	नी	ऽ)	E(त	दा	रे	दा	नी
×				२				०				३			
ध	सां	सां	ध	प	ध	—	प	ग	—	सा	ध	—	ध	सां	सां
दे	ऽ	रे	ना	ऽ)	F(या	ऽ	ली	आ	ऽ	ली)	ता	ऽ	न्ना	दे	रे
×				२				०				३			

अन्तरा

1	2	3	4	5	6	7	8	9	10	11	12	13	14	15	16
								—	गरे	ग	प	ध	[ध]सां	प	धा
								ऽ	तद	रे	त	दा	रे	दा	नी
×				२				०				३			
सां	सां	सां	सां	—	रें	सां	सां	सां	रें	गं	रें	सां	—	[सां]प	ध
दी	म	त	दा	ऽ	रे	दा	नी	त	दी	य	न	रे	ऽ	दा	नी
×				२				०				३			
—	रें-	रेंसां	धध	सांसां	धप	धसां	रेंगं	रेंसां	धप	गप	ध	—	ध	सां	सां
ऽ	दाऽ	रेदा	ऽनी	याऽ	ऽऽ	ऽऽ	ऽऽ	ऽऽ	आऽ	लीऽ	ता	ऽ	न्ना	दे	रे
×				२				०				३			

It need hardly be added that, with its visible emphasis on *dhaivata*, *gāndhāra*, *pañchama* and *ṣaḍaj*, and on the upper half (*uttarāṅga*) of the scale, the composition quite meets the technical demands of the *rāga*. It should also be clear that the **form** of such a composition, though quite non-verbal, may well be said to be **expressive** — at least for the singer himself. The **technical** (or craft) aspect of this form should reveal itself readily to a careful look at its notation. Perhaps, **its** most striking feature is its manifest self-division into ascending and descending segments. Overall, indeed the form of this composition is an integration of opposing musical passages, which not only heighten but conjoin each other, — partly, by means of glides — and an adroit blending of manner and meaning.

A formal detail of some value may also be noted regarding the passage embodying the words 'या ऽ ली आली'. The closed or इकार sound of ली provides a foil to the openness of ता which begins the access to the *sama*. The result is a pleasing mutual heightening of syllabic sounds by contrast.

The way is now paved to a study of form in the context of *khyāl*. Here, the *vilambit* composition that we propose to analyse is as follows:

राग पूरियाधनाश्री (विलम्बित) एकताल

स्थाई

1	11	12
		, (प) मंपध(प)मं गमं रे
		पा ऽऽऽ ऽ र ऽ क ऽ

1	2	3		4
रेग — — — ,	रेमंग रे — —	सा — — — ,	रेसानि	— रेग रे
रो ऽ ऽ ऽ ,	कऽरो ऽ ऽ ऽ	रे ऽ ऽ ऽ ,	ह	ऽ ज़ऽ ऽ
×		०		

5	6	7	8	
गमं पमं ग —,	गमंप — — -मं	प — — -प, (प)	मंपध (प)मं	गमंरे
रऽ त ऽ ऽ ,	ख़्वाऽऽ ऽ ऽ ऽऽ	जा ऽ ऽ ऽनि, ज़ा	ऽऽऽ ऽ ऽ	ऽमुऽ
२		०		

9 10 11 12

रेग — — —, निरेगमं धमं ग -मंरे ग रे सा —, (प) मंपध (प)मं गमंरे

दीन ऽ ऽ ऽ, औऽऽऽ ऽऽ ऽ ऽलिऽ या ऽ ऽ ऽ, पा ऽऽऽ ऽर ऽकऽ

३ ४

अन्तरा

11 12

,मंमं गग पमंमं धध

,खुश रंग कीऽ अब

1 2 3 4

मंधनिसां — — सां, निरें रें सां — रेंसांनि — रें — , रेंगं —रें सां -सांसां

लाऽऽऽ ऽ ऽ ज, तुम्ही ऽ हो ऽ तु ऽ म ऽ, ही ऽऽ ऽ ऽ मह

× ०

5 6 7 8

निसांऽनिसांसांऽनि धनि रें निध नि ध प -प (प) पमंप मंग मंरे, ग — — -नि

बूऽऽऽऽ ऽऽ ऽ ऽऽ, ऽ ऽ बे ऽई ला ऽऽऽ ऽऽ ऽऽ, ही ऽ ऽ ऽतु

२ ०

9 10 11 12

रेग रे गमपध प, ध मं ग -रे मंग रे सा —, — (प) मंपध (प)मं गमंरे

म्हीऽ ऽ ऽऽऽऽ से, आ ऽ स ऽल गा ऽ ई ऽ, पा ऽऽऽ ऽर ऽकऽ

Vilambit Khyāl

The opening words of the *sthāyī* "पार करो" as they are sung, obviously express the devotee-singer's yearning to be helped in crossing over the turbulent sea of life. The idea of 'crossing over' is conveyed not by the opening word "पार" itself, though it is obviously this word which really means 'crossing over', but by the way in which the word "करो" is sung, that is, as a gentle, concave curve which first descends from *madhyam* to *ṛṣabha*, and then rises to *gāndhāra*, appearing as a formal analogue of the idea of being carried along or beyond. Two points are here noteworthy. First, in vocal music the principle of sound-sense harmony is observed not as a direct correspondence of every word, musically uttered, with its own conventional meaning, but as a projection of the requisite significance through a conjoint working of words in a musical phrase. Second, the musical phrase in terms of which 'करो' is sung is also the catch-phrase of the *rāga*, so that the total purpose served by the musical utterance of 'करो' is not merely the observance of the requirement of sound-sense accord, but also the projection of the distinct character of the *rāga*. Incidentally, the other (grammatical) requirement of the projection of the *vādī svara* is also not ignored, for the very opening letter 'पा' is located at *pañcama*. What is more, the emotive essence of the song, which is a prayerful yearning, is also duly projected by the way in which the word 'करो' is sung, aided, of course, by the reposeful quality of the *laya* chosen. To conclude, the very opening phrase of the *sthāyī* (पार करो) meets the requirement of artistic form by integrating the various elements of musical sound, cognitive and emotive meaning, the aesthetic and grammatical character of the *rāga*, and aesthetic pace of *laya*. The way the *sthāyī* descends from the terminal letter 'रो' (of the word 'करो') to the tonic also serves a duly unifying function. It not only deepens the feeling of humility and surrender by virtue of its tranquil descending manner, but also rightly tarries at the *ṛṣabha* which is the *saṁvādī* of the *rāga* in question. The ascent from the tonic, after a momentary glimpse of the *niṣād* to the (*vādī*) *pañcama* where the word 'ख़्वाजा' ends not only appears as a reverential access to the presence of the holy personage addressed, but also continues to heighten the yearning of prayer. What is more, the utterance of the word 'निज़ामुद्दीन' is completed in such a way, in terms of a gentle upward passage from *ṛṣabha* to *gāndhāra*, that the manner of singing perfectly accords with the meaning of the word 'दीन' which, though it is itself but a part of the word 'निज़ामुद्दीन' enables the devotee-singer to deepen the pathetic feeling (or दीन भाव) of surrender. This, incidentally, is a clear illustration of the way in which a classical singer freely truns objective references into the material of his inner attunement with the spirit of the text of a song. The way we refer to Hazrat Nizamuddin in everyday talk is one thing; but the prayerful manner in which the classical singer saturates himself with the thought of surrender to the saint is quite another. Finally, the spiritual exaltation of the saint addressed is brought out by a slightly powerful, but yet not jerky or irreverent utterance of the *sthāyī*'s closing word "औलिया" which does not descend without, so to say, proclaiming the saint's exaltation at the *dhaivata*.

Turning to the *antarā*, the first noteworthy point may be put thus. The fact that it bestirs itself at the *madhyam* demands two comments. First, though it begins at this note which is two *svara*s away from the *ṣaḍaj*, the gap, whereas it certainly brings out the requisite otherness of the *antarā*, does not appear as an abrupt beginning. Second, this is so because in the closing phrase of the *sthāyī* it is the *gāndhāra*, the immediate neighbour of *madhyam*, which is projected, so that phenomenologically, or from the viewpoint of the experience of listening — rather than from that of mere grammar — the opening *madhyam* of the *antarā* does not seem to be so far away from the tonic as it would in the mere notation of the song. Here, we may note, an important truth of discriminating musical listening is suggested. Though the singing as such is an onward process, the listening of the right kind is at once an apprehension of the immediately given in the light of the **preceding** musical passage.

Further, the thought that the holy and exalted personage addressed is alone (तुम्ही) the protector of the honour of the singer-devotee: ख़ुशरंग की अब लाज तुम्ही हो is musically brought out in two ways: first, by means of a relatively nimble and ascending *tāna* which completes itself at the tonic, or the highest point of the *madhya saptak*; and, second, by projecting the *saṁvādī ṛṣabha* so noticeably that the insistence implicit in the words तुम्ही (Thou alone) is duly made manifest. The further ascent of the following phrase, तुम ही हो up to the *tāra gāndhāra* reinforces the thought of the exalted status of the holy one addressed, besides heightening the important phrase of the *rāga* 'नि नि रें रें गं रें ऽ सां'. In the descending part of the *antarā* (महबूबे इलाही) the musical flow rightly tarries at the *pañcama*, for this detail of manner serves two essential purposes. First, it duly projects the *vādī pañchama*; and, second, it may be said to provide a point of rest and assurance to the singer (/devotee). The utterance of the word 'ख़्वाजा' which follows, not only renews the act of adressing the saint, but also highlights the catch-phrase of the *rāga* (मं रे ᵐग. . . .).

The utterance of the concluding part of the *antarā*, तुम् ही से आस लगाई is adapted to the meaning of the text in two ways. First, the concluding letter of the words 'तुम ही से' tarries at the *pañchama*, suggesting, so to say, that in the Other addressed

(ख़्वाजा) a true locus of relief has been found. Second, the last two letters of the word 'लगाई' (following आस) are musically rendered in such a way, in terms of a 'गा रे सा' droop, that the requisite idea of utter surrender — and not merely the literal meaning of intentness of hope — is also duly projected. There is another point of detail which is here noteworthy. The letter which opens the word आस is so placed at the *dhaivat* that it at once seems to pray for relief, very much in the way of a look of entreaty.

In fine, the entire *sthāyī-antarā* twosome all along observes the requirement of sound-sense harmony, not of course, in the direct way of ordinary language where every word conveys its own individual meaning, but in that of bodily expression where a twinkle in a child's eye may at once mean mischief and liveliness. Above all, the gathering of sound and sense in this composition is also an instance of the way music acquires its form as art.

A Drut Composition

To turn, now, to the *drut* composition in the same *rāga*, we may first state its verbal text, and also outline its musical structure in terms of notation.

राग पूरियाधनाश्री (द्रुत) तीन ताल

स्थायी

1	2	3	4	5	6	7	8	9	10	11	12	13	14	15	16
									प	प	ध	(प)	-मं	-ग	रे
									बी	त	ग	ये	ऽऽ	ऽजु	ग
×				२					०			३			
ग	—	—	मं	ग	रे	सा	—	—	निरे	-ग	-रे	^मंग	प	प	—
वा	ऽ	ऽ	पि	य	र	वा	ऽ	ऽ	तुम	ऽरे	ऽमि	ल	न	की	ऽ
×				२				०					३		
^धपमं	—	ध	नि	धनिध	निध	मंग	रे	ग	प	प	ध	(प)	-मं	-ग	रे
आऽ	ऽ	स	ल	गाऽ	ऽऽऽ	येऽ	ऽ	ऽ	बी	त	ग	ये	ऽऽ	ऽजु	ग
×				२				०				३			

अन्तरा

									मं	[म]ग	ग	[प]मं	—	ध	[मं]ध
									चाँ	द	पि	या	ऽ	मो	हे
×				२				०					३		
मंधनिसां	—	सां	सां	[रेसा]नि	रें	सां	—	—	निनि	-रें	-गं	रेंगं	रें	सां	—
धीऽऽऽऽ	ऽ	र	बँ	धा	ऽ	वो	ऽ	ऽ	दर	ऽस	ऽदि	खाऽ	ऽ	वो	ऽ
×				२				०				३			
सां	निध	-निरें	निध	नि	ध	प	—	—	मं	मं	ग	[प]मं	—	ध	ध
ऽ	अब	ऽतोऽ	ऽऽ	आ	ऽ	वो	ऽ	ऽ	नै	ऽ	ना	नी	ऽ	र	ब
×				२				०				३			
पमं	गरे	गमं	धनि	सांनि	धप	मंग	रेसा	निसा	प	प	ध	(प)	-मं	-ग	रे
हाऽ	ऽऽ	ऽऽ	ऽऽ	ऽऽ	ऽऽ	येऽ	ऽऽ	ऽऽ	बी	त	ग	ये	ऽऽ	ऽजु	ग
×				२				०				३			

The first noteworthy, if simple, point about the *sthāyī* is that, though because of its quicker pace it is quite different from the *vilambit* composition which we have just analysed, it is yet able to retain its requisite character as a *sthāyī* (स्थायित्व) by abstaining from light-hearted flourishes. At the same time, it is able to keep true to the emotive meaning of the text — that is, a lament of the pathetic feeling of separation in love — by means of the phrase 'ग रे [रे]ग ऽ ऽ' sung in such a way that it seems to well up in the way of a sigh.

As for the *antarā*, it too seems to be designed quite suitably. The text of the song, here, is an appeal to the beloved to dispel the disconsolation of *virah* (विरह). So, whereas in accordance with the requirement of appearing different from the *sthāyī*, it rises up to the *tāra sa* (where the word completes itself) the wilful projection of the adjacent *komala r̥ṣabha* duly evokes the requisite suggestion of entreaty (सां [रेंसां]नि रें सां -- ब धा ऽ वो ऽ ऽ). The musical utterance of the words 'दरस दिखावो' is a tonal analogue of an intense prayer for a direct self-disclosure of the beloved, and so it rises even higher, that is, up to the *tāra gāndhāra*. The words which follow 'दरस दिखावो' rightly take the form of a descending phrase which appears as a kind of gathering the Other to self in a moment of serenity because of its stilling itself at the *pañchama*, besides highlighting the technical crux of the *rāga* (नि ध निरें निध नि ध प ऽ ऽ). Finally, the concluding *tāna* not only provides a decorative element demanded by the *rasa* involved, that is, *śṛṅgāra*, but may even be said to portray the uninhibited flow of tears.

Tāna

MEANING AND SOME PRINCIPLES

Besides the *sthāyī-antarā* twosome, the other important element of *khyāl gāyakī* which we now set out to analyse, from the viewpoint of artistic form, is *tāna*. As we know, this word is derived from the root तन्, some of the more important meanings of which are as follows:

To extend, spread, stretch (a cord); spin out, weave; to put forth, show, manifest; and, finally, to compose (say, a literary work).[15]

Now, by and large, the word *tāna* is today taken in the light of the first three meanings listed above; and so we speak of it as a kind of extension or development. But, here, a question at once arises. What exactly is that which a *tāna* must be said to develop? We can hardly say: the *rāga* chosen for treatment; for, it is the clear evidence of musical practice today that what brings out or develops the nature of a *rāga* is *barhat*, and not *tāna*s, though they certainly conform to the grammatical character of the *rāga* being rendered. Conformity is one thing; development, quite another. The evidence of practice rather is that *tāna*s are nothing but patterns that only rearrange the constituent *svara*s of the *rāga* in ever more decorative ways. Be it noted that whereas the first three meanings of तन् listed by us relate specially to something physical, such as a cord or a sheet of cloth, the other meanings, such as 'weave', and 'to compose' go well with works of art. So, we suggest that *tāna* may be taken as a composition or orderly weave which does not so much bring out the depth and dignity of a *rāga* (which is essentially the function of *barhat* or *ālāpa*) as the decorative possibilities within a *rāga*. In our view, even the most consummate kind of *ālāpa* cannot be said to be essentially decorative (श्रृंगारिक) though it may well be reposeful expansive and even sublime. The decorative quality of *tāna*s is perhaps the most important feature which distinguishes the *khyāl* style from the older *dhruvapada* form. Quite simply, the projection of *tāna*s is composition of decorative patterns in a *rāga*.

In our growing appreciation of the *hoary* form of *dhruvapada ālāpa*, let us not underestimate the value of pure decoration in music. Santayana rightly reminds us:

> That the ornate may be very beautiful, that in fact what is to be completely beautiful needs to be somehow rich, is a fact of experience. Decoration, by stimulating the senses, not only brings a primary satisfaction with it, independent of any that may supervene, but it furnishes an element of effect which no higher beauty can ever render unwelcome or inappropriate, since any higher beauty, in moving the mind, must give it a certain sensuous and emotional colouring. Decoration is accordingly an independent art, to be practised for its own sake, in obedience to (our) elementary plastic instincts. It is fundamental in design, for everything structural or significant produces in the first instance some sensuous impression and figures as a spot or pattern in the field of vision.[16]

But, one may wonder, is it at all proper to speak of decoration in music as an **independent** art? Is it not true that the more appealing *tāna*s of a *khyāl* singer conform to a linear pattern which can even be drawn out on paper? If yes, how does decorative music remain independent? Such questions, however, can be easily answered. Music is not a mere juxtaposition of notes, but their ordering in respect of pitch, that is, as higher and lower. In other words, the *svara*s make a passage, a flow. But any flow, be it that of a river or of the breeze, has its own natural manner; and the fact that it may be represented in a picture or as a passage in a thematic instrumental music composition is but a subsidiary matter. The *khyāl* singer does not consciously follow any prefixed visual pattern used in the formal visual arts; and the conformity of his *tāna*s with graphic patterns is but incidental, even as a particular formation of cloud may happen to resemble the map of a country. We must also remember that a *khyāl tāna* is not a mere undifferentiated flow of a particular manner but a succession of distinct (or distinguishable) notes. What is called *dānā*, (or the undimmed discreteness of notes) and uninterrupted flow are the two essential requisites of a good *tāna*, which is indeed why Ustad Bade Ghulam Ali Khan's *tāna*s may be said to be exemplary.[17] In other words, the form of every *khyāl tāna* is 'articulate' in the sense which S.K. Langer gives to the word; that is, it is an integration of notes in which the latter always retain a measure of individuality. There is one more requirement to which every good *tāna* in the *khyāl* style of singing may be said to be subject. It is the norm that a *tāna* should complete itself either directly at the *sama* with split-second accuracy or a little before that point in the *sthāyī* where the manifestly designed approach to the *sama* begins.

Within these overall requirements, however, it is possible and proper to distinguish the various devices which go to make the form of a *tāna* and invest it with its own unique look. These may be distinguished as follows:

A. Segmentation

This is the device by which the wholeness of a *tāna* is sub-divided into bunches of *svara*s so as to make for the appearance of inner orderliness. The segments, however, may either cover the whole *āroha* or *avaroha* of the *rāga*, or a lesser number of its constituents *svara*s. In the former case, the *tāna* assumes the form of an up-and-down contour of the *rāga*, and is satisfying because it is very easy to follow, provided, of course, the two overall requirements are also duly met; and in the latter case, the *tāna* draws our attention to, and focuses it on the inner tufts of *svara*s as well, instead of letting us merely flow along with the ascending and descending passages. The first kind of *tāna* merely embraces and traverses the *svara*s that go to make it; the second kind also projects them in a regulated way, and so may be said to be more articulate, and more deeply designed than the first one.

B. Accentuation

The suggestion of articulateness may also be heightened by accentuating or laying emphasis on some of the constituent notes. Here, though the singleness of the *tāna* may well be literally broken it will not appear so to those who are familiar with the grammar of the *rāga*, and are also able to follow the rhythm to which the *tāna* is set.

C. Interspersion with Formal Graces

The segments of a *tāna*, each comprising some *svaras*, may also be conjoined by means of formal graces like *sūta* and *mīṇḍa*. This device not only serves to keep the *tāna* undivided, but may heighten the beady appearance of the articulate parts of the *tāna* by opposing it to the undifferentiated flow of the formal graces in question.

D. Varying the pace or manner of flow

In so far as pace and manner are both inherent in a musical passage, the form of a *tāna* can be easily made to vary by changing its tempo or manner. Some *tānas* indeed look like a leisurely meander; others seem to gallop; and some may even seem to be meteoric. What is perhaps more satisfying to the discriminating listener is variation in the very way in which a *tāna* may seem to flow. It may appear to be simply curvaceous, or even curvilinear, or of involute segments.

E. Regulation of vocal volume

Aesthetically, however, perhaps the most likeable *tānas* are those which invest the whole pattern with a touch of feeling, and so make its form appear a little 'expressive', by means of the subtle employment of a gentle regulation of vocal volume. The *tānas* of maestros like Ustad Abdul Karim Khan, and Pandits Omkarnath Thakur and Behre Buwa are cases in point. Illustrations of such *tānas* cannot, however, be provided in writing, for the expressiveness in question, I repeat, is essentially a matter of practical singing.

But form in *tānas*, whatever be its specific look, cannot be dissociated from its material, that is, the *svaras* it builds upon, exactly as form of a painting cannot be extricated from the colours used, or as in sculpture one cannot divide the overall look of the work from the appearance of the marble used. The cramping of *ākāra* in *drut tānas*, or at higher *svaras*, is therefore a definite violation of the artistic form of a *tāna*. It turns the latter into a mere vocal **exercise**, and runs counter to the basic aesthetic requirement of **embellishment**. Ustad Bade Ghulam Ali Khan never lost sight of this requirement.

Before we proceed with our analysis of *tānas*, a remark of general value may be made. Every *tāna* has two aspects: one of **conception** and the other of **execution**. What the latter suggests is easy to see. Every *tāna* must be executed sweetly, and without any involuntary bedimming or obtrusion of its constituent notes. But the aspect of conception demands a little careful thinking. A *tāna* has to be so composed that it may fulfill the following conditions:

First, it must have a determinate and identifiable relation to the rhythm cycle. Second, it is also expected to be properly related to the *sthāyī* in the sense that the way in which it ends may seem to pave the way to the specific passage which constitutes access to the *sama*. Thirdly, in spite of being so related to both the *ṭhekā* and the *sthāyī*, it must have its own identifiable form and appear to be self-complete. Fourthly, it should also lay due emphasis on the salient notes of the *rāga*.

Some Tānas Analysed

These are probably the four more important ways in which a *tāna* forms itself. It is important to note, however, that a *tāna* does not form itself wholly by itself; and that it is really the musician who does it. And in so far as the matrix of all patterns is the *āroha-avaroha* arrangement of the *rāga* chosen, and also because the mind of the singer cannot but flow in accordance with the ascent and descent of musical passages, it is possible and proper — and is even demanded by the conception of aesthetics as a study of the ways of art-making — to indicate, in terms of linear diagrams, the flowing course of the passages. So, we have tried to supplement our verbal analysis of *tāna*s with their tentative visual-linear diagrams. With a view to avoiding disturbance in understanding, however, these diagrams have all been given at the end of the chapter, in the form of an appendix. (We may add that all the *tāna*s that we now set out to analyse will relate to the *drut Puriyā Dhanāśrī* composition that we have just analysed). Consider, now, the following *tāna*:

(1) From the third beat

1	2	3	4	5	6	7	8	9	10	11	12	13	14	15	16
		रेग	मंध	निनि	धप	मंग	गमं	रेग	बी	त	ग	ये	ऽ	ऽजु	ग
				२				०				३			

The first requirement is here visibly met, for the *tāna* moves at the same pace as the *ṭhekā* itself. Second, in so far as it ends with an upward twist of रेग, it seems (in the light of the *rāga*-form) to point to the *pañcama* from where the approach to the *sama* begins. Thus, it is also related to the *sthāyī* in the requisite way. Thirdly, the *tāna* in question certainly appears to be self-complete, and as having its own independent character. It seems to be self-complete because it both begins and ends with an identical twosome of notes, i.e., रेग; and it claims a measure of independence from the rhythm-cycle in so far as it neither begins nor ends quite at any *vibhāga* of the cycle. Finally, as demanded by the fourth requirement, the *tāna* in question lays due emphasis on the important notes and phrases of the *rāga*, say *niṣād*, *gāndhāra* and the **catch phrase** **मरेग**.

What we have said about a *tāna* so far is, however, quite incomplete. We have not made any mention of two very vital relations of a *tāna*: its relation to the listener and to the singer himself. What the listener finds very easy to follow, and so easily acceptable, is what may be called the up-and-down contour of a pattern. So, it is necessary for a whole recital to include some simple *āroha-avaroha* patterns too. Further, if a *tāna* ends at the tonic it enables the singer to test and keep his hold over the *ādhāra svara*, that is, the *ṣaḍaj*. This is all the more essential where fluent and intricate *tāna*s are executed, for in that case the risk of the singer's straying from the *ṣaḍaj*, and so from tunefulness generally, is greatly heightened. Another matter of detail which we have not so far noted is that the proper inter-linking of the *tāna*, as it ends, with the मुखड़ा (or approach to the *sama*) depends not only on the intrinsic suggestiveness of the terminal notes of the *tāna* itself, but also on how the singer himself modulates the beginning of the मुखड़ा. This creative act of the musician is extremely important because it can easily improve the look of the form of a *tāna* which may in itself be quite simple. No analysis of the form of *tāna*s can afford to ignore the singer's creative ability. Now, all that we have just said is borne out if we compare the following two notations of the same *tāna*, only if we bear it in mind that the second form (or b) is what we wish to focus on:

	1	2	3	4	5	6	7	8	9	10	11	12	13	14	15	16
(2) (a)	–	रेग	मंध	निरें	गरें	सांनि	धप	मंग	रेसा	बी	त	ग	ये	ऽऽ	ज्जु	ग
	×				२				०				३			

								सापमं	-प	-ध	(प)	-मं	-ग	रे
(b) —	रेग	मंध	निरें	गरें	सांनिधप	मंग	रेसा	बीऽ	ऽत	ऽग	ये	ऽऽ	ऽजु	ग
	×				२			०				३		

A flow, however, need not be a purely before-after successiveness. It may, instead, appear to organise itself, as it flows on, in segments of self-gathering flow. In other words, the adjacent segments may not merely exclude one another, but may repeat a part of each other's content. Thus, in the following *tāna* the second tuft of notes includes the complete first bunch of *svaras*; the third includes the last 2 *svaras* of the second bunch, and so on, so that there is no individual tuft of notes which does not include something of the preceding tuft's content. As it appears in notation, therefore, the form of the *tāna* is not merely successive, but in part repetitive in such a way that it seems to re-collect what it has just left behind. But when the *tāna* is actually sung it does not appear to gather itself in a curvaceous way, but rather strikes us, in the main, as angular, somewhat in the manner of the latter 'Z', because of its 1-2-3 manner. In other words, the form of a *tāna* as it appears in singing can easily differ from how it looks in notation.

(3)	1	2	3	4	5	6	7	8	9	10	11	12	13	14	15	16
										बी	त	ग	ये	रेग	रेग	मंग
	मंध	मंध	निनि	रेंनि	धनि	धमं	धमं	गमं	रेग	बी	त	ग	ये	ऽ	जु	ग
	×				२				०				३			

The form is like	रेग	रेगमं	गमंध	मंधनि	निरेंनि	धनिध	मंधमं	गमं	रेग
	1-2	1-2-3	1-2-3	1-2-3	1-2-3	1-2-3,	1-2-3,	1-2,	1-2

It should, however, be obvious that the 'Z'-like form to which we just now referred is not fixed at any particular point, but is seen to occur during the course of *āroha* and *avaroha*. What is more, the incidental moments of flow in the full range of a *tāna* can as easily assume a spiral form as the angular one. Thus, in the *tāna* which we are now going to present, and which interlinks note-names (or *sargam*) with little bits of *ākāra*, the pure vocal flow (or *ākāra*) seems a little undulating like the ebb and surge of a wave, if vertically in actual singing

a)	1	2	3	4	5	6	7	8	9	10	11	12	13	14	15	16
(4)	धनि	धनि	मंध	मंध	गमं	गमं	रेग	मंग	रेसा							
Sung as	धऽ	ऽनि	मंऽ	ऽध	गऽ	ऽमं	रेग	मंग	रेसा	बी	त	ग	ये	ऽऽ	ऽजु	ग
	×				२				०				३			

The flow which we have just now spoken of is not, however, relevant to music alone. Undulating flow is, in fact, a feature of the waves. If we wish to integrate such a flow more closely with the idiom of music, a good way would be to supplement a *tāna* of this kind with a brief *tiyā* which is, as we know, a typical feature of Hindustānī rhythm. This is precisely what is done in the *tāna* given below:

	9	10	11	12	13	14	15	16	1	2	3	4	5	6	7	8
(5)	निरें	निरें	धनि	धनि	मंध	मंध	गमं	गमं	रेग	रेग	रेसा	निरे	सा-	ऩिरे	सा-	ऩिरे
	सा-															
	०				३				×				२			
Sung as	निऽ	ऽरें	धऽ	ऽनि	मंऽ	ऽध	गऽ	ऽमं	रेऽ	ऽग	रेसाऩिरे	सा-	ऩिरे	सा-.	ऩिरे	
	सा-	बी	त	ग	ये	ऽऽ	ऽजु	ग	वा							
	०				३				×				२			

From the purely melodic viewpoint, however, another possibility may be availed of. The closing supplement can be such a simple flow that it may, by contrast, heighten the somewhat intricate character of the preceding flow. Thus, in the following *tāna* the little bits of a somewhat spiral flow which interlink some accented notes, are thrown into bolder relief by the simple descent of the closing melodic phrase

	1	2	3	4	5	6	7	8	9	10	11	12	13	14	15	16
(6)	निसां	निसां	निसां	निसां	निसां	धनि	धनि	धनि	धनि	धनि	मंध	मंध	मंध	मंध	मंध	गमं
	गमं	गमं	गमं	गमं	रेग	रेग	पमं	गरे	सा-	बी	त	ग	ये	ऽऽ	ऽजु	ग
	×				२				०				३			

Sung as	1	2	3	4	5	6	7	8	9	10	11	12	13	14	15	16
	निऽ	ऽसां	निसां	निऽ	ऽसां	ध़ऽ	ऽनि	ध़नि	ध़ऽ	ऽनि	मंऽ	ऽध़	मंध़	मंऽ	ऽध़	गऽ
	ऽमं	गमं	गऽ	ऽमं	रे़ऽ	ऽग	पमं	गरे़	सा	-बी	त	ग	ये	ऽऽ	ऽजु	ग
	×				२				०				३			

The ways in which the inner segments of a *tāna* can interact and heighten each other, or even the overall look of the form of the *tāna*, are almost infinite in number. The pattern that we are now going to focus on reveals how the *drut* character of a *tāna* may be heightened in subtle, little ways. To turn to its details, the first noteworthy feature of it is that it takes off from an unmarked point between the fifteenth and the sixteenth beat. This itself lends a touch of added sprightliness to the total pattern, exactly as a *bol* which falls between two adjacent beats in a rhythmic pattern, appears to be flighty (उचटता हुआ) in character. Further, the sudden descent from the opening phrase 'ऽ ध़ नि सां' to *mandra niṣād*, in the passage 'ऩिरेगम धनि. . . .' adds to the pattern's fluent character, aided of course by the uninterrupted character of its descending segment. It is as a result of the interplay of all these details that the *tāna* appears to be a little more fluent than it actually is. Yet, in spite of its own striking character the *tāna* in question does not seem to break away from the total singing because it ends with the catch-phrase 'मं रे़ ग' which at once paves the way to the utterance of the words 'बीत गये' that make the access to the *sama*. The following is the pattern in its rhythmic/notational form:

	13	14	15	16	1	2	3	4	5	6	7	8	9	10	11	12
(7)			ऽध़	निसां	ऩिरे़	गमं	ध़नि	सांरें	सांनि	ध़प	मंग	मंरे़	ग-	बी	त	ग
	ये	ऽऽ	ऽजु	ग	वा											
	३				×				२				०			

If, however, the catch-phrase itself is made the material of a *tiyā*, and if the latter forms the close of the *tāna*, it would not only make for a better integration of the rhythmic and grammatical aspects of the melody, but also predispose the listener's mind to register the clear rhythmical setting of the *sthāyī* which begins from a little after the off-beat, the momentary gap between the last note of the *tāna* at the *khālī* — and the instant at which the *sthāyī* begins — providing the requisite measure of distinctness to the *sthāyī* as it makes for the *sama*, so that the proper segmentation of the singing as a whole is not quite eclipsed by the uninterrupted flow of the *tāna*. This is, indeed, a clear feature of the *tāna* that we now turn to. We must at once add, however, that the *tāna* in question is itself duly subdivided into segments on its inside in so far as the last two notes of the first four segments (see the notation below) look like an incurvated hemming of the outer rim of the segment, so to say. In brief, the overall look of the form of the *tāna* is at once one of clear inner segmentation — so designed that the *tāna* seems at once to subdivide itself and gather the *svara*s it has just passed over — and of melody and rhythm.

The *tāna* in its notation and rhythmic form is as follows:

1 2 3 4 5 6 7 8 9 10 11 12 13 14 15 16

(8) 1)(रेग मंप मंग) 2)(रेग मंध निसां निध) 3)(मंध निरें गंगं रेसां) 4)(निरें गंमं पंमं गरें)

× २ ० ३

5)(निरें सांनि धप मंग) 6)(मंरे गमं रेग मंरे ग-) बी त ग ये ऽऽ ऽजु ग

In the *tāna* we have just analysed, we spoke of segmentation by means of an inward turn of the closing notes. But, to be sure, this is not the only way in which a *tāna* can appear segmented on the inside. Another way to achieve the inner sub-division of *tāna* is provided by what may be called the device of bracketing a musical phrase or a single note. In other words, as in the course of our next *tāna*, a particular note or phrase may be put between an indentical tuft of notes on either side (see the brackets within the different segments of the *tāna* given below). What is more, with a view to relieving the monotony of such bracketing, the descent of the same *tāna* may be made to assume the form of a coiled movement: see the portion marked out as [ ] in the pattern:

9 10 11 12 13 14 15 16 1 2 3 4 5 6 7 8

रेग गग रेसा (धनि निनि) रेग गग रेसा रेंगं गंगं रेंसां [नि(रें सां)नि][(धनि) ध)] [(ग (मं) ग]

रेसा बी त ग ये ऽऽ ऽजु ग

० ३ × २

रेग गग रेसा (धनि निनि) रेग गग रेसा/ रेंगं गंगं रेंसां [नि (रेंसां) नि]

[ध (नि) ध] [ग (मं) ग] रेसा

Another noteworthy feature of the present *tāna* is the fact that, though it embraces quite a few intervals between different segments of the *tāna*, it is yet able to seem, more or less, unbroken because the phrases which are held apart — and which serve as brackets — are identical in respect of their inner filling of notes. This is a clear illustration of the artistic truth — and also of the Gestalt law of similarity — that what is really divided and separate may yet be experienced as one, because of similarity.

Yet another way in which a *tāna* can acquire the look of clear inner segmentation is the simple device of putting a little emphasis on the first *svara* of every individual tuft of notes. However, in order to avoid the risk of monotony, this device will have to be tempered with some variations in the **extents** of the various segments. Thus, in the following *tāna*, whereas almost every individual phrase opens with a slight emphasis on the first note, the five segments of four notes each are relieved by one of six notes, and two others of two notes each. The result is that the overall form of the *tāna* wears a look of uniformity softened with a touch of variety. What is more, if the requirement of the accentuation referred to is duly heeded in the course of singing, at least during the ascent the first four segments will not only seem to follow, but to demand each other, making for an effect of what is called a look of सवाल-जवाब in musical parlance.

(10)	1	2	3	4	5	6	7	8	9	10	11	12	13	14	15	16
									गग	रेसा	निनि	धप	गंगं	रेंसां	पंमं	गरें
	सांनि	निरें	सांनि	धनि	धप	मंग	मंरे	गग	रेसा	बी	त	ग	ये	ऽऽ	ऽजु	ग
	×				२				०				३			

(गगरेसा) (निनि धप) (गंगरेंसा) (पंमं गरें सांनि) (निरेंसांनि) (धनिधप)

(मंग) (मंरे) (गगरेसा)

It would, however, be wrong to suppose that the requisite articulate character of a *tāna* cannot be achieved without the devices of inner segmentation and accentuation. The basic factor which makes for the articulate character of *khyāl*-singing is the balancing of the distinctness of notes with the successiveness of a flow. In a *tāna* which confines itself to this simple but fundamental demand, a touch of impressiveness may be imparted by its sheer range as manifest, we may say, in traversing all the three octaves. A good instance of all this is provided by the following *tāna*:

(11)	1	2	3	4	5	6	7	8	9	10	11	12	13	14	15	16
			रेग	मंध	निरें	गंमं	पंमं	गरें	सांनि	धप	मंग	रेसा	निध	पमं	गमं	धनि
	×				२				०				३			
	रेग	मंध	निरें	गरें	सांनि	धप	मंग	मंरे	ग-	बी	त	ग	ये	ऽऽ	ऽजु	ग
	×				२				०				३			

The distinctness of notes that follow one another can, however, assume different forms, according as the interval between the different notes is big or small. Where this interval is relatively large during ascent, the *āroha* part of the *tāna* will acquire a stepwise look. On the other hand, where the interval in question is small — that is, where the filling of notes in a *tāna* is close or intense — the *tāna* will acquire the look of a flow, even though the discreteness of notes may not at all suffer. A good example of this variegated look of the form of a *tāna* is provided by the following *tāna*:

	1	2	3	4	5	6	7	8	9	10	11	12	13	14	15	16
(12)									निऽ	रेऽ	गऽ	मंऽ	धऽ	निऽ	रेंऽ	गंऽ
	×				२				०				३			
	मंऽ	पंऽ	मंगं	रेंसां	निरें	सांनि	धप	मंग	रेसा	बी	त	ग	ये	ऽऽ	ऽजु	ग
	×				२				०				३			

However, where, the filling of a *tāna* is of even intensity, and flows at uniform pace, the whole pattern may come to acquire a satisfactory form by employing the simple devices of a repeated use of the *vādī svara* and employment of a *tiyā* at the end, as in the following:

	1	2	3	4	5	6	7	8	9	10	11	12	13	14	15	16
13)									पध	पमं	गमं	पध	पप	गमं	रेग	मंप
	×				२				०				३			
	धप	मंप	गमं	धनि	धप	मंध	निनि	धप	धध	पमं	पप	मंग	मंरे	गमं	पध	पप
	×				२				०				३			
	निरे	गमं	प-	निरे	गमं	प-	निरे	गमं	प-	बी	त	ग	ये	ऽऽ	ऽजु	ग
	×				२				०				३			

The interplay of melody and rhythm is, however, not so subtle a determinant of the form of a *tāna* as measured segmentation, repeated utterance which may directly make or call for some formal grace like *gamak*, and judicious pace which may impart a specific character to the very **flow** of a *tāna*. Thus, in the following pattern whereas all the segments excepting the last one (i.e., रेसा) comprise four notes each, the repeated utterance of the opening note of some segments (मंमंमंग, निनिनिग) directly demands a touch of *gamak*; and, what is more, a fluent utterance of four segments which make a part of the ascending flow of the *tāna* produces the look of a meander by virtue of the very nimbleness of the pace.

14)	13	14	15	16	1	2	3	4	5	6	7	8	9	10	11	12
	मंमं	मंग	मंग	रेसा	निनि	निग	मंमं	मंग	मंमं	मंग	मंग	रेसा	मंमं	मंगं	मंगं	रेंसां
	३				×				२				०			
	निरें	सांनि	धरें	सांनि	धप	मंग	मंरे	गग	निरें	गमं	रेग	मंध	गमं	धनि	मंध	निसां
	३				×				२				०			
	धनि	रेंगं	मंगं	रेंसां	निरें	सांनि	धरें	सांनि	धप	मंग	मंरे	गग	रेसा	बी	त	ग
	३				×				२				०			

Finally, where the segments are of inequal extent, a measure of uniformity, which is so essential for the seeming unity of a *tāna*, may be provided by the free employment of two identifiable devices: first, such a manipulation of adjacent notes as may generate the look of eddying around a common centre, and a sudden but controlled flight from an individual *svara* to its parallel in a different scale. The overall look of the form of such a *tāna* is surely not one of simple ascent and descent, but is rather one of encirclement, emphatic repetitiveness and flight. Thus, see the following:

	1	2	3	4	5	6	7	8	9	10	11	12	13	14	15	16
15)	पम॑	पध॒	पम॑	गम॑	पध॒	पम॑	गम॑	ध॒नि	ध॒प	म॑ध॒	पम॑	गम॑	म॑ग	म॑म॑	गम॑	म॑ग
	×				२				०				३			
	म॑म॑	गम॑	म॑ग	निनि	ध॒प	म॑ध॒	पम॑	गम॑	गम॑	म॑म॑	गम॑	गध॒	ध॒ध॒	गम॑	गम॑	म॑म॑
	×				२				०				३			
	गम॑	गध॒	ध॒ध॒	गम॑	गम॑	म॑म॑	गम॑	गनि	निनि	ध॒प	म॑ध॒	पम॑	नि़नि़	निनिध॒प		म॑ध॒
	×				२				०				३			
	पम॑	गम॑	ध॒नि	ध॒प	म॑ध॒	पम॑	गम॑	रे॒ग	रे॒सा	बी	त	ग	ये	ऽऽ	ऽजु	ग
	×				२				०				३			
	वा															
	×															

The segments of equal extent in this *tāna* may be shown by bracketing it as follows:

(पम॑ पध॒ पम॑) (गम॑पध॒ पम॑) (गम॑ ध॒नि ध॒प) (म॑ध॒पम॑)
(गम॑म॑) (गम॑म॑) (गम॑म॑) (गम॑म॑) (गम॑म॑ग) (निनिध॒प) (म॑ध॒पम॑)
(गम॑गम॑म॑म॑) (गम॑गध॒ध॒ध॒) (गम॑गम॑म॑म॑) (गम॑गध॒ध॒ध॒)
(गम॑गम॑म॑म॑) (गमगनिनिंनि) (ध॒पम॑ध॒पम॑) (नि़नि़निनिध॒पम॑ध॒पम॑)
(गम॑ध॒निध॒प म॑ध॒पम॑) (गम रे॒ग रे॒सा)

References

1. S.K. Saxena, *The Winged Form*, pp. 47-8.
2. Matanga Muni, *Brihaddeśi*, p. 81, *śloka* 283.

3. *Ibid.*, *śloka* 281.
4. *Ibid.*, *śloka* 280.
5. Bharat Muni; *Nāṭya Śāstra*, 74th *śloka*, 28th chapter, ed. by Pandit Kedarnath, 2nd edn.
6. George Santayana, *The Sense of Beauty*, p. 44.
7. Sir Monier-Williams, *A Sanskrit-English Dictionary*, p. 410.
8. S.K. Saxena, 'The Concept of Rāga — An Essay in Understanding'.
9. M.R. Gautam, *The Musical Heritage of India*, p. 15.
10. It is, in this context, interesting to note that absence of, or indifference to proper articulation of words, in music has not received universal approval. "The severer Greeks reprobated music without words; (and) Saint Augustine complained of chants that rendered the sacred text unintelligible". George Santayana, *The Life of Reason*, p. 348.
11. S.K. Saxena, 'Ālāpa in Dhruvapada Gāyāki', *Sangeet Natak*, July-December, 1986.
12. Sumati Mutatkar (ed.), *Aspects of Indian Music*, p. 79.
13. S.K. Saxena, 'Ālāpa in Dhruvapada Gāyaki', *op. cit.*, p. 50, Bracketed explanations added.
14. S. Mutatkar, *Aspects of Indian Music*, *op. cit.*, p. 83.
15. Sir Monier-Williams, *A Sanskrit-English Dictionary*, p. 435.
16. George Santayana, *The Life of Reason*, p. 351.
17. See, here, the following too:

    "Ghulam Ali's bass notes had matchless modulation and amplitude, while the notes of the upper octave were free from shrillness."

    Chetan Karnani, *Listening to Hindustani Music*, p. 78.

6

Conclusion

FINALLY, it would be appropriate if some remarks are made on the *khyāl* style of singing, first from the viewpoint of some general feature of art, because our approach is professedly aesthetical; and then by way of comparing *khyāl* with *dhruvapada*, in so far as we have taken the word 'form' also in the sense of **sub-types within the same art**. Now, a fairly general principle of art is the following one provided by John Dewey:

> Every art so uses its substantial medium as to give complexity of parts to the unity of its creations. . . . Take any art one pleases, and it will appear that the medium is expressive because it is used to individualise and define, and this not just in the sense of physical outline, but in the sense of expressing that quality which is one with the character of an object; it renders character distinct by emphasis. . . . In great art, there is no limit set to the individualisation of parts within parts.[1]

What Dewey here says in certainly true of the *khyāl* style of singing. The form of a *khyāl-sthāyī*, and of its numberless *tāna*s, arises from the incorporation of different *svara*s in such a manner that they are not only included and embraced, but also at once projected in respect of their individuality. What is called the *dānā* of the *svara* is required to be manifest all along. This is clearly not so in the case of *ālāpa* of the *dhruvapada* kind. My purpose here is not to make any judgement on the comparative **value** of the two musical forms, but simply to suggest that the distinctness of the individual *svara*s, as against their linkages, is **more** clearly manifest in a *khyāl* style composition than in *ālāpa*. In the case of the latter, the *svara*s are of course not absent, — how could they be?; but except when the singer tarries at a particular *svara*, the notes are **only embraced, not projected**, in an essentially flowing and undivided manner of singing. This is why, though *dhuvapada ālāpa* is admirably capable of working up the effects of seamlessness, flow and a musical atmosphere, it does not compare very favourably with the *khyāl* style in respect of investing music with **the suggestion of an abounding filling**. A manifest distinctness of details is indeed a key requirement of musical form in *khyāl*-**singing**. The meaning is not merely that the *vādī* and the *saṁvādī svara*s have to be kept duly manifest, but that every individual *svara* has to provide to the listener something of interest. It must appear as 'a moment of self-repose, an accent in a flow, a step to what is to come next or a merging into, or emergence from, another note in the space provided by the canvas of the *rāga*'.

Here, incidentally, a point may be made with regard to the distinctive way in which the suggestion of space is evoked in the *khyāl* **form**. The *dhruvapada*-singer's *ālāpa* evokes the suggestion of space as expansiveness; it seems to move on and on like a panoramic Chinese scroll-painting which presents 'a world in which ordinary boundaries are transformed into invitations to proceed.[2] In a good *vilambit khyāl-sthāyī*, on the other hand, space appears as roominess. Admittedly, quite a few different factors are here at work. The aesthetic pace is slow; the articulation of words is reposeful and (in principle) a little inward-looking; but the main factor which here evokes the suggestion of great (बड़ा or कुशादा) singing is the intervals of silence — or the thin, leisurely and luminous lines of singing (कण भरना) — which are made to punctuate, or fall between, the articulate utterance of the *bol*s of the *sthāyī*.

However, a *sthāyī* is not expected to unfold and establish itself in utter isolation. It is accompanied by a *ṭhekā* to which it is required to conform. Now, there is room within the *ṭhekā*, as there is within a *sthāyī*; and by availing of the roominess in the rhythm-cycle the *sthāyī* itself may gain not only in respect of roominess, but even by way of acquiring a touch of subtlety, say, when an emphasis in the *sthāyī* is made to fall in the interval between two adjacent *mātrā*s.

Finally, the *rāga*-**form** itself admits of suggestions of roominess in numberless ways. The most obvious of these ways is the inexhaustible filling of *tāna*s of various kinds that every *rāga* permits. Where patterning or *phirat* is not quite freely possible, as perhaps in the cases of *rāga*s like *Hiṅdola* and *Adbhut Kalyāṇa*, the suggestion of roominess can be evoked only in a limited number of ways, the more important of these being slowness of aesthetic pace or *laya*, steady articulation of individual notes, and their interlinking by means of simple and flowing curves, as distinguished from intricate and involute *tāna*s.

But we experience space not merely as something **in** which things are seen to be located, but also as a stretch or distance **from one point to another**, or as extent. Now, the most common device for producing a suggestion of extent in music is the employment of such *tāna*s as cover more than a single scale or *saptak*. What is more, if a *tāna* is somehow made to take off from a note in the *mandra-saptak* and to reach up to the corresponding note in the *tāra saptak*, the suggestion produced will not merely be one of a self-completing pattern, but of a pattern which seems to be considerably more extended than the space which its constituent notes take on a musical instrument. What is more, a suggestion of infinite distance can be generated through a skilful employment of but two adjacent notes. Thus, if in a *Sohnī* rendering, after a very brief utterance of the *ṣaḍaj*, the adjacent *r̥ṣabha* is projected in the way of a steady ray of light which seems to fade into quiescence, the cultivated listener will get the impression that the *r̥ṣabha* is looking far and deep into the distance.

The suggestion of extent can also be evoked by the number of *svara*s traversed by a *sthāyī*. There are some *sthāyī*s which traverse almost the entire musical scale. They naturally appear to be more extensive than those which comprise a lesser number of notes; the *sohnī tarānā* we have analysed is a case in point.

It is here necessary to add that extent appears in music not only as attitude but even as depth. The suggestion of depth can be easily evoked by a *sthāyī*, the *sama-bol* of which is placed in the *mandra-saptak*, as may easily happen in the cases of *rāga*s like *Puriyā* and Mālkauns. We must, however, hasten to add that this device of placing the *sama-bol* in the *mandra* is by no means the only way of securing a suggestion of depth in music. Most of the morning *rāga*s are admirably capable of producing a suggestion of depth. But, very few of them admit of a placing of the *sama-bol* in the *mandra*.

Further, in actual life space is experienced not merely as something which is **traversed** but as something which is **explored**. In the region of music this suggestion is easily evoked when two adjacent shades of the same *svara* are gently, but correctly embraced in a single, flowing passage.[3]

The lifelike quality of music as an art extends even further. It can project the major features of lived time too. In life we experience time quite variously, say, as repose and nimbleness, or as succession, simultaneity and duration. As for the first two of these, their distinct presence is clearly visible not only in *vilambit* and *drut khyāl*s but also in *tāna*s of varying pace. What is here important to note however is that, in music as contemplated, slowness and quickness of pace appear not merely as such but as invested with some extra suggestions, such as those of repose and contemplative quality, or of gaiety and ebullience. The point is clearly seen when we reflect that running on the track, whatever be its pace, does not appear to have these qualities. In the case of music, on the other hand, slow, onward movement may even come to wear a look of reverential access, as when we watchfully prepare the ground for a correct utterance of the *gāndhāra* in *Darbarī* or for the caressing descent of the phrase मं ऽ ऽ ऽ ᵐग in *Lalit*. It is also noteworthy that where leisurely pace appears integrated in a well structured *sthāyī*, the suggestion evoked is one of **stability**, in spite of the fact that movement across the various notes is actually there.

Simultaneity in music operates in three main ways: as a moment of attainment, as a process of confluence or as a background. The strains of the *tānpūrā* do not flow along with, but provide a steady vibrant **background** to the entire music. The *sama* is easily the most conspicuous moment of simultaneous **attainment** by the drummer and the singer. As a process of **confluence**, simultaneity is seen in the way the *sāraṅgī* player tries to duplicate the patterns of the vocalist or the drummer may seek to interweave parallel patterns with the various figurations of the vocalist (लिपटना).

As for duration as experienced in the contemplation of music, it is not the same thing as duration measured by our watches and clocks. When after attending a concert we look at our watches and say that the recital has taken a little more than two hours we obviously speak of duration from the practical, and not from the aesthetic, point of view. Duration thus regarded is only the length of time for which a thing lasts. In music, on the other hand, duration is necessarily the material of some effect, satisfactory or unpleasant. Thus, if an important note (*svara*) is not rendered long enough we tend to quietly protest against the unsatisfactory effect. A similar reaction may take place when the musician tarries at a note a little longer than is warranted by the grammatical nature of the *rāga* being rendered. Duration in music may also work as a determinant of balance between the various elements of a recital. Thus, if the weaving of patterns (or *tāna*s) is done for so long that the intervening utterance of a *sthāyī* is wholly ignored, the recital would come to appear ill-balanced. A similar effect may be produced if, as it is sometimes seen to happen in the music of the great Abdul Wahid Khan, the number of ways in which the various notes of a *rāga* can be permuted is highlighted at such leisure that the flowing form of music is sacrificed for the sake of merely calculative, analytical intent. On the other hand, where due care is taken in regulating the duration of the various parts of a recital, the ending of one distinct spell of music and the beginning of another may at once be felt as a mark of adroitness on the singer's part and a welcome change in the fabric of the music itself. Thus, if a brilliant *drut-khyāl*, following the opening *vilambit* one, is not overdone — that is, if its duration is kept within limits — a sudden switchover to a relatively leisurely *tarānā* (say in *jhaptāla*) may well strike the listener as a welcome relief, not in the sense of a riddance from something unpleasant, but as the complement of repose demanded by a burst of animated singing.

To conclude, not merely the various emotions, but many subtle details of felt life — and, what is more, the major general features of our experience of space and time — can all be projected in music with telling effect. It is indeed difficult to think of any other art which could be said to equal music in respect of appearing lifelike, **without necessarily making any explicit reference to life**.

References

1. John Dewey, *Art as Experience*, pp. 202-4. Italics added.
2. *Ibid.*, p. 209.
3. By way of illustration, reference may here be made to the use of *madhyama*s and *niṣāda*s in *rāga*s like *Lalit*, *Kedār* and *Minyā kī Malhāra*, or *Bṛndābanī Sāraṅga* and *Śuddha Sāraṅga*.

Linear Diagram of Tāna No. 1

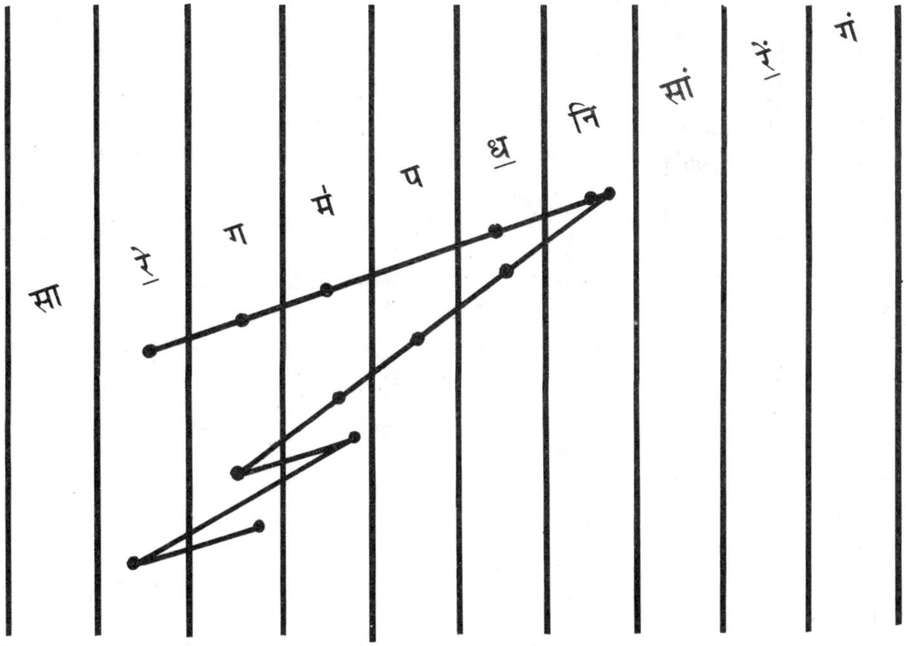

Linear Diagram of Tāna No. 2

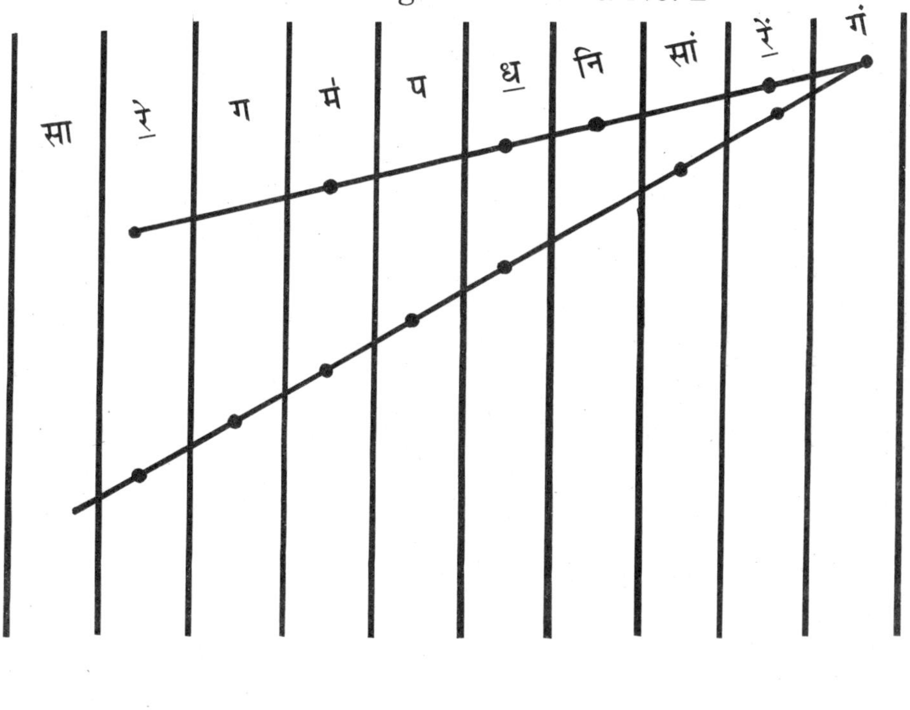

Linear Diagram of Tāna No. 3

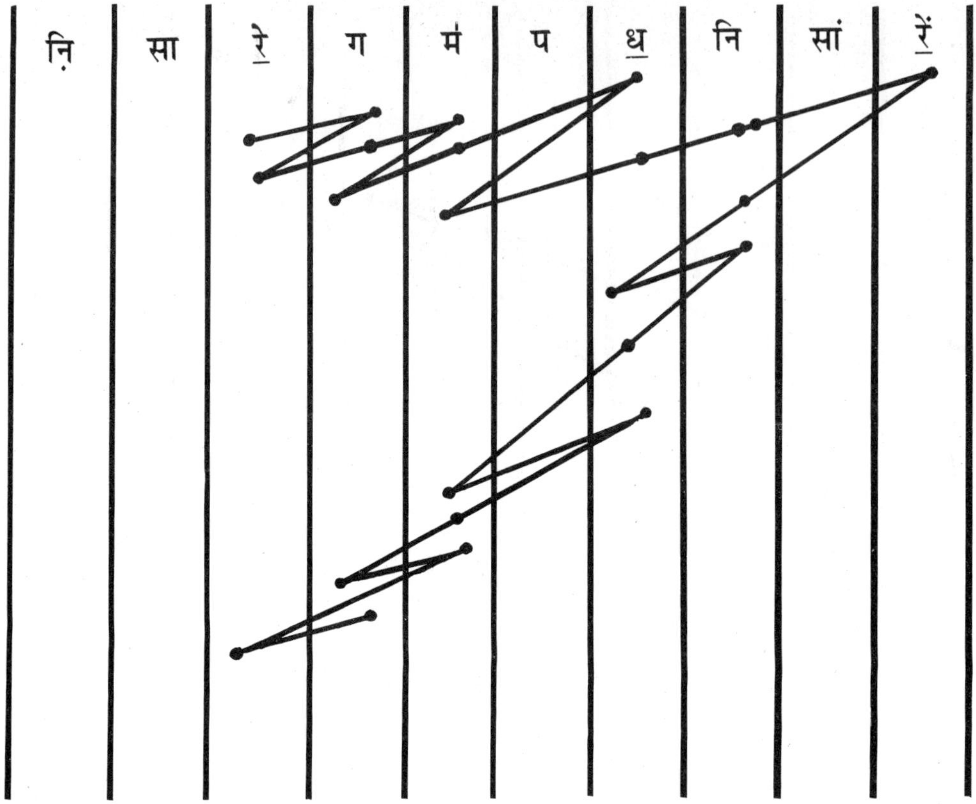

Linear Diagram of Tāna No. 4

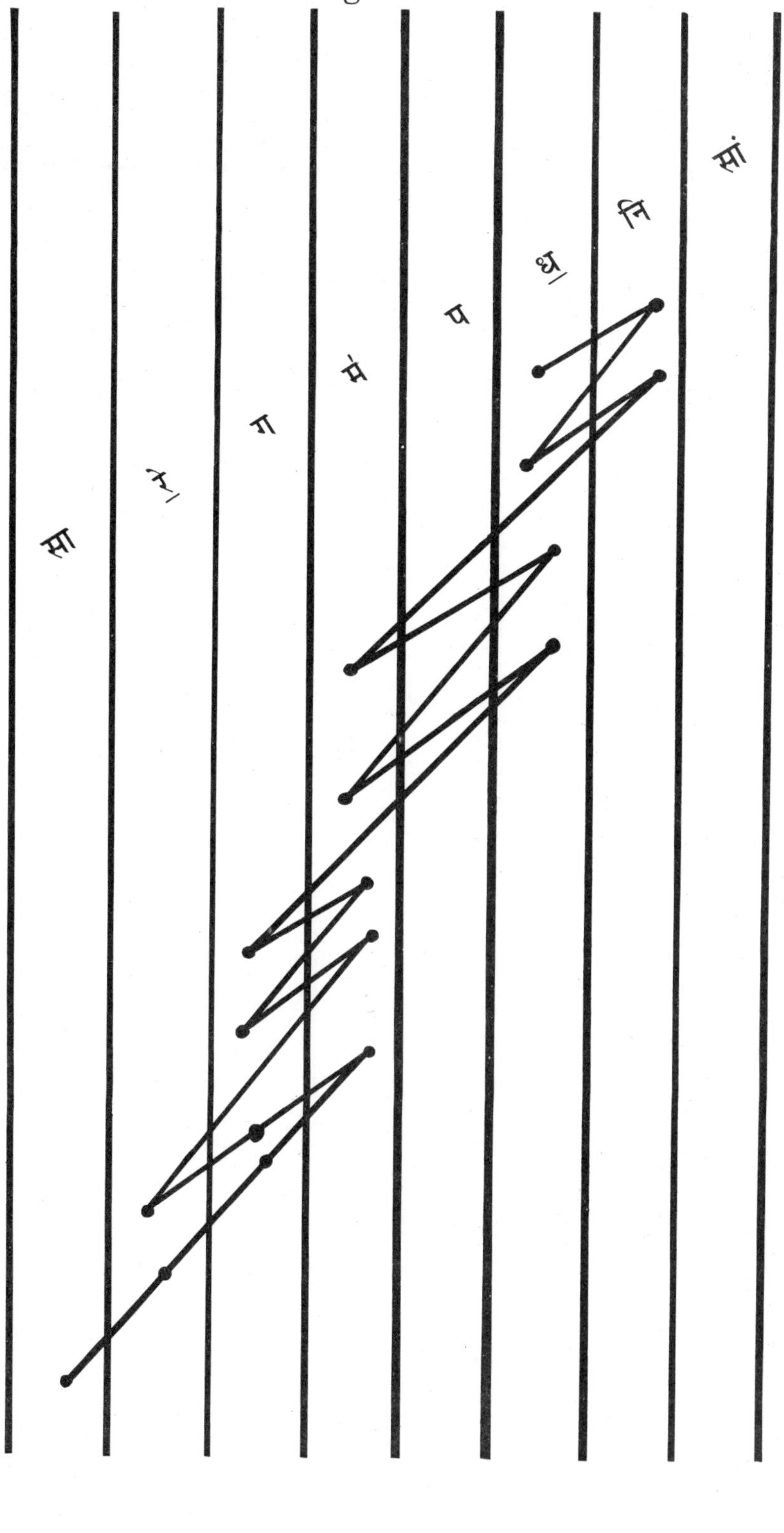

Linear Diagram of Tāna No. 5

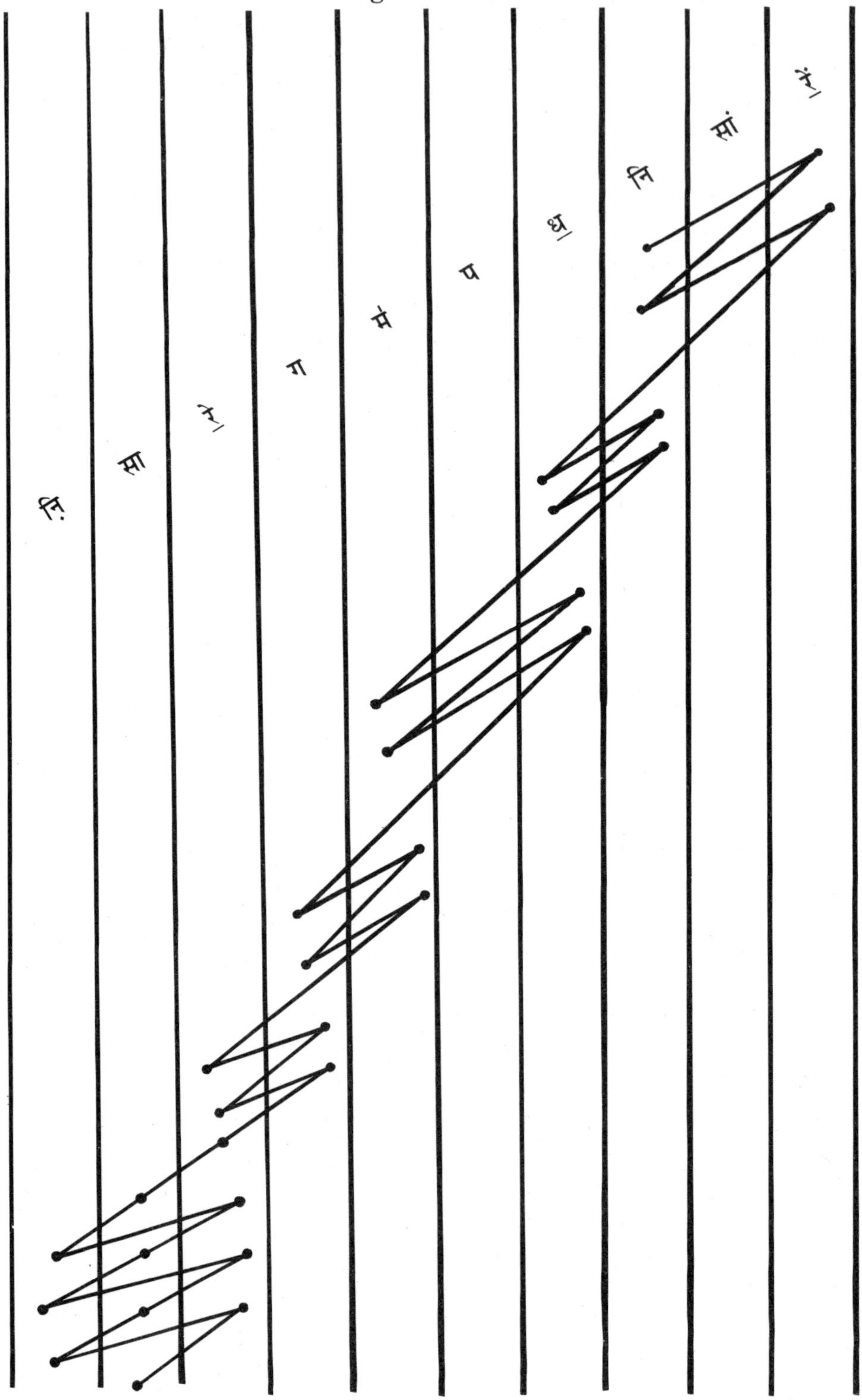

Linear Diagram of Tāna No. 6

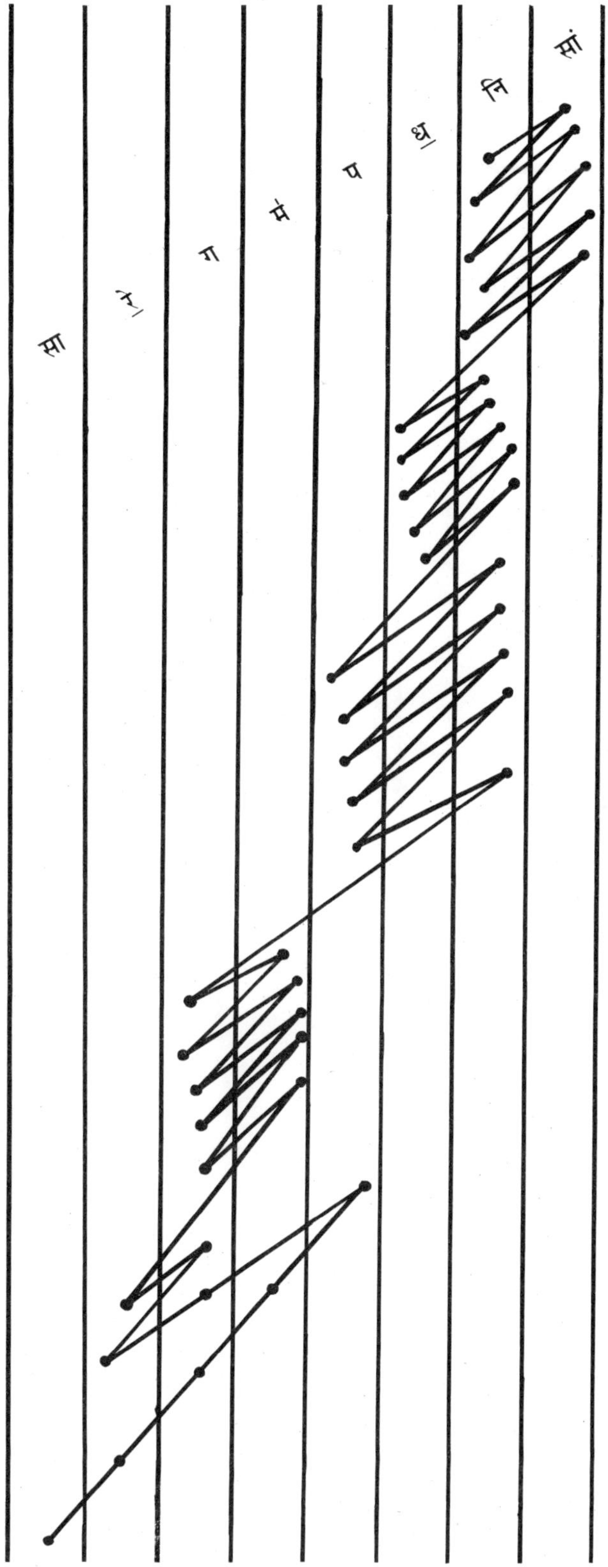

Linear Diagram of Tāna No. 7

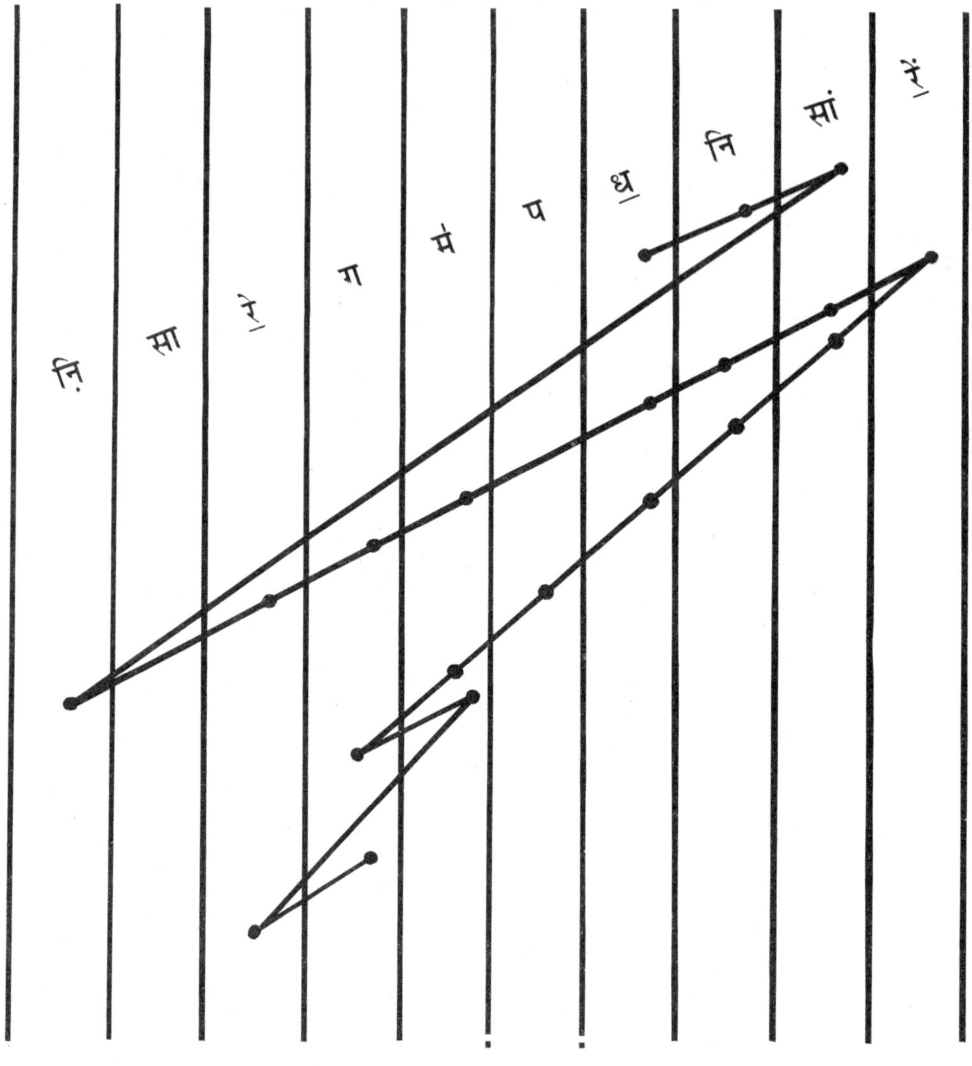

Linear Diagram of Tāna No. 8

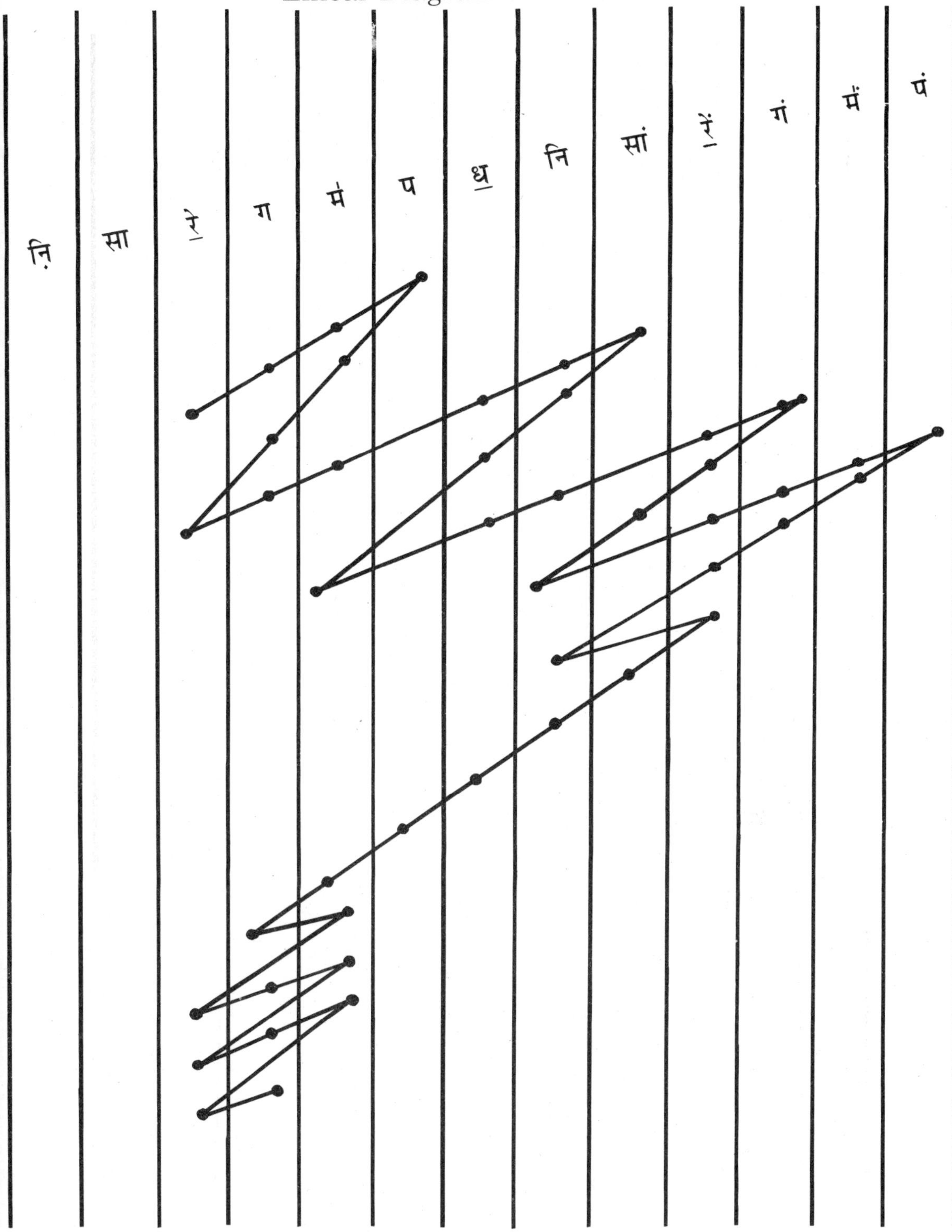

Linear Diagram of Tāna No. 9

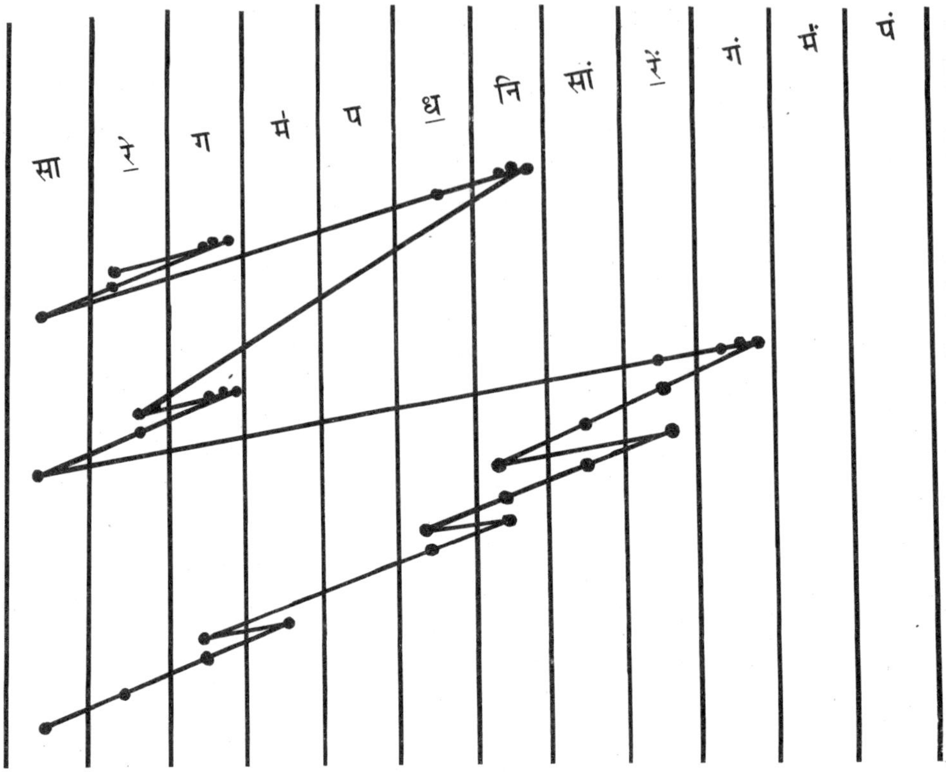

Linear Diagram of Tāna No. 10

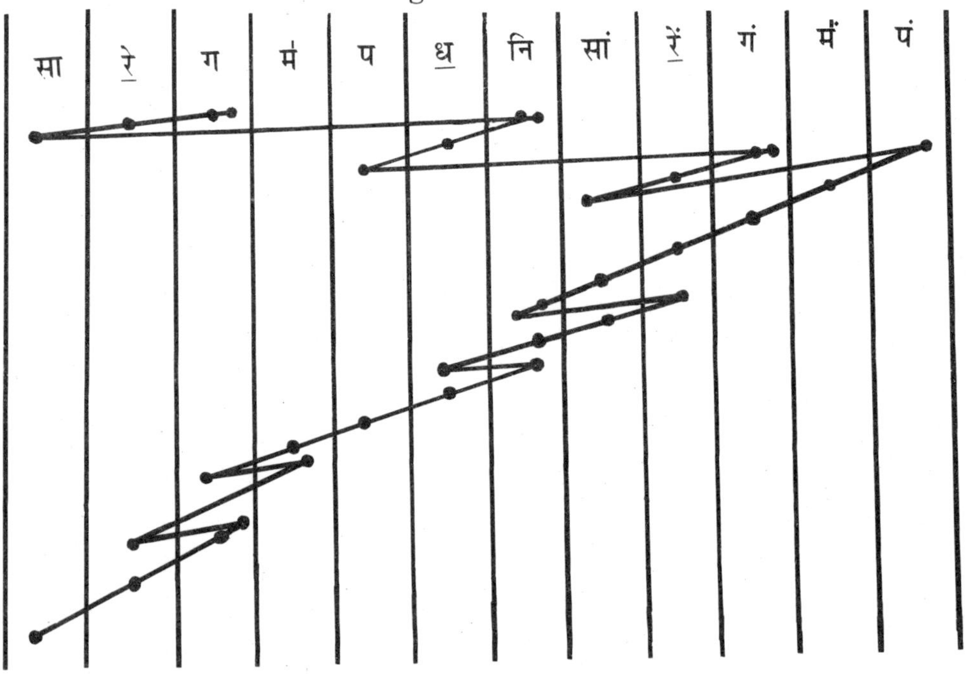

Linear Diagram of Tāna No. 11

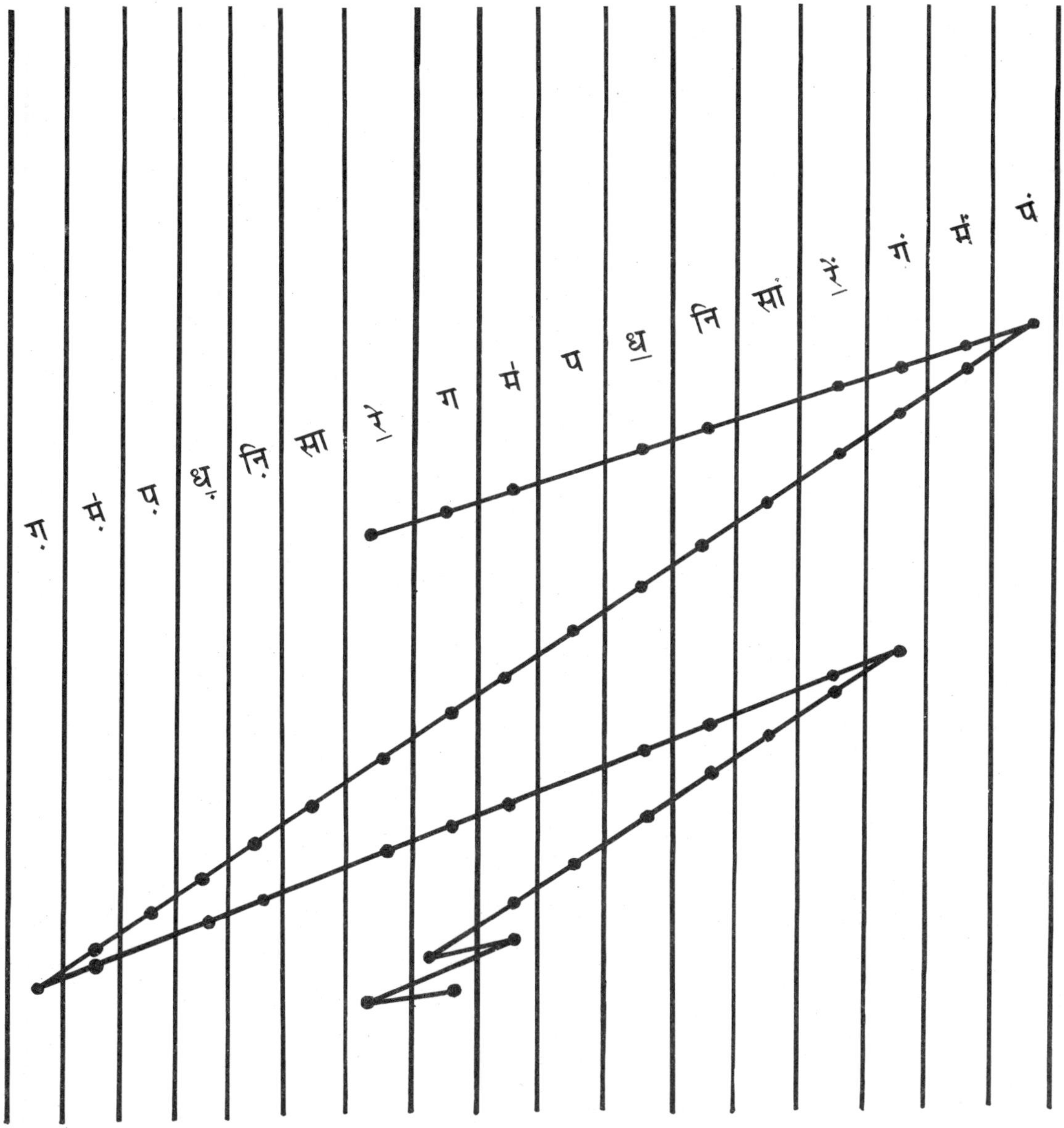

Linear Diagram of Tāna No. 12

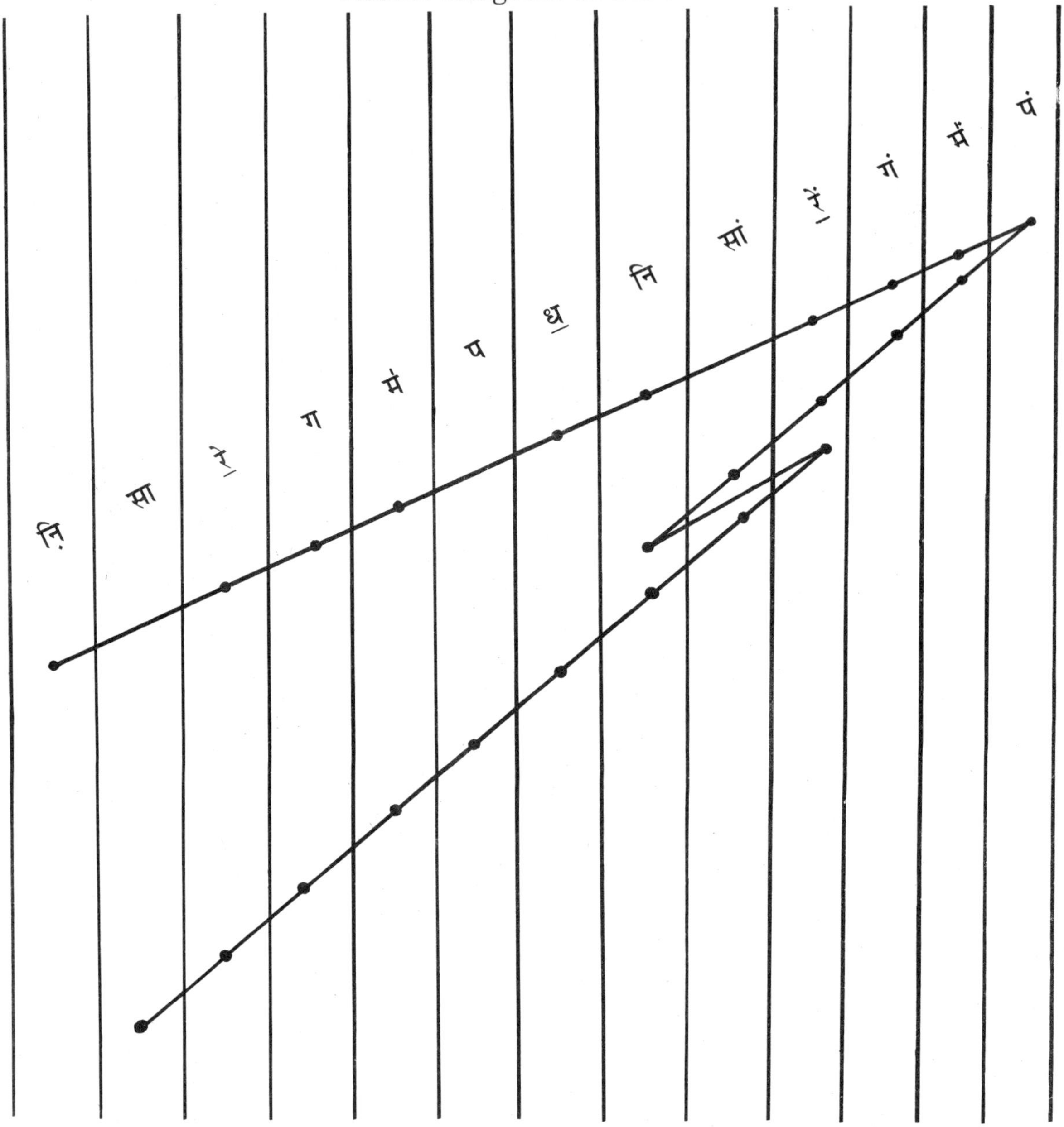

Linear Diagram of Tāna No. 13

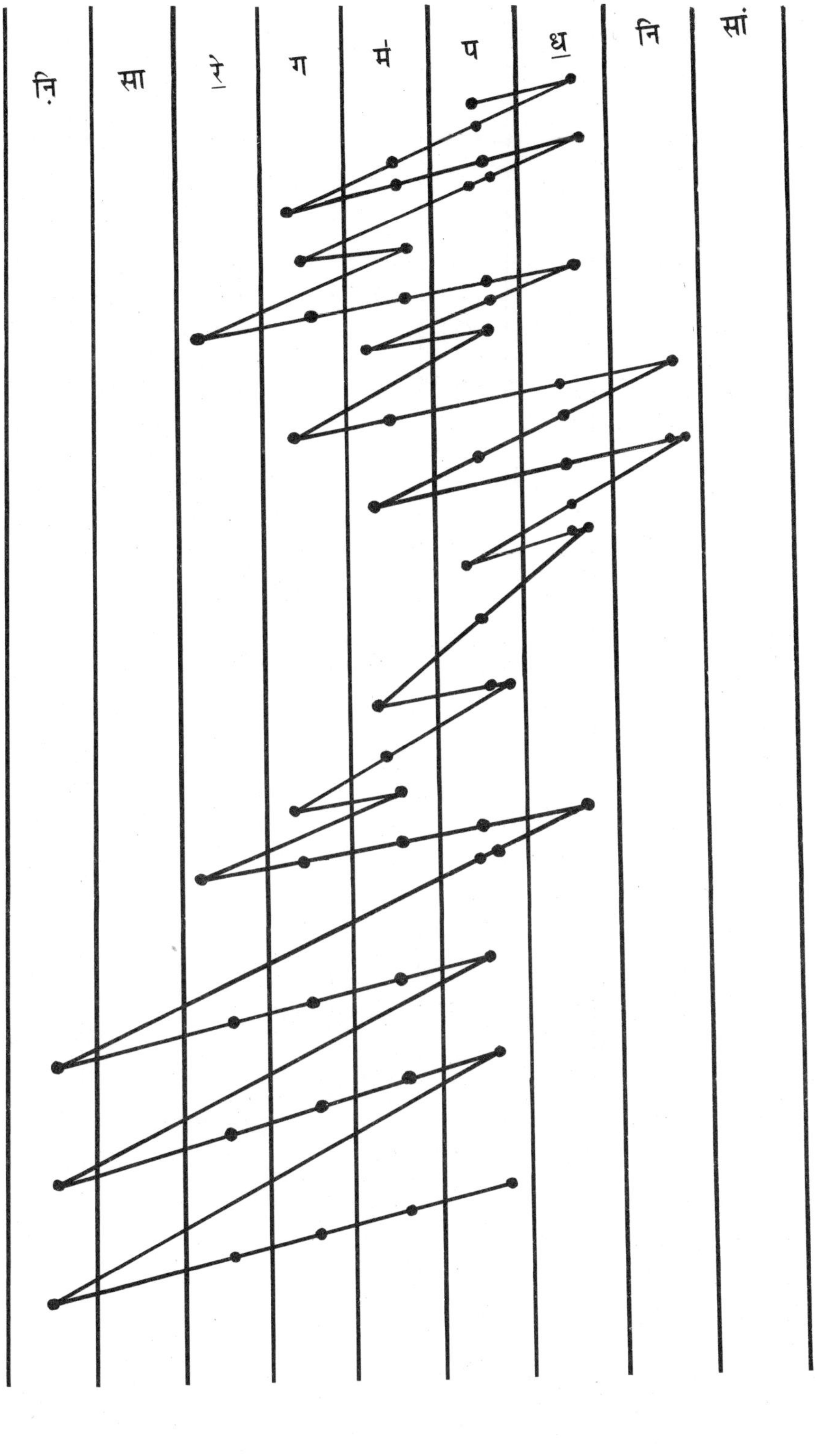

Linear Diagram of Tāna No. 14

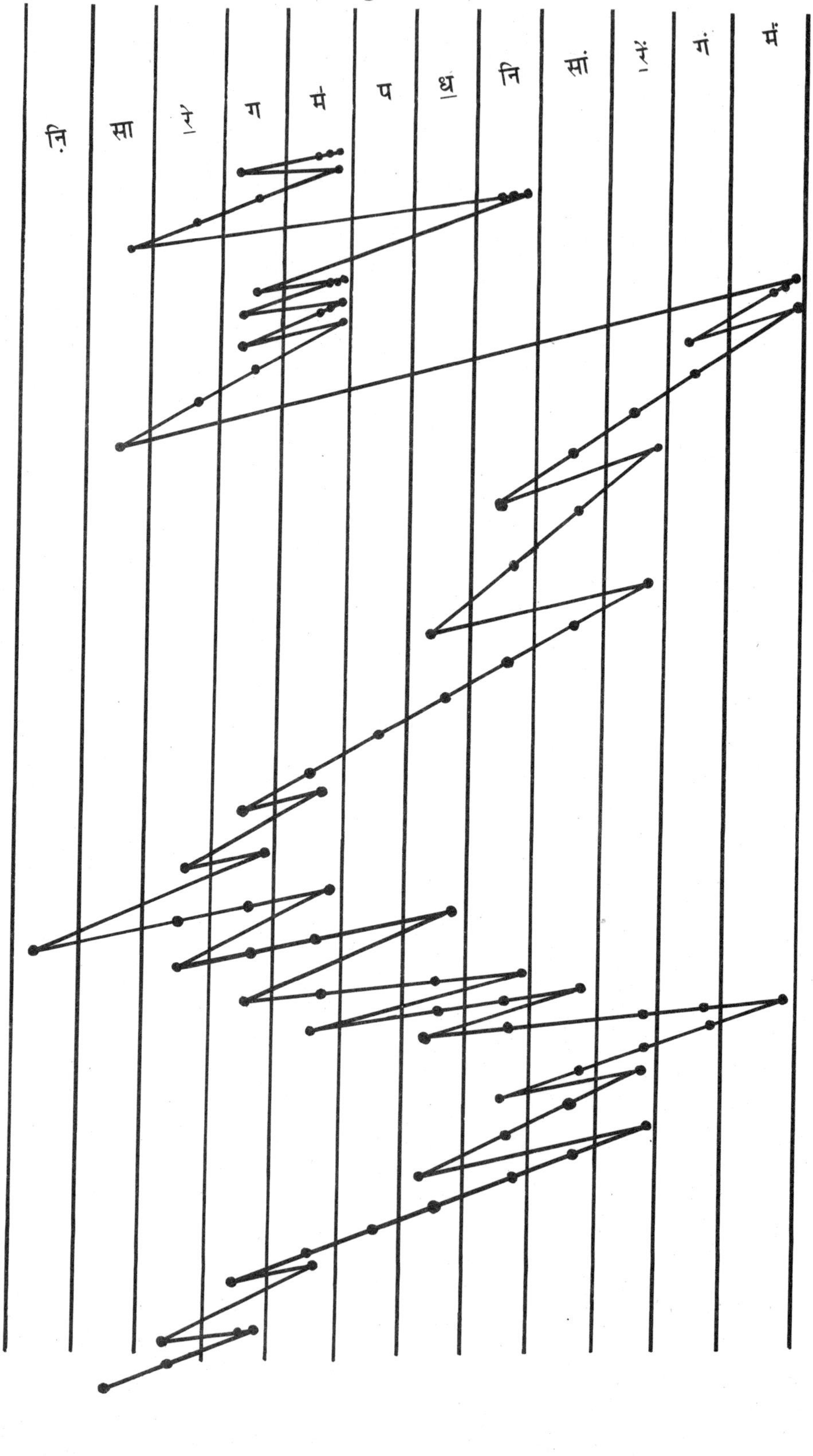

Linear Diagram of Tāna No. 15

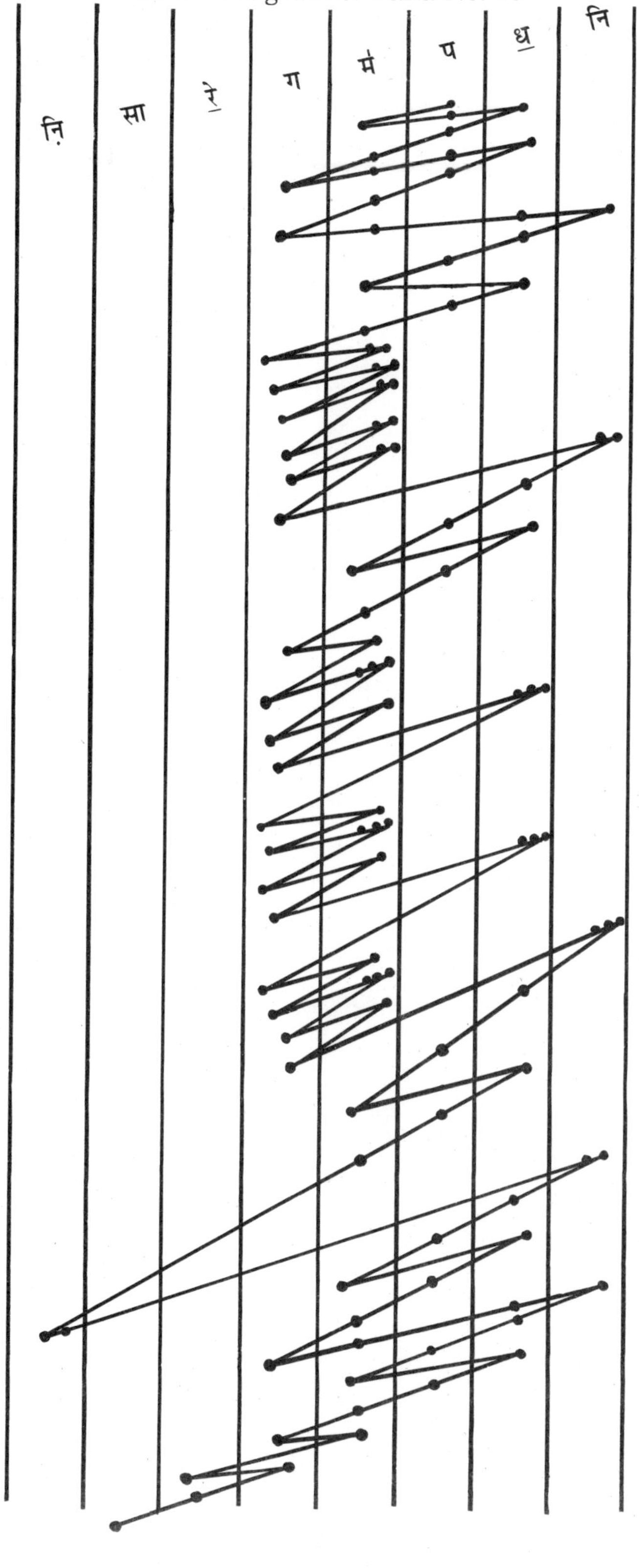

Glossary

ābhoga: A distinct segment of a *dhruvapada* composition which is generally put fourth in the order of singing.

ādhāra-svara: The basic note or the tonic *i.e. ṣaḍaj.*

ākāra: The voice as shaping melody only by using the vowel 'aa', instead of the solfa syllables or the words of the text.

ālāpa: Exposition of the *rāga* without the aid of both beat-measured rhythm and words.

ālāpiyā: One who specialises in the singing of *ālāpa*.

āmad: In many melodic compositions, a noticeable part of the *sthāyī* or the *gat* which appears as a well-designed approach to the sama.

āndola: Oscillation, a formal grace.

ārh-kuvārh: Two set forms of rhythmic variation.

ārohī: An ascending series of notes.

āvṛtti: A single round of the rhythmic cycle.

abhinaya: Acting, representational or expressive.

alpatva: Rarity in the use of a note; opposite of *bahutva*.

aṁśa: A predominant note.

anāgat: A rhythmic pattern of the *viṣama* (or displaced-from-*sama*) kind of which the last syllable or vocal emphasis is designedly made to occur a little before the *sama*-instant

aṅga: The body as adapted to the needs of dance.

antarā: The second section of a composition usually containing notes from the upper tetrachord and the higher register.

anubhāva: The third constituent in the evocation of *rasa*. It projects some movements, gestures and speeches which are seen to occur; makes *vibhāva* (situation) come alive.

anunāsika: Patterns/words in pronouncing which the hind part of the nose is used, such as the following: *ananta*, *mangala*. 110

anuraṇātmaka: An *alaṁkāra* or formal grace which provides to the notes sung a vibrant quality. Where it is used skilfully during the course of *ālāpa* by a *dhruvapada* maestro, a delightful melodic effect is evoked, resembling the sound of swaying temple-bells which appear to approach and recede alternately.

ati: Excess or excessive. In the context of music, the word signifies notes which are too high or too low.

atīt: A rhythmic or melodic pattern the last emphasis of which ends just a little after the *sama*-instant.

avarohi: A descending series of *svara*-s (notes)

bāj: The distinctive style of a *gharānā* of instrumental music or of an individual musician.

bahutva: Prominence or frequency in the use of notes.

bandiśa: An integration of notes — and also of some words in the case of vocal music — which embodies and reveals a *rāga*; is set in a particular rhythm-cycle; and so appears to be complete in itself.

barhat: Patient and rising unfoldment of the grammatical and aesthetic character of a *rāga*.

bedam: Non-intervallic or incessant; a rhythmic pattern the constituent syllables of which do not admit of any pause.

bhajan: A devotional song.

*bindī*s: dots; here, over letters.

bol: Words or mnemonic (nonsense) syllables used in a rhythmic or melodic composition.

Brahman: A religious/philosophical term for Ultimate Reality.

calan: The way of melodic or rhythmic progression.

camak: sparkle, glitter, alacrity.

caugun: Four times as fast as the original speed.

cautāla: A *tāla* of 12 beats used for *dhruvapada* songs.

cakradāra: A type of rhythmic composition longer than a *tiyā*, which completes itself as a kind of wheeling around three identical segments.

dānā: Individuality or discreteness of notes.

dāyān: The right hand drum of the two-piece drum, *tablā*.

dagar: In music, a formal grace which has the look of an ascending meander.

dhaivat: The sixth note, *dhā*.

dhamār: A composition in a rhythm of 14 beats (5+2+3+4) which is also called *dhamār*.

dhruvapada: A classical genre of singing. Its melodic structure has four segments: *sthāyī*, *antarā*, *sañcārī*, and *ābhoga*.

dhvani: Sound

dohā: A verse of two lines which rhyme with each other.

drut: Allegro; quick, lively rhythm.

drut gatkārī: Playing the basic *gat* and patterns across it, at a lively pace.

dugun: Double of the original speed.

dyut-vedāṅga: Two ways of singing a note which make it seem to throb and sparkle.

ek-tāla: A *tablā tāla* of 12 (2+2+2+2+2+2) counts used for vocal and instrumental recitals.

gāndhāra: The third note of the scale (gā).

gāyakī: A distinct style of classical singing.

gamak: Ornamentation in general; or a specific *alaṁkāra* (formal grace) which produces effects of depth and inwardness.

gat: The basic melodic line of a recital of instrumental music duly set in a particular *rāga-tāla* frame; it looks complete structurally.

gharānā: A traditional school of music possessing certain characteristic stylistic features, which generally arises as the concern of a particular family.

ghazal: A very popular form of Urdū poetry which specializes mostly in projecting human love and beauty.

greha: In traditional musical theory, a note from which compositions in a particular *rāga* should begin.

guṇas: The three basic qualities recognised in traditional Indian philosophy: *Sattva*, *rajas*, and *tamas*. They are believed to produce, respectively, the following attributes of human life and conduct: peace, tranquillity, righteousness; activity, desire, endeavour; and sloth, viciousness and ignorance.

Hindustāni music: North Indian music, as distinguished from music of the south which is popularly called Carṇātic Music.

jhaptāla: A *ṭablā tāla* of 10 (2+3+2+3) counts used for *ḳhyāl*/instrumental recitals.

jhūmrā: A slow and serious *táblā tāla* of 14 (3+4+3+4) counts used for *vilambita khyāl*.

jugalbandi: A distinct way of presenting Indian music — vocal or instrumental — as the joint contribution of two artists.

kaṇbharnā: The artistic device of bridging the space between the words of a *sthāyī* as sung with thin melodic lines which are made to puncuate or fall between the articulate utterance of the bols of the *sthāyī*.

Kathak: North Indian Classical dance.

khāli: The off beat in a rhythm-cycle.

khyāl: Today, the most popular genre of classical Hindustānī vocal music featuring a composition of two parts (*sthāyī-antarā*) followed by melodic and rhythmic improvisation.

komala: Flat.

koorh: Ignoramus

kuśādā: roomy, spacious.

lagāv: Manner of applying voice to musical notes.

laghu mātra: A beat of brief duration.

lahak: One of the many formal graces. It lends a measure of lightness to musical flow.

laya: Pace of melodic flow, with or without measuring with the help of *mātrā*-s or beats.

layakārī: Rhythmic variations.

lehrā-thekā: *Lehrā* is a simple, set tune played repeatedly to serve as a rhythmic anchor for a *Kathak* or solo *tablā* recital. *Theka* is a rhythm-cycle as drummed.

lipatnā: Intertwining, say of the *tablā*-player's rhythmic patterns with the melodic ones of the main artist, almost simultaneously.

mātrā: Single count or beat. Serves to measure the flow of melody and rhythm.

madhyama: The fourth note of the octave (*Mā*).

madhya laya: Medium tempo.

madhya saptak: Middle register or octave.

mandra saptak: Lower register or octave.

mantra: Any sacred word or syllable used as an object of concentration and embodying some aspect of spiritual power.

mīnd: A slow gide connecting two or more notes.

mr̥dangam: A double - headed barrel shaped drum akin to *pakhāvaj*, popular in the south, used for both solo recitals and as accompaniment with Carṇātic vocal and instrumental music.

mughlai: A *tablā tāla* having 7 (3+2+2) counts.

mukhdā: The first phrase of the *bandiśa* which completes itself at the *sama* (सम)

nāda: Sound in its broadest sense.

nāma-japa: Devout recitation of a Holy name.

navarasamālīkā: A rosary of the 9 basic sentiments (*rasas*).

nigāh: A trained and discriminating eye or way of regard.

niṣāda: The seventh note of the octave: *Nī*.

nyās: A final note at which a phrase or composition in a particular *rāga* is required to end.

pakhāvaj-bol: mnemonic syllable meant specially for *pakhāvaj*-playing.

pañcam: The 5th note of the *saptak*: *Pā*.

paran: An elaborate rhythmic pattern which distinguishes *pakhāvaj* from *tablā*-playing.

paṣto: A *tāla* cycle having 7 (3+2+2) counts.

quāyedā: The most highly valued pattern in the art of *tablā*-rhythm. Its structure comprises two lines, roughly in the way of a couplet. The first line or segment starts from the *sama* and ends at *khali*, while the second one takes off from the *khāli* and terminates at the *sama*. The terminal syllables of the two segments have to rhyme, without being identical. Thus if the last *bol* of the first line is *tīnā kinā*, the terminal *bol* of the second line has to be *dhinā ginā*.

rāga: A melodic form in Indian classical music comprising some specific notes of the scale having an identifiable melodic character and associated (in principle) with a particular mood, may be gay or sad, or just lively.

rāga-rūpa: Form of the *rāga*.

rañjan: Entertainment

rūpak: A *tablā tāla* of 7 (3+2+2) counts.

rasa: Aesthetic emotion as creatively evoked (in drama) through a proper integration of *sthāyībhāva*, *vibhāva*, *anubhāva* and *vyabhicārībhāvas*.

rasānubhūti: Rasa-experience

rasa-siddhānta: The theory of *rasa*.

rasika: One who is trained and attentive enough to experience *rasa*.

r̥ṣabha: The second note of the sapak: *Re*.

sāhitya: The (verbal) text of a vocal composition.

sama: The first and focal beat of a rhythmic cycle.

samvādi: The consonant; the note which makes an agreeable twosome with the *vādi* or main note of the *raga*.

samvāditva: The quality or state of *samvāda* or consonance.

sañcarī: The third segment of a *dhruvapada* composition.

saṅgīta: A comprehensive term covering both music and dance.

saptak: Graded series of seven notes; octave in Western music.

sargam: Series of note-names.

sawāl-jawāb: Melodic or rhythmic patterns which appear to rejoin or complement each other.

sawāri: A *tablā tāla* of 15 beats.

ṣadaj: The first note: *Sa*.

śṛngāra: The sentiment of love; the most popular of the *navarasa*-s.

sthāyī: The first section of a composition *usually* consisting of notes from the middle register excluding those that are highter than the upper tonic.

sthāyitva: The quality of being settled or fixed.

sur: *Svara*; the musical note.

sūta: A formal grace in the way of a quick sweep.

svara-samūha: A tuft of musical notes.

tāla: Rhythm, as measured with the help of beats.

tādātmya: Intense, imaginative identification with the essence of the other, say, the ongoing music.

tāna: A fast melodic pattern, longer than a mere phrase. Aims at imparting some decorative beauty to the ongoing music.

trivat: Similar to the *tarānā* in most respects, except that it employs sound-clusters of the *pakhāvaj* and does *not* use any words.

tānpurā: The drone used in Indian classical music generally. Provides a seamless melodic background to the whole recital; has to be tuned differently in accordance with the grammatical character of the *rāga* chosen.

tār sā: Tonic of the higher register.

tār saptak: Higher octave.

tablā: A two-piece drum used to provide rhythmic support and accompaniment to Hindustānī music, excluding the *dhruvapada* and *dhamār* forms.

tarāna: A distinct genre of classical vocal Hindustānī music which is duly set in *rāga* and *tāla*, but the peculiarity of which lies in making the most of vocables and rhythmic syllables, with but an occasional use of meaningful language.

teorā: A *tablā* tāla having 7 (3+2+2) counts.

thumrī: Essentially, a genre of light-classical vocal music. Puts emphasis on bringing out the meaning and emotional content of the words used, through varying and duly adapted singing.

tiyā: A brief cadential pattern having three identical segments, sometimes at varying *laya*, but sung (or played) in quick succession.

tīgun: Three times as fast as the original speed.

tilvarāh: A cycle of 16 (4+4+4+4) counts. Mostly used for *vilambit khyāl* singing.

tivra: Raised or sharp; in music, refers to the higher form of a note, such as *tīvra Mā*.

tukdā: Generally speaking, a segment or piece of a whole. In our rhythmic system, the word signifies a segment segregated from some lengthy *paran* of *pakhāvaj*, but yet appearing to have a relative wholeness of its own.

uttarāṅga: The upper tetrachord.

vādī: The sonant or the most important note of a *rāga*.

varṇa: Character or quality of a *svara*.

vibhāga: A group of *matrā*-s subdividing, but not fragmenting the *tāla* cycle.

vikrit: Altered, not *śuddha*; signifies flat or sharp notes.

vilambit: Adagio; slow in space.

virah: Separation in love.

vitavighna: Transcendent of obstacles.

vyabhicārī: Fleeting emotions: one of the three basic *bhāva*-s which have to be integrated for evoking *rasa*.

ẓarab: The impact of a *mātrā* or bol on the flow of *laya* or melody.

Bibliography

Archer, W.A., *India and Modern Art*, George Allen and Unwin, 1959.

Bell, Clive, *Art*, Arrow Books, 1961.

Bharat, Muni, *Nāṭya Śāstra*, ed. by Pt. Kedarnath, 2nd edn., Bombay, Nirnaysagar, 1943.

Bratu, H., and I. Marculescu, "Aesthetics and Phenomenology", in *The Journal of Aesthetics and Art Criticism*, Spring, 1979.

Croce, B., *Aesthetic* — As Science of Expression and General Linguistic, tr. by D. Ainslie, Peter Owen Ltd., London, reprint 1962.

Ducasse, C.J., *The Philosophy of Art*, Dover Publication, INC. New York, 1966.

Gautam, M.R., *The Musical Heritage of India*, Abhinav Publications, New Delhi, 1980.

Indian Painting Today, 1981, Jehangir Art Gallery Publication.

J. Stolnitz's essay, "The Aesthetic Attitude" in *Introductory Readings in Aesthetics*, ed. by J. Hospers, The Free Press, New York, (PB), 1969.

Karnani, Chetan, *Listening to Hindustani Music*, Arnold Associates, New Delhi, 1999.

Langer, S.K., *Feeling and Form*, Routledge and Kegan Paul Ltd., Third Impression, 1963.

———, *Problems of Art*, Routledge and Kegan Paul Ltd., London, 1957.

Leo Tolstoy's essay, "The Communication of Emotion", in *A Modern Book of Esthetics*, ed. by Melvin Rader, Holt, Rinehart and Winson, INC, 1973.

Matanga Muni, *Brihaddeśī*.

Mitias, Michael H., "What makes an Experience Aesthetic". Essay in *The Journal of Aesthetics and Art Criticism*, Winter, 1982.

Osborne, *The Art of Appreciation*, O.U.P., 1970.

Reid, L.A., *Meaning in the Arts*, George Allen and Unwin, London, 1969.

Santayana, George, *The Sense of Beauty*, Dover Publications, 1955.

———, *The Life of Reason*, Constable and Co. Ltd., London, 1954.

Sanyal, Ritwik, Philosophy of Music, Somaiya Publications Pvt. Ltd., 1987.

Saxena, S.K., 'Ālāpa in Dhruvapada Gāyaki', *Sangeet Natak*, July-Dec. '86.

———, *The Winged Form*, Sangeet Natak Akademi, 1979.

Sir Herbet Read's, "Critical Appreciation" in *Vermeer* (The Masters, 2), Knowledge

Publications, Purnell & Sons Ltd., Paulton, Nr. Bristol, 1965.

Sir Monier Monier-Williams, *A Sanskrit English Dictionary*, Oriental Publishers, Delhi 6, 1899.

Sparshoot, F.E., *The Structure of Aesthetics*, Routledge and Kegan Paul Ltd., London, 1963.

Sumati Mutatkar (ed.), *Aspects of Indian Music*, Sangeet Natak Akademi, New Delhi, 1987.

Swami Prajanananda, *A Historical Study of Indian Music*, Anandadhara Prakashan, Calcutta, 1965.

The Oriental World (Landmarks of the World's Art), Paul Hamlyn, London, 1967.

Veron, Eugene, "Art as the Expression of Emotion" in Melvin Rader's *A Book of Esthetics*, Holt, Rinehart and Winston, 5th edn., 1979.

Index